TIME STORY

TIME STORY

W.W. MARPLOT

WAXING
GIBBOUS

TIME STORY

Printed in the United States of America

Cover Design and Interior Layout by Claire Flint Last

Waxing Gibbous Books
www.WaxingGibbousBooks.com

LCCN: 2022923088
ISBN: 978-1-7347583-5-1

For those who paint what they can't see.

If time travel were possible, we would already know about it.
And now you do.

—W.W. MARPLOT

My inheritance how wide and fair!
Time is my fair seed-field, of Time I'm heir.

—GOETHE
"Wilhelm Meister's Travels"
(tr. in Carlyle's "Sartor Resartus")

When Rememberance wracks the mind,
Pleasures but unveil despair

—ROBERT BURNS
"Frae The Friends And Land I Love"

The Saint and Sinner Fool and Wise attain
An equal Share of Easiness and Pain.

—THOMAS CHATTERTON
"Happiness"

And aye, methinks, this hoary Pile,
Subdued by outrage and decay,
Looks down upon her with a smile,
A gracious smile, that seems to say,
"Thou, thou art not a Child of Time,
But Daughter of the Eternal Prime!"

—WILLIAM WORDSWORTH
"The White Doe of Rylstone"

But the downward glide
and bias of existing wrings us dry—
always inside me is the child who died,
always inside me is his will to die—
one universe, one body...

—ROBERT LOWELL
"Night Sweat"

The Child is father of the Man

—WILLIAM WORDSWORTH
"My Heart Leaps Up"

CHAPTER ZERO

"*Hi! What's your name?" the young man asked a small, prim, and proper little girl. She was at play in a park, apart from a group of others who looked and sounded very much like her. Blonde bumpy pigtails spun outward and whipped the air when she heard the voice, which seemed to pop out of nowhere.*

"Sally," she answered, looking at the man's face. It looked familiar, as if he was famous somehow. A woman was with him; she didn't speak.

"No—your full name," the young man requested curtly.

"Sally November Thirtieth Two Thousand Five Hundred And Nine."

"Thanks, kid. Gotta go."

"Where?" the little girl asked, quite innocently, even fondly—the man seemed like an old friend. She trusted him, as if his face was the very one on the statue in front of her school.

The man answered. "Back to my dorm room…uhhh…keep up the good work…" while wondering why he bothered to answer at all, notwithstanding polite habit. This girl and all those in this world meant nothing to him, and, he believed, most likely didn't even really exist in the way, say, his dorm room existed. He would ask a physicist when he got the chance.

Then, he and the woman clasped hands and disappeared. Gone, removed, erased, as the girl watched and blinked at the nothingness left at the spot. Her eyes adjusted and saw again the trees of the playground beyond where the two had stood. The disappearing act looked fake, like the cartoons she watched each morning with her sister on one of eleven twelve-foot television screens in their house. There had even been a "vooooop!" sound, a lame one, and the girl realized that it came from the man's own mouth. That sound, of course, was cut off as abruptly as the vision, and both only barely lingered in the little girl's mind.

"You can't keep him. I agree that he is cute, and pathetic, and sad, and he needs help. But you can't keep him." A young man was addressing an older man, pointing out something that should have been obvious.

"But…" was the only response. For now.

The two were looking down at a little boy, who was wearing very large eyeglasses, had chocolate stains all over his lips and cheeks, and was squeaking to them that he wanted to stay with "my Unkie" and "Unkie's funny friend."

"That's cute but you can't, kid," came the response. "Why is he squinting like that?" the young man asked the older one.

"Turns out his glasses are the wrong prescription."

"Then take them off him! For god's sake…"

This was done. But then they were quickly replaced. The little guy giggled. "Me ugly," he squeaked.

The young man spoke again. "Okay, it is sad, but really you have to put him back. It will be alright. In a few years. But!"—a new thought came—"don't tell him his future, you both might go blind. Just tell him to go back and wait for the silver truck. It will come. All his dreams will come true if he waits for the silver truck."

"Mom and Dad's! Wow, that brings back memories, that big old SUV."

The old man smiled, the young man did not. He never smiled when his brother smiled: not when they were kids, not yesterday when they were young men, and especially not today that they were forty or so years apart.

"Yeah whatever. He just needs to wait, like everyone else."

"No one wants him. No one is nice to him."

"Is that why you brought him here?"

"There are a lot of reasons...." The old man looked and sounded as exhausted as the infinity of time.

"None of them good. Go take a nap."

Besides, the young man thought, a college dorm room is no place to keep a kid.

<hr/>

The bodies of many strange characters gathered both on and around the couches of the dorm room, the place where each had landed having been pulled from time. They waited with great anticipation for a solution they were told was coming; they danced and partied while they waited.

<hr/>

"I can't."

"What do you mean you can't? Just tell me what happened, in order, and starting from the beginning."

"That's the problem, the timing. In a time story, it only makes sense to tell it in the order it couldn't have happened, you know what I mean?"

"No. Just tell me...."

But it wasn't a simple matter, and one brother needed time to tell the other brother about time. "If I stuck to strict chronological order," he went on, "the first thing would be like a 'Chapter Negative Five,' narrated like this: 'These plants are huge!' the hero said, then escaped the attack of a lamb-sized mosquito by hitting the yellow button on his time-travel belt. The girl followed, using her own powers...'"

"I am stuck in a dorm with a madman," the older brother spoke to a vacant, pensive face, "and it's wasting time, the time I could be using to generate cash and personal pleasure. Now you—my younger brother—I command you to answer the question—"

"That too! Good point. Am I your younger brother, if I have lived more years? See how time is relative? We need to have an 'agreed upon normal time' in order to-"

"I wanted an 'agreed upon normal' brother, but the adoption agency found a family of chimney sweeps from under the powerlines who never weaned off rat's milk. Give me the device, I will show you how it is supposed to be used."

CHAPTER ONE

Friday late morning, the brothers Woby
and Plunkett, the latter's college dorm
room, and an initial trip to the past
where yellow hats are seen.

The older brother referred to was Plunkett.

The time of the philosophical argument with his younger brother was also matter for philosophical argument. From Plunkett's point of view it took place a short time after their first failed adventure during what they came to call "agreed upon normal time" or AUNT, in an effort to keep things straight.

For example, from Plunkett's many plans and notes, this excerpt: "It is Friday, 2:00 p.m. AUNT, and I am really pissed at that imbecile, and I am not rich yet. Because I am not rich yet, and it is already 2:00 Friday AUNT."

The dorm room referred to, the most famous of all time(s), was Plunkett's. It would be studied by many a physicist, many an enlightenment-seeking mystic, and many a psychiatrist. Though it lacked color, and was in fact quite drab, it was a colorful place.

Truth be told it was a disgusting mess.

Plunkett's roommate, and older brother, was Applemon. Applemon was a genius. (More on Applemon later.)

Plunkett was not a genius, yet he was a comfortable fit for the school he attended, the local University, which served those students who were sufficiently above average to have fairly regular displays of studious intelligence. In between those flashes, however, for such young adults, came brown sinkholes of mediocrity that pitted and pocked the vocational landscape, disturbing any track of serious achievement or distinction.

For Plunkett, life was mostly spent looking to cheat and lay around.

Cheat: in a general manner; whatever happened to be nearby, he would find a way to treat it like an annoyance and steal from it if possible, if easy. He liked life best when he was getting away with something.

Lay around: in order to play video games or look for simple excitements that might be on TV or internet.

Mostly: yet not always.

Plunkett had the same blood as the genius Applemon after all, and did have swells of ingenuity and insight, like rising waves, though they of course died once they hit land. Plunkett would not ride these waves, however, he made his other brother—Woby, the aforementioned younger brother—row him through them. (We will get back to Woby.)

Applemon was three years Plunkett's elder, and attended the local university only as required to help advise gifted graduate students on their research while he completed his own in comfort and near to home. He was, at twenty-two years of age, finishing his third PhD at Princeton, 100 miles to the west—and a million miles to Plunkett's intellectual west, and farther north. Each found the other reassuringly dull, though with different definitions of the term.

Plunkett's parents thought it would be a good idea for the brothers to room together, and be together, when possible. This would serve as motivation and direction for the younger sibling and get him away from his preferred social circle of slackers, losers, and their future ex-girlfriends. This might also break his emotional backward slide: He hung out with Woby a lot, still. Too much.

For their part, their parents were skeptical in a very realistic way.

Though they were loving and nice. And they had certainly set the scene: by bringing forth a locally legendary genius; by giving birth to a plain old mortal with questionable hygiene and goals that were the texture and color of hard Swiss cheese; and by adopting a third boy who really, really needed adopting.

That was Woby; though *Woby!* expressed it better. Woby had a hard life early on, the particulars of which belong in a serious, tear-wrenching narrative, far from this one. Any story with Plunkett and Woby at its dramatic center would not make passion in the gods or propel men to climb mountains. Suffice to describe it this way: During AUNT, Woby was eighteen, and a junior in high school. Most of his friends were even younger, from middle school. The two were best friends and as close as any brothers could be since the adoption, but they were smaller between the ears, above the chin, and below the haircut. Woby missed a lot of school, and school missed a lot of him.

But Woby was okay. And being okay had helped him to get along, in the way that a family of plump groundhogs avoids evisceration by human landowners because they are non-threatening, are oblivious, are harmless, and eat bugs.

His adopted parents loved him and did a very nice thing in giving him a good home and a real chance in life. But they felt that Woby presented a bad temptation to Plunkett, since college men should not have human pets. For his part, Woby liked being petted, was comfortable under Plunkett's lash, and spent a lot of time at the college dorm to see his brothers, Plunkett and Applemon.

And now to the scene that started it all, a point in time within a story of time, and where "points" of time have become lines, planes, hyperplanes, and more.

But to start somewhere, without philosophical argument, the story starts in agreed upon normal time with the following historically fixed, historically significant, and momentous event.

Woby entered the room!

The dorm room, referred to and described earlier, the drab and colorless one that lacked color—but that was merely to one's eyes. The other senses were pelted: with scents that only a full carnival could leave behind, sounds that combined heavy metal music with amplified disharmonious but inventive chords that originated from bodily functions. And to the touch: What feels might come!

The dorm room Woby entered was actually four rooms: a large open kitchen, living and dining area, two bedrooms, and a bathroom. It was layered in many directions with direct evidence of college-boy life. As Applemon the physicist could explain: complexity, and even life, could be born of chaos, and in this dorm room foraging-cockroach-life had an especially distinct evolutionary advantage.

In he went! Woby's own blobby life made it through the front door and into the kitchen area, where awaited a counter, a sink, a fridge, an oven, some wooden stools—all but the stools were a pale, unambitious white. Color came only figuratively.

The boy's slow-heavy eyes glanced around through slow-droopy lids. Today's was a general, nondescript mess with, yes, macaroni and cheese boxes, both empty and new, both standing and tipped; and inescapable, obligatory empty beer bottles and soda cans whose imbibers were long gone.

As usual, the light was dim and depressing, not reflective of the motions of the Sun or Moon but matching the scheme of most dormitories. This much was not Plunkett nor Applemon's fault; the single window in the kitchen was large but covered with thick, closed curtains. This cast a drab imprint onto the lack of color. Even the artificial light sources seemed distracted, some covered with socks or towels.

Woby himself looked dejected, yet he always did. He carried a thin notebook, the sole record of his own school day, of his eighteen-year-old razor-stubbled giant presence in the public high school. The book is bent in half and scribbled-on beyond usefulness. He put it on the kitchen counter, pushing over a pile of textbooks and folders until it almost fell over the counter edge. He then picked up an open macaroni and cheese box, shook it, heard it was full, and put it down into its own dangerously tee-tering position.

Noticing a white sheet of notebook paper taped obtrusively to the curtains above the sink—a note left for someone to read, as he could well see—made no immediate impress on the tough skin of his mind, so he ignored it. He picked up the mac and cheese box again. He looked at the floor for numerous underwhelming seconds.

Only then did Woby walk over to the sink and read the note.

For Woby, reading to oneself entailed a certain percentage of reading aloud, and mumbling, on average, maybe two out of every five words. So he did. The note was addressed to him, and he read: *Woby you fat idi...Put on the belt...hit...green button...don't worry, it is a time machine. Apple used it...to a better place...me, too...lots of babes here, wow look at that one! Do it...it's Plunkett, here.*

Our oversized high schooler then looked at a walled corner of the kitchen counter to find, among more colorless refuse, an odd-looking corset-shaped apparatus—certainly hand-made, and sloppily done, yet adorned with an impressive array of electronics: wires, LED displays, circuit boards, computer chips. And a few large round colorful buttons—a red, a yellow, and a green—all very bright even in the dull lifeless tile of the dorm room kitchen.

Woby returned to the note: *Just do it*, it read, *all your dreams will come true...and whatever. Plunkett.*

He thinks I'm stupid or something, Woby thought. Though, like when reading, sometimes Woby would think out loud with simple words and an unsure voice.

Placing the note down, he noticed more message on the note-paper's reverse side: *If you don't believe me...proof...World War I... Royal Fusiliers Company C...I was just there. Do it!...yellow button.*

This made no impression on the young man, a state which he found easier than being confused. So Woby moved on, returning to the box of macaroni and cheese and its own notes and instructions.

While clearing a space within which to cook, he found, han-dled, and eyed curiously a metallic shell, a casing, a bullet. It was small. Woby rolled it in the fingers of his right hand as he rubbed his temple with his left. Connections were forming, and though it took a little time, eventually a conclusion was born.

Applemon's time machine. Cool. I wonder how Plunkett found it. But—Plunkett at a war? Yeah right—he learned that—"Royal Fusiliers"—from that Pink Floyd song. Huh, thinks I'm stupid. If that thing worked he'd be at Woodstock to see Jimi Hendrix. He thinks I'm stupid, Woby thought.

Mac and cheese a-heating, Woby opened the fridge, considered its cool emptiness, and grabbed a can of Diet Coke. As he moved to crack open the tab, the sound preceded the action, that is, he heard the snap before his fingers pulled.

Woby was startled at this—was this perhaps a time warp? This thought died as the realization came that the sound had come from elsewhere, from Plunkett's bedroom in fact. Walking toward its open door Woby saw the top of a baseball cap exposed above the level of the bed mattress. The hat tilted back, and Woby heard a sipping sound.

He announced himself to his brother Plunkett who sat beneath the hat. "Jerk," Woby said, "you think I'm stupid."

Plunkett's nasally aggressive voice rose from the floor in response. "Man, no, it's real. That's what Applemon was doing all those times he didn't come to parties. We always wondered what. I always figured it was a time machine—either that or a belt for the XBox."

"That would've been cool..." Woby replied, referring to the possibilities of video game enhancement given Applemon's inventive prowess. Such was their leveled understanding of the potentialities of true genius.

"Yeah," Plunkett added, "for that belly dancing game."

"That would have been awesome," Woby said.

Plunkett rose. Ignobly, sure, but the brothers then moved together to the common area of the kitchen, and both leaned on the counter, awaiting the completion of macaroni and cheese.

Plunkett spoke again, thumbing toward the apparatus and its pretty wires. "Well, we've got the time machine. I think Applemon used it, it must work...."

"Yeah—but you wanted *me* to try the thing?" Woby answered. "I could've been killed, or a dinosaur could've fallen on me. You probably don't even know which button or what the dials do."

"No—it's Apple's, Wobe, it must be safe," Plunkett pleaded, aggressively, playing his role as commander of the two-man ship they'd launched afloat since they were kids. "He's so careful and detailed and everything. It's cool. Think about what we could do with it."

This was not an easy thing to request of Woby.

"What?" Woby asked, though in his case sometimes simple questions were more comfortably posed as statements. "What."

"Anything we want," came Plunkett's reply.

To this Woby nodded, and as he stirred the mac and cheese mixture Plunkett hopped himself a seat on the kitchen counter. The brothers sipped their sodas in quiet contemplation and with the rhythm of synchronized tramps. It was obvious to Plunkett that Woby's thoughts must have been running deep indeed. Relatively speaking.

"Yeah." Woby said, expressing the inexpressible, then went back to idle, reading the blue and yellow mac and cheese box near his face. Then he put it down. Then he lifted it to read again.

Plunkett moved to the common area couch and was soon either in serious penetrating thought or had fallen asleep.

Woby turned off the stove and moved to the second couch, shoving aside various flotsam to clear a seat among its fading brown and green threads.

A full minute went by, but time had no meaning here. Slovenly, college late-mornings flowed like cold molasses.

Another minute, perhaps, passed, at one second per second, at most.

Then Woby spoke. "Well. What *do* we want?" he asked.

Plunkett sat up at this, looking tired, but quickly answered his younger brother. "What does anyone want? Wine, women, song, sex, drugs, rock 'n' roll. That seems universal enough. Let's go back to the first Woodstock and bet on fantasy sports leagues, starting with the first Super Bowl. We'll be heroes."

"Yeah." Woby said, then returned to his stovetop pot, the scent of burnt cheese floating about. Plunkett turned on the TV, and the sounds of generic sports reporting filled the room with a background buzz of artificial, manufactured excitement. "When was that?" Woby asked.

"What?"

"The first Super Bowl? Like in the 1940s?"

"No, way off. I think 1969. Same as Woodstock."

"They were at the same exact time?"

"No, gnat-brain." Plunkett pressed aggressively, but all in careful measure: He was glad to have Woby's interest now, the hook was baited with a large, slow worm to catch a fish.

"Don't you have to know the exact time to set up the time machine?" Woby asked and pondered. "There are dials on it—no keyboard. You can't put in 'Woodstock.'"

"Hey, good thinking, Wobe," Plunkett said, visibly pleased with this progress. "I don't know exactly when Woodstock was, but you can get close enough and then wait for it. Put in January 1, 1969, just to be sure. You could see the moon landing also that way."

"The heck with that! Wait around all year? It could be in December!"

"Well, what do we know the exact date of, then? When did the Beatles play on that roof?"

"Let's just Google it…" Woby responded, and having scraped out the black and amber coal-lumps of his lunch from the pot, he now searched the dorm room's jetsam while asking, "Where's the iPad?"

"Psilocybin," Plunkett answered, of no help to any third parties listening in.

"Where?"

"Microdosing," Plunkett reiterated.

"Oh yeah," Woby said. "Applemon's gonna be pissed."

"Yep, the poop is going to hit the propeller." Plunkett thought he expressed it better. "It was worth it though." He smiled as the two enjoyed a grinning private remembrance of things vomitous, until Plunkett went on.

"Forget it," Plunkett said, "don't you know when *anything* was?" Plunkett's tone was aggressive, with admonishment. Everything Plunkett said to Woby had some percentage of aggression and admonishment, determined as appropriate to the situation and Plunkett's immediate goals.

"Let me think…" Woby answered, the very words partly funny whether anyone was there to laugh or not.

"What is high school teaching you?" Plunkett pressed. "You know no history. I raised you a classic rock fan, in the face of lots of pressure from the modern world. And you don't know any specific dates, even of Woodstock? Or the Stones at Altamont?"

"You're in college!" Woby struck back.

"Exactly—so high school was a whole year ago for me. You have no excuse." Plunkett moved his focus to the TV, still volleying off-hand ideas over his shoulder and back at his brother. "What about Live Aid? Led Zeppelin at Madison Square Garden? You like Zep. When was that?"

"I don't know *exactly*. You have to know exactly, right? To time travel somewhere?"

"Well, *you* do, apparently, your Holiness, because you are lazy and spoiled and don't want to earn it or have to wait when you get there." Chiding Woby like this came easily and naturally to Plunkett, given years of practice. The point here was to wiggle the fishing line a bit, to tempt the fish, to look like dinner. "I offer you a trip to Woodstock, the moon landing, and the first Super Bowl, and you whine about having to wait a little."

Woby did not respond, he was using his smartphone to try to access the Web to find some hard data, but there was no signal in the room, the cellular airwaves perhaps blocked by the cinder block-based architecture, or maybe purposely blocked by university authorities based on the small likelihood of important transmissions emanating from the area.

Plunkett continued from the couch. "You can't think of *anything*? I did the hard part, swiped the machine from Applemon.

He has two PhDs, but his little brother doesn't know anything. Shameful. Hey, when was the Normandy invasion? I might want you to see that, too."

Woby, frustrated by the distractions, blurted, "Everything you're saying applies to you too—what do *you* know? Any history at all?"

"Okay, okay," Plunkett eased off, careful not to rip the hook clear out of Woby's drooping mouth and lose the catch. "Okay. Then let's just test it, do something easy. What do we know of, for sure? I mean something recent, something definite, something local."

"I'd like to retake my science test," Woby said, his face as bright as if it had fingers to snap. "It was last Wednesday morning, eight-thirty."

Plunkett did not share the enthusiasm. "Look," he said, "our time machine has to be of more use than being a digital streaming service for your failing life. We have to be able to use it to get rich. Or at least happy." Plunkett stood up and leered at a beer-sponsored pretty-girl-emblazoned calendar on a beige, otherwise barren, wall. Studied it.

Woby, misunderstanding Plunkett's purpose, and in doing so extending a streak of consecutive days of misunderstanding things, said, "Look how easily you are distracted."

"I'm looking for the exact date of something, moron," Plunkett responded with his usual amount of brotherly patience. "There's nothing today. But yesterday was the first bikini contest, 1960."

"Really? Where?"

"Doesn't say."

"Probably Florida."

Plunkett then lit up in an expression of Eureka! Exclaiming, "Perfect! John F. Kennedy's assassination, 1963. Perfect. Says so right here. And this way at least you could solve who shot Kennedy while we figure out how to get wealthy and adored."

"Wait! What do you mean 'me'?" Woby asked. "Why do I have to test it?"

"It's gotta be you. The belt is an extra large. And I have to stay here and work the box so you can get back."

"What box? There's a box?" Woby I-didn't-know-thatted.

"Yeah there's a box!" Plunkett of-coursed.

"Nuh uh, no way—I'm bringing the box with me." Woby said, sounding distrustful, but Plunkett took this, and his victory, in stride.

"That's the spirit!" he said, and he reached overboard to pull his large blubbery catch into the boat. "Look, you'll make history. The first time traveler!"

"What about Applemon? He must have used it. He was first."

"Then you'll be the first underachiever to do it. Or go back in time farther than he did, and then you'll be first."

"Hm?" Woby said with rarified clarity.

"Yeah, it gets confusing. Let's try it. Hurry, I'm going to be late for work."

"I'll do it if you clean up the kitchen for me."

"Fine." Plunkett agreed and leaned back against the couch in a comfortable position with which to watch either history-in-the-making or a disaster of mind-blowing proportions. His mind had competing thoughts, those based on greed versus those of a more general, slouchy, scientific thrill, as he watched his brother Woby try on the belt and begin to adjust parametric settings on dials that were dumbed down an epic, mountainous amount.

Regardless, Plunkett thought he himself should take over the controls, and he did, allowing Woby to stand there.

Plunkett spoke his adjustments aloud. "Eleven…twenty-two…nineteen…sixty…three. Seven a.m.…Wait, it would be central time for Dallas. The return time we'll set to be now—what time is it?"

"No idea." Woby answered. "Like 12:30."

"There's no 'like' switch."

In answer to this, Woby twisted on a sudden impulse to reach for his cell phone, and the action caused the belt to pop off his wide girth. After being aggressively admonished by Plunkett who was seeking accountability for Woby's size, eating habits, and resemblance to certain unattractive mammals, the belt was re-fastened, re-parameterized, and Woby had time to rethink.

"Maybe we should rent a JFK documentary first," Woby offered, "to make sure we know enough."

"Relax, it's just a test. Put it on."

"Where's the box? Give it to me," Woby directed. Plunkett handed it to him, a cube about the same size as Woby' head, yet weighing much more, and Woby's arm drooped. The box exuded a grave impression of indestructibility, which comforted Woby. "Is it the green or yellow button that I hit?"

"On the belt, yellow. Alright? Do it. I'll be right here. Keep your head down."

"Why?" Woby looked worried. Only now.

"You are going to an assassination, jackass."

"Okay." Woby was resigned to go. "One more sip," he said and finished his Diet Coke. He rolled up his bulky flannel shirtsleeves, and without fanfare pressed the green button near his navel with the fingers of both hands.

He then straightened up, shaking and breathless, panting and crazy-eyed.

Plunkett, eyebrows all a-crinkle, watched as his brother looked around wildly and then took the belt off in a panic. Woby then grabbed his empty Diet Coke can, and also the mac and cheese box, and held them like teddy bears during a thunderstorm. He dropped the heavy cube as if it were the anti-teddy bear.

Seeing Woby fluster always made Plunkett laugh, but he fought against the rising joy and steadied enough to ask: "Dude, what's wrong? Nothing happened."

"Screw you, 'nothing happened.' I was almost killed." Woby replied, his face contorting in interesting patterns.

"How?"

"Screw you, 'how.' Where did you send me? I almost fell off a ledge," Woby replied, his face contorting in bizarre patterns still.

"When? What are you talking about?"

"Screw you, 'when.' When you sent me. Where you sent me."

"You never left…." Plunkett began, but stopped short as new and clearer thoughts waved their arms in front of him.

"Screw y—" Woby began, but Plunkett interrupted him.

"Holy wow! You mean it worked? Where were you?" he asked his larger yet smaller brother.

"You said it was Dallas." Woby replied. "But I was on a ledge. I almost fell off."

"You mean a knoll? Was it grassy? Did you see Kennedy? Zapruder? Marilyn Monroe?"

"I saw construction workers. I hate you. I hate you with all my—"

"No convertibles?" Plunkett mused, leaning further back in body and mind. "Slow down," he continued to Woby, "tell me everything. How long were you there?"

"Hold on a second," Woby said, and walked off to Plunkett's bedroom, returning after a moment a changed young man—his jeans were replaced by brightly colored shorts.

Then he told his tale, slightly calmer than before, and certainly drier, but still confused. "I was there like twenty seconds. I was here. I hit the yellow button. Then I was there—in the middle of a big construction site. I was on the edge of a pit, like the basement of a new building they were building. Some of the workers started yelling and running toward me. I tried to use my phone, but then…I don't know, I think I just hit one of the buttons again."

"Historic!" said Plunkett. Woby had calmed, so Plunkett went on. "What was it like? The trip itself I mean. Was there a tube? With long, stretchy lights? Loud? Did your body morph?"

"No, nothing. I told you: I was here and scared and then I was there and nauseous. No trip. Instant." As if to answer Plunkett's last and misunderstood question, Woby stretched. "Where was I?" he asked during the last of his post-trip warmup. "And when?"

"1963, I guess. See—the dial still says that. Did you see anything that looked like Texas? Or Lee Harvey Oswald? Anything?"

"I saw yellow hats and flannel shirts and cement." Woby answered, still shaking at the thought. "But wait a minute…" he stiffened, "that's right! Yeah, I remember: I also saw the radio tower—yeah, but, the one from here on campus, with the wildcat logo. I thought it was strange, but I thought I was in Dallas, so..."

Woby trailed off, re-hugging the mac 'n' cheese box.

Both young men pondered.

Plunkett, out of long conditioned habit, wandered to the couch and looked dumbly at the TV. Woby moved the belt to the kitchen counter, reverently, and sat on a stool.

Plunkett then snapped the TV off with a deft movement of wrist and remote. "Oh," he said, then also, "Yeah!" and finally, "Well, guess what?"

"What?" Woby asked emphatically.

"You were here." Plunkett explained. "On campus, but like fifty years ago. This building must have been built around 1963. Right. Doesn't it say that on the bricks in front? It says 1964 actually—where you smashed your head that time—remember? I said it stood for how many stiches you would need? Remember?"

"No."

Plunkett went on. "But this makes sense. It's a time machine, not a place machine."

"Well, I could have been freaking killed. Popping into the middle of anywhere like that."

Demonstrably exhilarated and clearly encouraged, Plunkett got up, and spoke in an inspired flurry as he dressed for work. Woby didn't know where his brother's new job was, but apparently it required wearing yellow.

"Are you kidding?" Plunkett spoke as he dressed. "This is awesome—you never left here, but spent twenty cowardly seconds somewhere else, in a different time. With all the bad crap that could have happened to you—you could have come back eighty-five years old, or been vaporized, or married—you made it and should be excited. We had no idea what was going to happen. So relax. Next time we just need to be more specific. At work I'll do some research for your next trip."

"Alright then," Woby said, reassured for a bit. Then, as if the wild horse of his thoughts had angrily reared up, "Whoa whoa whoa– why can't *you* go next time?"

"Technical reasons," came Plunkett's trailing words as he left the dorm room.

CHAPTER TWO

Friday, later afternoon. In which there is another trip to the future, and from whence their friend Ariel is texted.

Woby spent a lot of time at the university when he could; he liked being with his brothers.

And they liked being with him, despite Plunkett's sometime exasperation.

"I wish you would hang out with your own friends more," Plunkett would lie, or tease, when small things went wrong. Time travel is a big thing; small things include impressing a popular fraternity brother, or impressing a popular sorority sister, or convincing a professor not to give Plunkett a deserved grade, or manipulating the cafeteria and meal plan for better and more snacks for late at night.

"I like it here," Woby would reply. "You guys protect me."

"From...?" Plunkett would ask.

"Nothing yet," Woby would say.

Woby's adopted parents encouraged time with his siblings. Applemon was certainly a role model. Plunkett was definitely company—and at least served as a first level of protection and oversight. Plunkett was streetwise enough to stay out of real trouble. So far.

Due to his unfortunate early years, Woby was still in high school and still immature, and in fact preferred the middle-school mentality. Caught in between, he would escape and lose himself at the college, among the buildings, at the gatherings and parties, within Plunkett's schemes and under Applemon's penumbra, and in their never-dull, hue-limited dormitory.

Woby wandered the campus the rest of that Friday and awaited his brother's return from his yellow job, whatever it was. The time-travel belt was not a temptation, and, hard as it might be to believe, he had almost forgotten about it after a time. He was dozing when Plunkett splashed and crashed in through the front door, his shirt noticeably stained with browns and reds.

"Wobe, listen, I got it. I have a great idea," he said.

Woby replied and awoke simultaneously. "But listen, it's your freaking turn," he blurted. Only brothers as close as these could continue a conversation from five hours earlier as if no time had passed.

"Come on," Plunkett answered him, "do you really want to be remembered that way? That you time-traveled for twenty seconds to see post-historic steelworkers?"

To this Woby frowned, sighed, and thought.

"Oh, and I got your text." Plunkett threw his cell phone to his brother, instructing him to scroll all the way to the top—to the *oldest* of his messages, where Woby read, "*I hate you, Plunkett*" in a blue message bubble dated from 1963.

Woby stared at the phone's glass screen until it was obvious that he was stuck in some infinite thought loop, so Plunkett broke through to retrieve it. "And you did call me—and I got a warning from the phone company, a warning that my account was going to be suspended if I break the contract again."

"Sorry," Woby said, staring at his hand where the phone had been.

"Don't worry, you're new at this. Now if you'll listen," Plunkett offered, "you'll hear that I have an idea that will make us famous."

To this Woby's face changed and perked up, signaling his openness to persuasion, once again. Plunkett—brother, master, fisherman, trainer—could read such signs, though they remained imperceptible to others, and he did so unconsciously. He would push his argument further, just enough, as he knew instinctively, to close the matter.

"You need to go this time," Woby repeated.

"No. I'll clean the kitchen," Plunkett said, "and I found the thing, so you owe me. And if I go, I am not coming back for you—screw you. Do you want that?"

"No, but…yeah, well…" Woby offered lamely, letting Plunkett go on.

"Do it!" Plunkett said.

"No."

"Do it. As a punishment…for…" Plunkett faltered, not for lack of deserving offenses, but for the abundance of choices.

Woby's mind reviewed a similar inventory, but he held his ground. "No."

"Do it as a reward then," Plunkett said.

The 180-degree turn from Plunkett made Woby a little dizzy. "Hm…maybe…"

"Just listen to the idea," Plunkett continued. "Go back five years. There was no new construction, and everything was the same here as it is now. Go to the student store—Established 2009—and buy all the newspapers, grab any flyers you see, and anything with information. Anything that will give us accurate data on the scene five years ago. Just as a test, but then we'll be able to plan better. It's hard to get that info on the internet from AUNT."

"Aunt?" Woby asked, as he ought. "Beverly?"

"'Agreed upon normal time,' remember? The here and now. Anyway, we need printouts, paper. I don't trust the Web, and we need to keep this secret."

"What about the library?" Woby asked, stretching and twisting away the couch-shape that his body had assumed while napping.

"Fine, go to the library, too, that's better actually, go to periodicals and get what you can. Newspapers, magazines. Don't use your phone this time." Plunkett went to his bedroom.

"No, I meant we could get that stuff at the library now, and I don't have to go all the way to the past."

Plunkett took this suggestion as just so much procrastination, excuse, and delay. "Look, do you want to time travel or screw around?" He shot his replies louder as he wandered the adjoining rooms. "I don't have time for that. I'm tired, and I was hoping to be rich by tomorrow night, latest. Just listen to the rest of my plan." He came back out, bare-chested, clutching a ball of a shirt.

"Sorry." Woby was sitting up now, alert, behaved, ready.

"We can get the lottery numbers," Plunkett went on, while his upper half swam awkwardly into two layers of clothing at once—a shirt and sweatshirt cocooned within each other as if destined to be so. "And then you can go back to the same place a day before and we can start to collect." Plunkett ended his oration and threw both hands into the front sweatshirt pocket to show dramatically that this was the plan, the whole plan, a terrific plan, and proof of his own genius.

Woby, nodding in agreement, went into motion immediately and secured the clackety time travel belt from the kitchen counter. He strapped it on expertly. Then he noticed and seriously considered the strong-looking, grave, metal box—the one that complemented the belt technology somehow. But Woby shook his head, refusing to take it with him this time.

Shuddering involuntarily, he was ready.

Woby looked up at Plunkett, the former's face wearing a new idea. "I am going to leave from the bathroom this time," he declared, and an astronaut could not have stated it better. "Just…because." Maybe an astronaut would have stated that part better, but still: Woby was strapped in and ready to launch.

"Whatever. Have a nice trip," Plunkett said from the couch, TV remote in hand.

"Cool," Woby answered, as he walked into the bathroom with as much dignity as he could summon from its unfamiliar hiding places.

Then, suddenly, from mission control, that is, from Plunkett: "No, wait! Man, I just saved your ass! If you leave from there, you are going to land in Dirty Dan's bathroom. Remember that guy?" Plunkett yelled to reach Woby in the bathroom. "Applemon told us about him. He had this dorm before us, five years ago." Woby did not reply. "You really have to start thinking like a time traveler, dude." Plunkett clicked on the TV.

The sound of a flushing toilet was heard. "I'll leave from the hall then," Woby said, emerging with a few cubic centimeters less dignity than before.

His one-man procession left the door of the apartment…and in three seconds returned in a similar panic as hours earlier, struggling to catch his breath.

Plunkett sat up. "What?" He sounded annoyed.

"Hold on. I ran all the way back. Damn!" Woby was bent over, clutching for air, pushing his words through exhausted lungs.

"From? The past?" Plunkett asked.

"From the bookstore," Woby wheezed, "and yes, from the past. Oh, man. Geez…"

"Breathe, dude. Where's the stuff you were supposed to get?"

Woby breathed, yes, but at an increasing pace.

"I meant *slower*, Woby, breathe slower. Relax…" Plunkett said, faking an air of concern and, perhaps, caregiving love, but it came across as aggressive and admonishing.

Woby calmed a few cubic centimeters' worth and went on with his science-nonfiction story. "I got some newspapers and went to pay. It wasn't the usual girl at the register. It was an older guy."

Plunkett bounced his head back and forth to show that he was following Woby's account so far, and that, so far, it made sense. But Plunkett did not speak, so Woby went on.

"I showed your school ID to get the discount. And the guy said 'What's your problem?' It was cruel."

"You lost me." Plunkett slowly shook his scrunched forehead.

"He looked at me. For like a minute. A whole one," Woby said, his wheezes turning to whimpers, combining exhaustion with pain and mortification.

"What are you talking about?" Plunkett scrunched.

"Then I ran," Woby went on. "I kept running until I got to the hospital."

"The hospital? That's like three miles from the bookstore! Why did you go there?" Plunkett asked.

"Its doors opened for me. That felt good, reassuring." Woby started panting again in remembrance of his Olympian sprint.

"I'm still lost. Why did you run?"

Woby calmed enough to answer, then didn't. "God," he continued, "now what am I going to do? God, god…"

"Since when are you so devout? Can you tell me what happened now, please, Sister Woby?"

And to finally add the clarity that Plunkett's brow so desperately desired, Woby handed his brother the university ID—a copy they had procured so that Woby could use the campus facilities more easily. In the present day, that is.

Plunkett stared at the ID for a minute, waiting for the lamp to turn into a lady's face. "I don't see what the problem is…Oh!" he eventually said. And, cruelly, he turned his face away from Woby, hand over mouth, laughing uncontrollably and every few seconds looking at the ID card again—especially at the large shiny 2014 printed across it—to reenact the joke, enjoy it all over again, and refresh his cackling uproar.

Woby finally had caught his breath and used it toward a new goal, that being to defend himself. "Oh, you're a genius," he said. "I can't leave here, they're probably looking for me…for forgery and counterfeiting…"

"What?" Plunkett's laugh continued.

"I was going to pay with money from today, 2014, new bills," Woby said.

"I doubt any of this would stand up in court."

"Aha! Well, I thought of that, so I dropped the evidence—the fake ID—in the mailbox on my way back. Maybe *you* should start thinking of things, instead of me taking all the risks."

"*What!* Why did you mail it?" Plunkett said, as his laugh decelerated to a giggle. Though this very question yielded a few newborn guffaws. "*What?*"

"Your ID card says on it '*Guaranteed postage*' and '*Drop in any mailbox,*' so I did. I figured I would then have proof when you got it back five years ago that now it had the future date so that we could then defend ourselves if we got caught now." Woby finished, apparently content with such a sentence.

Plunkett, now face to face across from Woby, was inconsolable, however, and doubled over in hysteria and stomach pain. All he could manage to say for a long period was essentially just a list of synonyms for "stupid" and "man." Finally, and only after a few false starts, he was able to verbalize this utterance: "The ID would get mailed to the school, not to me." And he wiped away many tears.

"Oh." Woby said. "Then I wonder..."

"*Don't*. Don't wonder. Don't think. Don't ponder, don't contemplate. Don't do anything except what I tell you to do, do it exactly, and don't improvise, ad lib, riff, rap, or jam. Okay?"

Woby was too tired to argue, and as he removed the belt, tossed it onto the kitchen counter, and plopped his bulk onto one ungrateful couch, he yielded. with three okays in a row.

Plunkett produced from a pocket his ID card like a magician his rabbit. "I have the ID, so life goes on."

Plunkett too went on—aggressively, admonishingly—and explained what he had garnered from movies and cartoons, namely that time travel could get complicated, especially if you try to predict or impact things. But this is where scientists always failed, and where slackers like Woby could actually succeed. The slow can become rich. The simple can inherit power over life and death. Beings like Woby can win—as long as they follow the instructions of their betters and 60/40 partners.

Woby only followed 40 percent of this argument, which is perhaps appropriate. He was still trying to reposition mind and acclimate body to the present time and place, to AUNT. It was Friday. It was dinnertime. It was today, it was now, he was here. To a time traveler, even a simple one, these were warming and comforting thoughts.

After new moments passed in peace—the only sounds were the rise in muffled, beat-heavy music coming from various directions of nearby dorm rooms, and of Plunkett's actions in reheating some cold pizza—Woby returned to the topic.

"One good thing is that I am getting better at coming back. I set the timer thing to leave early, so I could walk back and you wouldn't have to wait."

"Damn considerate of you," Plunkett replied, picked up a pen, and retrieved a battered notebook, flipping to the back and surely empty pages. "Okay," he began, "I'm going to put all this in my notes. We have a lot of experience now. Two marginally successful trips backward through time."

"Yeah?" Woby was happy at being called successful—no small praise coming from Plunkett. "And return trips," he added.

"True. Impressive. You didn't die, and you made it back and still a teenager. That was a big risk I took."

"Oh. Yeah, I guess. Thanks."

Plunkett wrote out loud. "Go back…seven…years…at least… for statute…of…limitations defense. Need to get…old cash…and forms of…ID."

"And can we go somewhere off campus?" Woby asked.

"I was thinking about that at work—but how are we going to get the belt on a plane? No way that thing gets past security. And, as I've said many times before, you look like a chubby terrorist."

Woby could not argue with that; Plunkett *had* said that before.

"But cheer up!" Plunkett said. "In the future, post-9/11 will be just a thing of the past."

Plunkett reviewed his notes and asked, "Is there anything else I should know? This all seems manageable and fixable so far."

"There's a girl…" Woby began.

"This I don't care about."

"No, at the hospital, I saw a girl. She looked at me." Woby recalled as best he could.

"They all look at you. Years and years of people looking at you. Finally they have a reason. Don't worry about it."

"This was different, she seemed to—"

"More paranoia," Plunkett said, "or insecurity, or whatever. Does this have anything to do with our real problems, like taming the wild wrath of physics, like escaping the iron jaws of time? I like that…" Plunkett wrote more down.

"Yes, that's what I mean, she was different somehow," Woby said carefully, "as if she was the one time traveling and I was standing still. Her name was Trice."

"That's nobody's name, that's not a name." Plunkett said distractedly, until Woby's words settled deeper. "And how the hell do you know that? Don't tell me you talked to people!"

"I guess it was on her hospital nametag, though I didn't think she worked there, she didn't look like a doctor or anything. She was our age. I don't know. I have to think about it, it was confusing and fast. I jogged and walked back to near the bookstore to come back. That's it."

Plunkett wondered why this girl stood out to his brother, but then recalled the time Woby followed a centipede for fifty yards studying it, reading it with his lips as it were.

"Okay, whatever, it's nothing," Plunkett reassured him. "The girl doesn't matter. If you had done anything causal and effectual, or paradoxical, we would know. You would come back to a world without hospitals, or they would be Woby-shaped, or something. But things are the same, don't worry, no new architectural paradigm shifts since you left."

"Okay, good," Woby replied. "But there are too many problems with that thing," Woby pointed at the belt on the counter. "So much can go wrong. I was thinking about it all day, too, before you got home."

"Yeah, you look beat," Plunkett said, ba-dum bum. "But there's that word again; just stop. Stop thinking. You are doing too much of that. We're a team—leave the hard stuff to me."

"I thought about it longer than you, technically, because my day was longer," Woby said, and it hurt him to do so. He lay deeper down into the couch, his head flat on the cushions, his feet necessarily dangling up and over its other side. He gazed at the parallel lines of the ceiling as if it were the abstract mathematical reaches of the spacetime continuum.

Something occurred to Plunkett. "Wait. While I was at work… you didn't tell anyone about this, did you?"

"No."

"Well, don't. Look, all we need to do is get old clothes, IDs, old cash, maps, and some newspapers from an exact date, with the lotto numbers, from somewhere near here." Plunkett patted his notes as he spoke. "Then we'll do the time thing, the ping-pong balls of the lottery will be at our command. We'll be masters of spacetime, we can pick somewhere convenient to live, pick up babes, think of new ways to spend money, be worshipped, and…done. No: *Then* we zip ahead to our ten-year high school reunions. It's all in the notes."

Plunkett held up his notebook. There were indeed many ideas memorialized there in a scrawling pen. Some text was underlined, some marked with symbols: exclamation points, dollar signs, question marks, a large round stick figure with messy hair.

Woby gave it a going over from his tilted head a few feet away. "Fine," he admitted, "those are good ideas. But where's Applemon? It's Friday, he's usually back from Princeton by now."

"We don't need him," Plunkett said. Woby expected this and was always apprehensive when mentioning Applemon—older brother and living legend—having lived with Plunkett's obvious and understandable envy, jealousy, and petty acrimony for many years.

"Knowing him," Plunkett went on, "his plan is nowhere near this one. He probably wants to go back and meet Einstein. Imagine the two comb-less weirdos hanging out near a whiteboard. That is not how to live."

"No," Woby's voice came straight up from the cushions, "I don't think he did. We would have read about it—I mean we would already know about it if he did."

"Hey! Now that's pretty smart, Wobe, good thinking!" Plunkett had to admit. "But don't, okay? I don't know where Apple is, but there were two boxes, and only one belt, so he might be doing some traveling himself, taking his white chalk to ancient Greece to compare triangles, or who knows where. Forget him. We have better ideas."

"But maybe we should get his advice, or someone's," Woby said. "Twice I almost got in trouble. We can't risk going too far, but staying around here is also messed up—what if I meet Mom or Dad? Or myself? I'm good at noticing things, like myself on TV collecting lottery winnings."

"We don't need anyone else. You're making this too complicated." Plunkett said. "Look, what's wrong with my plan? We have experience now."

"Well, why can't you go next time?" Woby asked.

"My stalking ex-girlfriend might see me. For one thing."

"When?" Woby asked, meaning "who?" but time travelers are more interested in questions of time than of people.

"There's lots of them. There's always one. The past has nowhere for me to hide. I'm too popular."

Woby moaned while circumscribing a frown.

Plunkett went on. "Don't you think I thought of going? Trust me, it's better if you go, especially now, and until we get things rolling with the cash. Then we'll both go, okay?"

Plunkett was sitting now, eating his pizza, cracking open another Diet Coke. Friday night.

Woby sat up with more questions. "And why can't we go to the future? That sounds easier."

"And do what? How can we get rich in the future?"

Woby found himself attracted to the pizza like a dog toward garbage in the woods. He moved nearer to his brother as he spoke. "We could be famous historians, or archeologists."

"Name one," Plunkett said slowly, pulling his pizza nearer to his heart. "Ever seen one with groupies? Fill a stadium?" As Woby thought about this and his rising, salivating hunger, Plunkett continued. "For example, look at Professor Steinway. Famous historian, a legend on campus. He has twelve cats and runs the Renaissance festival."

"Well, maybe he's happy," Woby said earnestly.

"Please. You don't watch enough TV."

"Look, can we ask Ariel? She could definitely help." While speaking, Woby cast his eyes downward. Even trickier than discussing Applemon with Plunkett was mentioning Ariel. The brothers, all three, had a complex mesh of relationships with Ariel. The young lady—a junior at the university—publicly puppy-loved Applemon. She famously had a crush on him and his legendary academic prowess since her freshman orientation two summers past, then infamously changed majors twice during their breakup, and ineluctably settled on Psychology.

Outside her heart, she admired Applemon as a scientist and a person. His overachieving work ethic, his local roots, his donnish but kinda-cool good looks, his quirky style during presentations to students, his messy attire and manner—all these attracted Ariel the nerdy moth to Applemon's cerebral flame.

Applemon, being older and focused on his studies, did not take Ariel, or any other fawning students, into his calculations or projections.

Invert that relationship, remove the purity, and you get the Plunkett/Ariel situation.

A curious and additional dynamic further confused myriad intertwining emotional posturing when Woby and Plunkett were together. Unbeknownst to the brothers—as many things were—Ariel was actually studying them as part of her academic coursework, observing them from a sociological and psychological viewpoint. And, from a scorned-woman standpoint, to keep an eye on Applemon.

The intertwixtedness of all this was beyond Woby's standard capabilities to fully understand or to act on, so he just tried to be nice to everyone and not use big words.

But Woby did use a small word, a name, and it still ghosted in the air between the brothers. *Ariel.* Woby curled up wimpily on his stool, having actually broken two rules: suggesting that Plunkett needed assistance and mentioning Ariel.

"Why do you keep saying that—to tell other people?" Plunkett grilled his brother with a lack of syntax but his tone said more than his words. "*Did* you tell anyone, today? Especially her?"

"No. But I had been thinking about it."

"And every time you do that, I say '*don't.*' Even before your time adventures, we've discussed how dangerous that is, you thinking. Remember that party last week? Remember that smell? Stubborn, persistent, etcetera?"

"What does that have to do with—" Woby tried to ask, genuinely curious.

But Plunkett interrupted him. "And remember when I caught you surfing the Web for pictures of the Kardashians? And you couldn't find any? Stop thinking. I'm telling you—forget Ariel. Just listen to me."

"But she has good ideas about this." Woby stated, abashedly afraid, bent over and trying to look deep within his own navel as he did.

"*You.*" Plunkett said.

"*You.*" Plunkett repeated.

"*Are you telling me.*" Plunkett didn't ask.

"*You.*" Plunkett said again.

"*You told Ariel*!" Plunkett observed, finishing with barely controlled force that, while impressive, served to spit pizza pieces out from his lips. "I knew it—you're going to blow this. I was only gone a few hours, and it cost me billions of dollars. Mom didn't like the leash idea, but she'll agree now. Damn it! You. You! Her!"

Woby endured another minute of his brother's rage and rambling, but at a pause he perked up, sat straight, and presented his defense, one he was obviously pleased with. "I *didn't* tell her," Woby explained, "but I got her talking about time travel, and we got into it a little bit."

Plunkett responded with the same force, consternation, and pace as before. "You. Got her. Talking about. Time travel." He stopped to swallow, lick his lips, to force down and digest the dyspeptic smile on Woby's round face. "And just how did you. Get Her. Talking. About Time. Travel?"

Woby replied, "She read my text message. From the past."

"Tell me either that you're joking or that I can garrot you." Plunkett said.

"Well, I also got confused when I saw The Girl." The way he said it made the term capitalize in midair. "So I thought," he went on, "I should ask Ariel about it. But she was too young. At the time. Ariel."

"So you sent her a text. A note. To the future. A text." It made sense to Plunkett, so he nodded to Woby that he expected a reply presently.

"Yeah."

"And you don't think Ariel, the nosy, busybody, know-it-all, suspected anything?"

"No."

"You know how weird she's been since Applemon dumped her? Meddling, snooping…and you don't think she suspected anything, can I ask again?"

Woby responded, "No," though he wasn't settled on which question mark he was responding to. "It's okay, she likes us. She's smart. I had a lot of questions for her, but I left it casual."

Plunkett took a moment, and then answered this: "No offense, Wobe, but advanced physics does not naturally roll off your giant and fuzzy tongue. Time travel is about math and probability theory and quantum mechanics and more math."

"Not in the movies it's not."

"You watch too much TV," Plunkett declared. "Ariel sees right through us every time. She will find out everything, and she'll want to share our time travel belt with everyone, for the good of the world. She's one of those. I am surprised she isn't here already."

Within a short second sounds came from the front door of the dorm, and one of those was Ariel's soft but indomitable knock.

CHAPTER THREE

Friday late afternoon, but before
Ariel's knock on the dorm room door. In
which we meet Ariel the erstwhile PHY
but now PSY major and her roommate
Nancy the resident wordsmith.

Ariel was a serious student, with a detail-oriented and process-loving scientific bent. Her interests had changed with her academic majors: from tadpoles, to chosen-ciphertext security, to astronomical spectroscopy, and finally to psychology.

And, thereby, people. The odder the better. She was naturally insightful into human nature and behavior, she found. The odder the better. And for as long as she could remember she felt she understood the motivations and inner conflicts of others. She did not feel sympathy, empathy, or any emotional attachment to subjects under observation. These instincts grew over time from curiosity to a hobby, and were refined as part of her formal study as a transfer to the university's already overcrowded but well-regarded Psychology department.

Applemon was an inspiration, knees-knocking perspiration aside, so that Ariel was doubly driven to be as successful in theoretical psychology as Applemon was in theoretical physics. The two had dated, for a short time, and the tempest was on the campus' collective lips for a short time.

So she knew all three brothers well, growing closer to them over her past two years at the college, initially jealous of Plunkett's time with Applemon, of his access to the great man. The relationship between those eldest two seemed typical enough on the surface: an overachiever, his average and jealous younger brother sent by parents to try and follow the role model lead.

Ariel's research exposed that the two underling, younger brothers and their lack of accomplishment moved and originated in dynamic and fascinating ways. While one couldn't say that Ariel *enjoyed* watching the two never-will-bes (her word) within their odd, schlubby, mediocre world, their typical extended adolescence and silly immaturity, their frat-boy mentality that mixed with lonerism and loserism (her words), she did find it fascinating and worth watching in the shadow of the great and handsome (her word) Applemon.

Others, all and any others, did not find Woby and Plunkett all that interesting.

Professor Chatterton was her unofficial but personal guide. The man—whom his inner circle called Aris, simply, oddly, Aris—had numerous advanced degrees, like Applemon, though he was a decade older, stiffer, and considered by students to be much less cool. Their interests, at the cutting edge of advanced physics, made them rivals, bitter ones in fact. Aris was on a par with Applemon in the eyes of all the illustrious faculty, though, again, was definitely not as cool.

The evening of Woby's first, risky, unproductive time traveling, Ariel was putting the finishing touches on a report, a presentation for her professors that sought approval for continued study of the brothers. It outlined the psychological framework behind the observable behavior of all three men, alone and in their varying social combinations, what Ariel sought to achieve, and why it was worthwhile as research.

She called it: "Three Star Constellation: Close Patterns Among the Mentally Distant," this after rejecting numerous alternatives such as "Brilliant, Mediocre and Plain Stupid," "Genius Imperfectly

Copied," "Big Shoes for Tiny Feet," "Same Roots, Different Leaves," "Psychoneuroimmunologicality Done One Syllable at a Time" and "Epic Versus Not—Parallel Subconscious Processes."

Ariel's roommate Nancy offered her own title: "Communication by a Disgusting Type of Mental Allorubbing: Why Woby and Plunkett are Not Worth the Time." It summed up what others thought about Ariel's strange hobby.

At Ariel's dorm room desk was a gentle light, a very small plant, fanned out folders, and her laptop glowing with the bulleted text of the major points of her presentation.

Behind her was a similar scene: Nancy, at her own desk, clicking away in short bursts on her own device, and in between returning to thoughtful study over the book in her lap.

Quietly, Ariel rose, undoing her long, sleek, midnight-black hair from its ponytail, shaking and scratching at it, and with a few deft manipulations returning it to a tidy, tight braid. Her bare feet then shuffled quietly to the clean, orderly kitchen to make some green tea. Everything on the counter and within drawers and cabinets and nooks and spaces sat in its place—tea kettle, tea bags, teacups, and teaspoons—so that she made her drink with simple movements that sustained the silence. There was only the peaceful waterfall from the spout and the short clicks of opening and closing to disturb the air.

Teacup in hand, Ariel sat over a printout of her presentation, swishing her spoon in the cup and her eyes over her work. Nancy came to join her, removing her eyeglasses and rubbing her eyes—and stifling a yawn.

"Almost done?" Ariel asked, getting a nod from Nancy. "I am, too. I'm going to head over to Plunkett's."

"Oh god, why?" Nancy said, her voice betraying that the last thing she herself would want after a long day would be a night with Plunkett, and where Plunkett was, Woby might be.

"They're up to something—something that might affect my work," Ariel said. Nancy sighed, ugged, and snorted, but Ariel continued. "I call them 'sophomoric semiotic signals': when something starts, when the boys are up to something that copies an Applemon pattern. That is what my research is about: how they mimic and how it morphs. It starts as a small signal, an idea, an accident, it could be anything. I got a definite signal from Woby before. If this is a good one, it is just in time to get into my presentation."

Ariel poured Nancy some tea and offered her a comb.

"Thanks—that bad?" Nancy asked, referring to her own long and curly, thick, black hair, which she immediately began to tame with the comb.

"You going for beehive?" Ariel said.

"Ha, no." Nancy answered, then refocused. "Are you sure you want to use those guys for your work?" she went on. "It's kind of strange, like creepy. What kind of signal?"

"A clear signal, check this out: Woby texted before and said, '*What's up?*' and then immediately followed with questions about time travel, out of nowhere, asking what I knew about it-"

"Yeah?" Nancy interjected, resting her combing arm and allowing the wisps steaming tea refresh face and eyebrows. She sipped loudly.

"Yeah, and," Ariel continued, "specifically he was wondering whether it would make someone grow old and if it was legal."

"He's a little, uh…you know…not an idiot, but…" Nancy was a nice person, an English major who believed that words and their proper use and accuracy were important. She often struggled to satisfy both qualities.

"Oh, he's an idiot," Ariel offered helpfully.

"He probably got it mixed up with something he saw on TV or in a video game or in a cloud."

"Nuh-uh," Ariel shook her head slowly, keeping her hair steady, "no. That's the point, this was a strong signal—note how specific he was with those questions, as if this was something he was, well… with anyone else you would call it pondering…" Nancy laughed into her next sip of tea as Ariel went on exuberantly. "And that ties to my research in two ways. One: When Woby tries to do any deep thinking it is a very subconscious thing, he can't control it. And Two: Applemon's last two lectures were about non-unitary physics and closed timelike curves."

Nancy assumed that these things had to do with the science of time machines and so she immediately took the point and agreed that this was a good case to support Ariel's theory. It was perhaps a parallel fantasy, as Ariel called it, where Applemon did something, and then the younger brothers reshaped it into something moronic, as Ariel called it. Nancy still searched for nice, but correct, terminology.

"I am not saying your research isn't right," Nancy said, "it's just that your subjects are, you know, underachievers. And messy. And are your motives, you know, in the right place?"

"Oh my god, this again?" Ariel laughed, but it had become boringly repetitive, Nancy's constant revisiting of Ariel's rocky breakup with Applemon, her decision-making during it and since. "Listen, Aris says this is viable, so it has nothing to do with Applemon. Okay?"

"Studying Applemon and the two dilatorily-witted, bovine-brained gaping-apes he has for brothers has nothing to do with Applemon?"

"No. It's viable," Ariel repeated, ending with a loud sip from her cup.

"Says Professor Chatterton?"

"Aris. Yes."

"Aris, sorry. The same Aris who encouraged you to change majors, was there to help you and guide you, and become your new crush? A new crush but only as in a 'let's see if my old crush notices' kind of way? Apple hasn't noticed, and neither has Aris, right?"

Ariel shook her head through a half-smile. "What do you have against Aris?" she asked. "You don't like anyone I, um, like. Lately."

Nancy laughed, backing off a little, Ariel appeared dejected, despondent, and depressed, and Nancy did not want that—the girl might change majors again and bring the aquariums of mud back into their dorm.

"Sorry," Nancy said, "I like Aris, I'm just looking out for you, you know that. He's a little old, and I—as a language expert—do not like the way he talks."

"Well, give him credit, the guy's a genius."

"Yeah but," Nancy explained, "he has an impressive vocabulary, but he chooses terms at random, from what I can tell. It's as if he could care less about them, the words, and it's all fake. Same way he is with people, from what I heard, that's all. I always take that as a bad sign. The way people treat animals and words says a lot about them."

"And you think Plunkett is weird?" Ariel smiled, but her head sank. "What else do people say?"

"Sorry, Ariel," Nancy resumed, milder in tone. "Nothing. I'm being protective, you know. I just see that your other psych-major friends get to be around mice and monkeys. These guys are the worst of both… do you really have to go there tonight? Get so close to them?"

"Yes," Ariel resigned, clanking down her cup and rising.

"Will Applemon be there?" Nancy teased, as Ariel wandered off to her bedroom to pick out a change of clothes.

"I hadn't thought of that. At all." Ariel said, coming back with a nice sweater, perhaps her nicest, as Nancy knew well. "I need to pursue this. Woby's clear and probably completely subconscious sophomoric semiotic signal is an early psychotic projection of their warped understanding. I need it documented."

"Their understanding of what?" Nancy asked.

"Of that insufferably callous jerk's, I mean, *Applemon's*, latest work," Ariel added. "The mention of such a sci-fi notion as time travel makes it a juicy one, too, uncharacteristically complex. Usually Woby and Plunkett only constellate with very homologous connections to their older brother's inferior lysic archetypes." At this point Ariel was talking as much to the nearby mirror as to Nancy.

"English version please…" the roommate said.

"The boys usually do simple, obvious things. Like when that thoughtless, single-minded, headstrong scoundrel, I mean Applemon, was publishing his paper on supernova heat diffusion, I heard that Plunkett had Woby stay in the sun all day, until sunburnt sufficiently, so he could peel him."

"And Professor Chatterton—sorry, *Aris*—thinks this is worthwhile? You sure?"

"He thinks it might be my big chance to…" Ariel sputtered, "… make a name for myself."

"Big chance to impress Applemon, and upstage him? And Aris would love that for how many reasons? Are any of them *good* reasons?"

"Oh my god," came Ariel's familiar refrain, "you could never be a psychiatrist, jumping to so many unwarranted conclusions and seeing only the worst in everyone, and only their top layer. In fact, Aris believes in me, and these were all my decisions, he only helped me a little in fact. I told him my ideas, and he said…"

Ariel winked at Nancy who accepted the invitation to lighten the mood.

"Do it! Do the voice!" Nancy enthused.

For her roommate's enjoyment, Ariel adopted a deep, leathery voice, pulling her chin inward and neckward for effect, and boomed, "'Yes, yes, superb! More of the inchoate, fluvial dreamings of the young brothers! Follow them, Ariel, follow! This improves on the usual pro tedio publico twaddle that passes for psychological research today! Toothsome! Neat! No slatterns here! You will make your mark!'"

"He should be shot at dawn, every dawn." Nancy said. "The man tortures my favorite language. Did you tell him about the time travel, this latest, dopey 'signal' from Woby?"

"Nope. But he'll love it."

Nancy scoffed amicably but shook her head for so long that Ariel mistook it as disapproval of her own hair now being styled up.

"And," Ariel went on, reshaping her raven-feather tresses with a more than typical fuss. "I don't think anyone's ever studied multidisciplinary underachievers from this standpoint before."

"There's a reason," Nancy answered, nodding now in approval to Ariel's choice of top and hairstyle. "You shouldn't get too close.

The boys are going to think you like them, you know, romantically. You're using them, also, you know, which isn't very nice."

"Only in the way a biologist uses flowers or something. Come on, it's so interesting! Look at how much Freudian and Jungian context there is, so much inflated individuation, so much classic psychoidal typology, if you know where to look."

"Yeah, in empty beer bottles and in the holes of T-shirts...." Nancy spoke loudly; Ariel left to go to her room and soon returned with competing garments: gray pants versus a skirt that blazed with color.

"That's the point." Ariel said. "Woby and Plunkett are alive and real and in the present and melded with their surroundings. I admit, most of the rest is 'Spongebobian.' Don't laugh, this could be my PhD dissertation."

Nancy giggled and pointed to the skirt, voting for it, as Ariel nodded unanimously. It went without saying, and therefore without arguing, that she hoped to run into Applemon at the boys' dorm.

Ariel draped the skirt carefully across the back of a kitchen chair, walked to her desk, and returned with one of the colorful pages of her presentation. "Look," she said to the bleary-eyed Nancy, who did not want to look, but rather to shower, or perhaps just go to bed.

She looked. On the page were brightly graphic concentric circles. Ariel began a practiced narration, adopting her most professorial lecture voice: "If you were to cut Plunkett or Woby open," she began as Nancy winced, "there would be layers—"

"And it would smell like eel—"

"Stop." Ariel tilted her head to ensure, via guilt, her audience's seriousness. "Say the first layer is their consciousness, like an outer skin, the part the normal people like us see and converse with." Ariel indicated the page at appropriate times and in the right places on the circles. "Once you get to know Woby and Plunkett..."

"Nope." Nancy said.

"Stop! I'm trying to practice!" Ariel said and went on. "You'll find a layer under that where there's evidence of failures, psychological scars that are close to the surface, the results of excessive daydreaming or mental mishaps. Another mental layer deep are the artifacts that were pushed down and repressed, deeply unconscious memories of unsuccessful attempts at sports, guitar, photography, sales jobs of four different consumer products, the desire to be famous for being famous, and a whole layer dedicated to misunderstanding social relationships, especially sexual ones."

"Typical college males," Nancy replied, "What's to study? Did Professor Behmen approve this?"

"Yes," Ariel said emphatically. "Well," she added not emphatically, "he didn't not approve it."

"Uh-huh. And Barfield?"

"Yes, and he's more important." Ariel handed her paper to Nancy. "In fact, he actually suggested that I get more into the games they play, to look at them as an unconscious communication mechanism; very encouraging. I like Barfield, he's very smart, and-"

"What games?" Nancy interrupted, "What do you mean? Games-games?"

"Well, yeah, sort of. This is where the in-the-field research pays off."

"Gross."

"I know, but they're known to sit in their underwear and release spiders from a jar and see who moves first. On windy days they spit in Russian-roulette-determined directions. Another one is a solitaire game called 'Where'd my sneeze land?' And their use of social networks is a whole treasure trove of odd behavior. Can you imagine their followers?"

"Nope." Nancy said.

"Fascinating, isn't it?"

Nancy checked twice, but saw that Ariel was indeed serious.

"It's either groundbreakingly original," Nancy said, "or you are one of them. But good luck, and don't ask me for help." She handed the paper back to Ariel, adding, "And 'marsupialic' is a nice try, but not a word. Otherwise, it looks good, I suppose."

"I'll look it up. Thanks. I have to get over to their dorm. I'm sure they're up to something!"

"Okay, but please, please keep a straight head? And call me?"

"Yes, I will. And that reminds me: We got a call about the phone bill. I paid it but there was some warning about breaking the contract, or something. We might have to switch it back to your name."

CHAPTER FOUR

> Friday night. In which Ariel witnesses
> a third trip, to a future with a "cause."

At the dorm room door, Ariel's reflection winked at her from the oval of her small handheld mirror. She replaced the mirror into its proper pocket within her bag. She knew when she looked pretty. She knew when she is smart. She readied herself for the possibility of seeing Applemon, the object of an ever-changing, conflicting expanse of varied affections, and seeing Woby and Plunkett, the subjects of her research.

She knocked with a trill of cascading knuckles.

"Yeah?" came Plunkett's cracking voice in answer, "Who is it?"

"It's Ariel," a sure voice answered, another round of taps accompanying.

"Damn it! I knew it!" Plunkett whispered to Woby in a hoarse, threatening growl. "You—"

"I didn't tell her anything, I told you," Woby whispered. "Let's ask for her help though, come on."

"No!" Plunkett snarled. "Take the belt and the box and go hide in Apple's room. Get in there. I'll get rid of her! Don't come out."

Woby had never known Plunkett to get rid of Ariel until he was already rid of himself. "Yeah, right. I know you won't." Ten years prior this would have been expressed, actually sung, like so: *Plunkett loves Ariel! Plunkett loves Ariel!*

"Yes, I will," Plunkett said in defense, "this is more important than her. She's old news." Plunkett was convincing nobody. He shoved the unwieldy belt and the clunkily cubic metal box into his brother's arms, but Woby stood his ground.

"Come on...tell her. She can help."

"No." Plunkett tried, but realized, as more knocks struck the door, resolute rhythmic knocks, that he would have to make a deal. "Fine, Woby. We'll try the future next, and we'll both go. Just let me get rid of her for now." His words were amiable but inexorable whispers aimed at Woby's ears as the latter was shoved into Applemon's bedroom. "Get in there. Don't come out unless a fireman tells you to."

With Woby away and quiet—which took a horrible extra few seconds as timed by the incessant door banging—Plunkett returned to a counter stool and said, "Alright, come in."

Ariel entered the dorm, where few overachievers had tread more than once. She adjusted to the dirty sock climate with an expression of disgust as she looked, listened, and sniffed around.

"It always smells like reheated something in here," she observed— not as a scientist, but as a woman—and entered the kitchen area.

"Hey, Ariel, what's up?" Plunkett said with fooling-nobody enthusiasm. "Woby's not here. Did you just want me? Need me for anything?" Plunkett offered with helpfulness, fooling nobody. "Uh...want a drink? Diet Coke? Beer? Hey—I think we actually have some wine..."

"And from what fruit, I wonder?" Ariel said. "No thanks. I was just in the neighborhood. What are you doing? Anything interesting?" Ariel wandered about, led by her widening eyes, observing small and large evidence.

"Wobe's not here," Plunkett said again. "I was just going to go out, probably to the student union. Wanna come?"

There came a racket, some bumbling, rustling, shuffling noises from Applemon's room, then some wheezing, and then silence. Plunkett had to engage in a plain-face-to-pretty-face stare-down contest with Ariel that lasted a few awful, dreadful, painful seconds. He lost.

"Applemon's here?" she asked, feathery black eyebrows afloat.

"No, no one," Plunkett answered. "I haven't seen Applemon in a while. Woby's not here, either."

"Yeah, you said that, greater-than-or-equal-to three times. Come on, what are you guys up to?" With this Ariel walked determinedly toward Applemon's bedroom door. With a quick couch leap and adroit slide Plunkett was able to arrive himself between door and girl.

"Okay," he said, blocking her gaze toward the bedroom where Woby lay noisily hidden, "I know Woby was asking you funny questions, but you know how he is." Ariel looked at him, her eyes a laser, her aspect overwhelming. Within a second, Plunkett continued with, "Okay, he wanted to ask you something, but it's nothing, and he's not here." Ariel looked at him for another hour-long second, and Plunkett countered, "Okay, he is up to something, you're right. But it's nothing, and I don't know what it is, and he's not here…"

Given that Plunkett had effectively now melted into a puddle of weak, foundationless ooze, Ariel easily walked around him/it and knocked on Applemon's bedroom door.

Plunkett lifted his arms in surrender, and mumbled a frustrated, "Fine, whatever," knowing that she would find Woby, and she would be told everything.

"Applemon? Are you here?" Ariel said at the door. There was no response. "Woby? I got your texts, did you see my mine? Hello? Anyone in there? I know there is. I'm coming in." There was no response. She looked at Plunkett while she turned the doorknob to enter, and Plunkett repeated his arms up surrendering motion and moved to the kitchen, annoyed and defeated.

Ariel entered. Plunkett cracked a Diet Coke.

But then Ariel came out, silent and alone.

She and Plunkett looked at each other, both confused; this was not another contest of wills, however. Both their faces were arching in question marks.

Then! Woby entered—staggered—through the front door. He was carrying the time machine belt in front of him, covering his wide midsection. *"Don't look!"* he shouted. His knees buckled; the belt dropped to the floor. He used both his hands on walls and furniture to accomplish a banging zigzag toward, and into, Applemon's room.

Ariel and Plunkett obeyed, and turned away, still looking at each other with angled eyes and peripheral confusion. Ariel was still considering the empty bedroom she had entered, what the noises might have been, and what might have caused Woby's distressed entrance.

And behind them both, they heard the young adventurer emerge. *"Don't look!"* he shouted again, and another door slammed, that of the bathroom.

Out Woby came once more—*"Don't look!"*—and bumped his way onto a couch where Ariel and Plunkett watched him land and lie and pull a blanket over himself.

They did not turn away.

"Keep don't looking!" Woby shouted.

"What?" Ariel asked, in summary. In fact she wanted to know the answers to many whats.

"Shit," Plunkett said, in summary. Things were not going well on many levels.

"What happened to him?" Ariel asked Plunkett.

"Einstein only knows," Plunkett answered, still clinging to some hope that he could keep the truth secret from Ariel. "Can we call you later?"

"No." Ariel stepped to the couch and gently shook Woby by the shoulder. "Woby? Are you okay? What happened?"

Woby did not look at her, he was gazing far away in space and time. He spoke in fits and starts. "I don't know." Fit. Start. "I tried to get to…" Stop. Start. "…a few minutes ago…" Stutter. Fit. Start. "…so I wouldn't have to hide." Only then did he move, lifting his face up toward Ariel's. "You need to help us."

Woby sounded so earnest, so weak, so pleading, that Ariel actually moved her face away a few inches in a search for words to match the emotion.

"Pfff...drunk again," Plunkett lied. "So sad."

Ariel ignored Plunkett. "What are you talking about, Woby?" she asked gently. "Tell me."

"It's okay," Woby answered, "it's a time machine. But I went to the future this time."

At this Plunkett almost spit out his Diet Coke and wished he had since instead it sought and found many an interesting internal route.

*The future...*Plunkett mused, and washed his Diet Coke down with Diet Coke, swallowing hard. He moved to the couch next to Ariel and directly above Woby the unpredictable, chubby explorer *par excellence*. The two brothers stared at each other, Plunkett with refreshed interest.

"Really?" Plunkett burst out. "Awesome! Awesome. What happened?"

"No. It's horrible." Woby bent his midsection to force the choppy syllable up to his brother.

"How famous am I?" Plunkett persisted.

"Pretty famous. How did you know?"

"Destiny. Told you." Plunkett said, and added sidelong to Ariel, "Never told *you*." And he tried to wink.

Ariel grimaced, then refocused. "What's going on? What are you talking about?" In her mind were many scenarios, and all of them held deep psychological meaning; this could be a goldmine of discoveries. Was this a brotherly-paired hallucination? A fantasy game? A hypnagogic dreamworld? A regression to a twilight reverie recalled from mental infancy? Do they believe it? Is it drug-related, or, more likely, mold-related?

Woby answered as best he could, calming by the second. He tried to sound reassuring. "It's okay, it's okay," he said, "but I'm not going back there."

Plunkett injected himself as Ariel got tangled in her own rampaging thoughts. "Get back to it," he directed Woby, "why am I famous?"

"We're both famous."

"And rich?" Plunkett asked. His delight visibly carbonated.

"Well, sort of…" Woby answered Plunkett, but with quick round-trip eye movements toward Ariel.

"Just tell it. I don't care if she knows." Plunkett burped.

"We are famous donors," was Woby's reply, "apparently we donated a few hundred billion to *The Cause*." 'The Cause' was emphasized strangely, stiltedly, in the young man's voice. *The Cause*.

"The Cause…The Cause?" Plunkett mused, scratching his chin with the possibilities. "Billions? That's a good number, give or take… that left me with how much, then?" he asked, but quickly added, "Was I dying?" The future was wide open, and Plunkett's analysis was developing fast.

"No, I don't think so," his brother answered. "But you don't understand, we had to. We had to donate. It's a different world." Woby looked away from Plunkett's intense face and added lamely "They looked at me…"

Plunkett said to Ariel, "He seems to have a problem with that every trip we take."

"Trip?" Ariel asked slowly, processing Plunkett's choice of words. "To where?"

"Not *where*. *When*." Plunkett said.

"Don't worry, it's a time machine," Woby said, bobbling his head like those aptly named dolls do. To Plunkett he said, "I saw that girl again. She said something to me and then ran."

"Geez, usually they don't run until you speak," Plunkett said.

"Haha, but she was being followed, she called me 'penthos,' like wondering if that was my name, 'Penthos'…or maybe it was where she was going? I don't know."

"Forget her, it's a hallucination, how much money did I—" Plunkett began, but Ariel, PSY major, pounced on the term.

"You said he was time traveling. Why do you say hallucinating now?" she asked.

"He can do both," Plunkett answered. "He's a whiz. Forget it, Woby, just rest and let me think."

Ariel retrieved her pen to write with, but failed to find something to write on that wasn't cardboard or wet.

"Penthos…" Woby mumbled repeatedly.

"Hm," Plunkett joined him. "Maybe it was pantyhose? Or penthouse? Yes! That makes sense, see? This is excellent. Finally a decent standard of living for us."

"I don't know, I don't know." Woby looked forlornly at Ariel, but the blankness of her stare scared him so he looked back at Plunkett. "And there were others, those guys, you know, the fat ones, the quiet ones, all in purple. Happy ones."

Plunkett and Ariel looked at each other, eyebrows going up, then down, then across, and back.

Woby said impatiently, "you know; they chant and cross their legs in purple. They were following her, and he was following them."

"Who?" Plunkett asked. Ariel nodded slowly in solidarity, so slowly in fact that it was not perceptible. "He who?"

"A guy, he looked familiar, I tried to follow him to see why they were all following each other. But the girl from the past! And a guy from nowadays! But it was so far in the future! It makes no sense. They would be dead."

Woby joined the others in some quiet time. Then, just as Ariel finished her nod, he blurted, "Buddhists!"

Ariel burst free from her many interweaving thoughts. "Why didn't I bring my laptop!" She directed Plunkett to retrieve a some paper.

"Here, use my notebook, add to my notes," Plunkett replied. "If you're going to know, you might as well help. Help the future rich men." Plunkett tried to wink again, this time with his other eye.

Ariel began jotting words furiously, but soon was distracted and overcome by the snatches of Plunkett's own scribbles on the page.

They described time travel planning tips, like those one might find on an internet vacation-planning website. Examples were, *"Bring extra towels,"* and *"Convert to local currencies beforehand,"* and *"Make sure to try the local music scene,"* and *"Bring Jimi Hendrix bio."*

While Ariel digested this content, Plunkett was continuing to debrief a Diet Coke-refreshed Woby.

"Now, Woby—my man!—forget about the guy and the girl and the yogis and tell most importantly why I gave my money away."

"Man, it's really weird there." Woby sat up. "We weren't very old, or dying, but you have to give everything to"—here Woby changed his voice again—"*The Cause.* But I never figured out what that was. I came back after an hour."

"An hour?" Ariel asked.

"Not AUNT, an hour my time I mean, not the here and now but the there and then." Woby said, and unpacked the acronym, their abbreviation for the collective point of view, to Ariel's delight and fascination,

"Wow," she said, and wrote, and began a page of glossary notes.

"Don't distract him," Plunkett said. "Keep going, Woby. What else?"

"Yeah, more," Woby continued to his brother. "There was statue of us. This campus is some sort of headquarters named after us, too."

"Okay, that doesn't sound too bad, at least things are cushy. I want to go see…" and Plunkett stood up straight and strong looked as if he literally wanted to put on the belt and leave at that very instant.

"No! You don't! It was our turn to plough. I'm telling you," Woby implored, "there's a lot you need to know. It was our turn. Everyone takes turns, everyone's equal."

"Why would a billionaire need to plough!?"

"Uh—they tried to explain it me—it was a big word—" Woby stammered.

"That's horrible…" but then Plunkett stood up straight and strong again, saying "No—you screwed it up. That can't be right."

"I agree, it's impossible. The guy I followed was following the Buddhists and the girl, and he said something about Apple."

"Applemon?" Ariel leapt up. "What? What guy?"

"Tall, skinny guy, dressed like for work at a library, had a bowtie, a blue one. No moustache but it looked like he should have one. Might have been wearing shoes."

"We have to work on your observational detail," Plunkett said. "Next time take a video, like I'm going to."

"Okay, but no. It can't be right," Woby said.

"No, it can't be…" Ariel agreed from far away. Was it Aris he was talking about?

"Like I said, Woby must have screwed something up. We can do better."

Woby replied with a surprising and plunging earnestness that drew Ariel's attention. "You need to let it go. Trust me," Woby said directly into his brother's eyes.

"Look, Woby, I need to find out for myself…" Plunkett began, but Woby's face twitched with concern.

"Please!" Woby almost begged. "Don't go. Why do you have to go? Is this a midlife crisis or something?"

"What?" Plunkett asked.

"Forget it," Woby answered.

There passed a few minutes of silence as each of the three considered their futures: Ariel's one of astounding psychological discoveries and a career that overshadowed that of her yet-to-be-determined husband; Plunkett's of undonated billions; and Woby's of a safe stay in the present for all—or, at worst, the recent past.

Plunkett looked up *penthos* with his phone, but did not share with Woby its possible meanings or applicability.

Then, looking up from the notebook, Ariel, pen between fingers and legs crossed in earnestness, asked, "What is all this, do you think? Can you explain what it means, Woby, and how you feel right now? Also…" She walked over to the belt. It lay on the floor where Woby had dropped it while Ariel and Plunkett were don't-looking.

She handled it like a sack of laundry. "Do you believe that this is Applemon's? That he made it?"

Plunkett found her attitude impertinently disrespectful. Ariel was mistreating his ticket to a better, more deserving, more dictatorial life. He relieved her of the belt, though he was careful not to put his hands near the buttons nor his waist within its dangling, open perimeter.

"We don't believe it, we know it." Plunkett replied. "Why?"

"And that, using it, you can travel through time?" Ariel continued.

"Yes!" Woby squeaked. "Oh yes."

"Perfect." Ariel said calmly, aloud, but to herself.

Plunkett spoke heroically, or thereabouts. "But Woby keeps screwing it up. I'm going next. I want to see what's going on. What's *going to* go on."

"This is great." Ariel said calmly, aloud, but to herself.

Woby rose fully from the couch. "Ariel—help. Tell Plunkett he can't use it anymore. We've tried, and time travel is more complicated than it sounds."

"Yeah. Listen…" Ariel began. She was thinking briskly and thinking like a psychiatrist. Her plan was to go along with this fantasy, whatever it meant, yet still try to control it, to slow it down, to isolate it from their other cerebral defects. In this way she would study it, carefully, and in hilarious but scientifically sound detail.

She spoke in a kindly voice. "The continuum of spacetime is not something that is easily dealt with. The latest theoretical physics show that time itself might not exist the way we think, and Holographic-String Theory also seems to indicate…"

During these sentences, and more, all of which might as well have been in a Swahili braille sign-language dialect over semaphore flags, Plunkett walked over to the couch, sat, swung his legs around, stretched, lay down, and turned on the television via remote—all in one complete motion like a practiced gymnast, ignoring Ariel. Rude, and yet too ignorant to consciously be so.

Ariel adjusted her lecture and focused anew on Woby, continuing her exposition on Lorentz transformations, Bohm coherence, and the physical and philosophical difficulties of using a time-travel device, concluding with "…and so unless there is a perfect vacuum, Einstein's cosmological constant might come into play unexpectedly."

She had run out of things to say, and though still thinking on her feet was anxious to further her analytical study in a more clinical, clean setting.

"So don't do anything until I get back," she said. "Okay? Promise me. Woby! Promise me."

Woby came out of his faraway state, having heard words he knew. "I promise," he said. And walked away.

Ariel moved over to Plunkett and couch and addressed them as one.

"You. Promise. Do it. Or I will tell everybody." Her tone was direct and firm, and Plunkett apparently liked it and the fact that he could have such an effect on Ariel. "You need to listen to me," she went on, "I'll keep this between us only if you let me help you. Otherwise you're going to kill yourselves or do worse harm to the planet, the human race, or the universe." Truly, she was thinking, they could do harm only to their own sanity, if it wasn't too late already.

"Impressed, huh?" Plunkett offered.

There was then a blast of background noise. Woby was vacuuming, inexplicably.

"Promise me. Say it, " Ariel pressed Plunkett. Woby came nearer, bumping the couch as he worked.

Plunkett had to yell over the sucking, motorized din. "Fine, yes, I promise!" he said with a smarmy voice and the smarmiest of looks.

Ariel's mind was racing with plans and ideas that she had to organize. She left in a hurry, but it was obvious she would soon be back.

"She loves me," Plunkett said.

Woby shut off the vacuum. "Yeah? She is popular, she has that retro sub-goth done-punk look."

"Dude, she's Swedish geek-chic pruppy-Asian, if anything." The two exchanged blank stares for a moment, like they had done almost daily since they were, physically, kids.

To Woby's surprise Plunkett sprang up, dangled the belt on one forearm, and resumed his energetic excitement. "And she's wrong!" he announced. "Let's go! Where's the box?"

"In Applemon's room. Go where?" Woby asked.

"When! Go *when*? you should ask. Go *when*, young man!" Plunkett declared. "They used to have room out west, but it's not 'go west' anymore, it's go when!" Plunkett declared, and almost raised his finger to the air.

"Oh. No—didn't you hear all that stuff Ariel said? She's right. We need help."

"All bogus, everything she said. Watch this." And Plunkett practically danced off to Applemon's room and practically skipped back, holding the box.

"No, please, I'm too tired." Woby moaned. He leaned against the couch.

Plunkett selected the demeanor wherein he knew he could rule over Woby, and knew he was better at it than Ariel. He spoke.

"It was bad 'cause you went alone. We'll both go, like I said before. Apparently we made big money between now and then, an important point that you and Ariel-the-Wise both missed. We were rich in the future. How far ahead was that?" Plunkett asked rhetorically and looked at the dial on the belt for an answer. "Looks like two hundred or so years, according to the setting. But the rest you must have screwed up. Or maybe," he reached for a few chin hairs, indicating a shift into deep contemplation, "that's the future with you and Ariel in charge. Yeah, that's it." He looked back directly at Woby, who did look very tired. "Let's do it my way. I'm the captain here now. Hear that, future?" Plunkett yelled to the sky, though the future was not that way, it was actually straight ahead.

"Okay—you'll see," Plunkett continued, moving a step closer to his brother. Then another step. "Watch how much better it is going to be…." With a third step, he whipped one end of the belt out to lasso, partially, Woby's large waist, and timed that move with a firm press on the green button.

CHAPTER FIVE

> Friday night. In which Ariel updates
> Nancy on her research breakthrough:
> that Woby and Plunkett are
> hallucinating about time travel. Nancy
> implores Ariel not to obsess. Aris,
> Ariel's new mentor and love interest,
> is impersonated. Ariel goes back to the
> dorm after promising not to.

Ariel—serious, intent psychology student—typed, her fingers a ten-person ballet on the tiny keyboard tiles.

"Plunkett is not unattractive. Woby is not unduly large. Plunkett is not wholly underachieving. Woby is not completely unintelligent. Woby is not unaware of how others perceive him. Plunkett is not undertly anti-social..."

She sat with tiring but correct posture at her silvery and simple laptop. Both her and her machine were centered on the desk, papers placed in parallel, the chair in its slot between symmetric drawers, and two plants straight in two rectangular pots at the corners. Tired and starting to slack, she adjusted her position *twice*, and the tea-containing coffee mug *once*, so that its handle would also align satisfactorily.

It was Friday night, her mind was on her subjects, Plunkett and Woby, and not on relaxation or ease or partying.

Her ideas were coming a million a minute, and from brain to digits her nervous system struggled to coordinate a consistent rhythm with which to stream her thoughts to the page with any consistent fluency.

There was also a growing to-do list. One task was to email Professor Barfield to arrange to meet and to ask his advice on getting more time so that she could expand on her original research ideas, the ideas that Aris loved, but Barfield had to approve. She was sure that he would; the psychological oceans that Woby and Plunkett were now swimming in ran much deeper than she ever expected. There was a lot to investigate.

In the brothers' minds—or their integrated one-mind as it sometimes seemed—they believed they were time traveling. They had taken a concurrent course alongside Applemon's latest super-advanced and world-class work, which was a true study into the theoretical limits wormholing within the bounds of proper and real physics. But the two slackers childishly competed with their— here she crossed out emendations like "wonderful but self-absorbed and selfish and callous"—older brother in a fantasy-world only. The simple ideas and naïve approach to time travel came out of their sad and shaggy heads.

And: Note how they could not even do it right….

Even after their psyches removed the physical impossibility and obvious paradoxes by inventing a lame device—a belt! Why not suspenders?—they still failed to succeed, and succeeded to fail. How telling….

New handwritten notes flew all over the printed pages. She would need extra time to do all the experiments, and psychoanalysis, required to fully understand the many dynamics of the boys' psychotic relationships. She listed those hurriedly across the clean yellow prairie of new notepad pages.

Her efforts should have warranted extra credits toward a degree, perhaps even served to replace her remaining coursework, a rare dispensation that required even more approval from even high higher-ups than Barfield, but Ariel smirked with the knowledge that with Professor Chatterton's—Aris'—help, she would get everything she wanted.

But what about Applemon? Ariel wondered how much she could directly involve her ex, knowing that he and Aris were rivals. Yet Applemon's input and cooperation were key to the whole project. She needed to interview him, dig further into his relationship with his younger brothers, whom she assumed were an embarrassment to him, though, to her recollection, he never spoke of them in such terms. But she knew not to presume anything; she needed to proceed only empirically. *Who knows? Maybe the three brothers all feed off each other somehow, and maybe the older was as nuts as the younger,* she thought, *and maybe Applemon was even the reason, the impetus, the head of the snake. If not the whole snake, the jerk.*

She then emended away her personal feelings with a stiff smile, accompanied by a vision of her ignoring Applemon as he stood in line to congratulate her on her third Nobel Prize. His clothes looked ragged. Were the rumors of his heartbreak and mental collapse true?

She noticed that these words had made it onto a page, and crossed them out, ashamed, but still smiling.

Next Ariel needed to get Woby and Plunkett "on the couch" of course, to psycho-analyze them the way a psychiatrist would. Like Sigmund Freud. Or better, Carl Jung.

Tiring, and amid strengthening yawns and widening arm and finger stretches, she listed the questions she should ask, cross-referencing the therapeutic approaches and techniques in play. Should she analyze Applemon also? Did Applemon know about Aris? Would she need two couches? Ariel put her head down, but her thoughts still raced. Nancy wouldn't allow a second couch in their small dorm room, so Apple and Aris would have to duel—yes, they were both world-class and equally brilliant—but only the winner was deserving to accompany Ariel into her future house in Vienna and father her two wunderkind prodigious prodigy children, and set up book tours…

Nancy entered the dorm room. *Good thing,* Ariel thought, her eyes opening, her head jerking upright—she had fallen asleep and had even typed the equivalent of a long string of *zzzzzs* onto the drool-spotted page in front of her.

Nancy gave Ariel a look; it clearly expressed a knowing disappointment. Nancy observed immediately that her friend was mucking around with that Woby and Plunkett *stuff* instead of taking a weekend off. With uncompromising zeal she stomped to Ariel's desk and read from the laptop monitor.

"Knew it," she said, shaking her head.

"I have a call with Aris in a few seconds and was preparing. Good thing you reminded me."

"Woke you."

"Yes."

Nancy looked up from Ariel's notes. "Honey, *undertly* is not a word."

"I will change it back to *mediumness,* thanks." Ariel said.

"Don't," Nancy advised. "And can't you give this a break? Come out with us, we're going into town."

"I can't, I need to get ahead of this. It's going in new directions. You should see what they—"

"*No!* I should *not* see anything of those two. They're just plain-old goofs, irremediably so. You're wasting your brain. *And* your other attractive qualities! Focus on Applemon if you want, but leave the little boys to themselves."

Ariel took a sip of tea that had gone cold; she wanted to answer this challenge and needed energy to do so. There was so much to say in her own defense.

Nancy walked off to her own bedroom, tossing her voice—words conciliatory, offhand—over her shoulder. "I need to change. Please come with us. Let your boys play their games without you.…Did you ever pick up the laundry? I can't find my red—oh, here it is.…"

Ariel spoke as Nancy reentered. "They think they've traveled through time. Do you know what this means? This is a serious development. It takes my ideas in a whole new direction. They're exploring other consciousnesses, other points of view. This is great stuff."

"Easy," Nancy said. She did not like hyperbole, inexactness, or exaggeration. Especially using the word *great* when *sufficient* was more apt. She believed that Woby and Plunkett could not be described such a way without insulting, say, Beethoven, Newton, Wordsworth, and people like that.

Ariel changed strategy. "I need to help them. You don't understand, they really believe they have a time travel belt—"

At this Nancy laughed aloud and mumbled a small personal prayer at the end of it, but Ariel forced her way onward, and more loudly.

"*And* that the belt thing works. *And* that Woby has gone to the past *and* to the future. *They really* believe it. Even forgetting my research, they can do themselves serious psychological damage without help. They could come back with psycho-somatic smallpox or bubonic plague or something, start a pandemic. Who knows what their minds might contrive."

"Simple things only," Nancy replied, "a pimple from 1947." She was now behind Ariel and reading from the notepad on the desk.

"You don't understand," Ariel said, "you weren't there. They need help."

"Yes, that I agree with." Nancy said, then: "and *mediocrify* is not a word, though it might be by the time you are done with your patients. And replace *slackify*, too; use *vitiate* instead."

"Oh, that reminds me, what does *penthos* mean?" Ariel asked.

Nancy paused but was not stumped. "In what context? How did it come up?"

"It was in Woby's time-travel fantasy, a girl said it to him, called him that, I think like a subconscious moniker or perhaps name-letter-effect resembling-outcomes is at play here..."

"It doesn't mean anything in psycho-babble?" Nancy asked.

"No."

"Well, it actually makes sense that Woby would be called that. It's Greek, it means grief or sorrow. An appropriate first reaction to his Woby-ness. In fact, in the Euripides play, Pentheus was killed, torn apart actually, by—"

"Okay, thanks." Ariel jotted more notes. "Fascinating, right? All this from his mind?"

"Nope."

They were interrupted by a ringtone. Ariel gave a quick look at the wall mirror, moved two flumes of hair that were out of place, and rubbed her front teeth with a forefinger.

"Aris?" Nancy asked. "Or—?"

"Aris, yes. Shush! I need to get organized…" Ariel grabbed her phone, as the tone—a feathery piano melody apparently assigned to Professor Chatterton—played on.

Nancy grunted something about Ariel having to mind her own signals, was hushed, so tiptoed away over-dramatically, staying within earshot. While it was hard to listen to such fawning from her otherwise confident, driven, woman friend, Nancy increasingly knew her own role, and right now it was to eavesdrop.

First she heard a summary of the Woby/Plunkett research in Ariel's voice, and much encouragement from the older, donnish advisor, the worldly and wordy Aris.

Nancy squirmed at his responses, they seemed fake and manipulative. When told of the brothers' acts of idiocy and the fantastic yet believed time travel explanations, Aris grew audibly impressed and enthusiastic.

"Yes, yes!" Nancy heard, Aris' voice humming like a vacuum cleaner, pumping syllables as if backfiring accumulated dust, "Indeed! This is unexpected, but expected, if your insights are adding to what I think they are amassing to."

Nancy winced at the anaphoric solecism—*Take that!* she thought—while squirming at Ariel's reply: "Really? I mean, why yes, yes, I believe so, too."

When told of the Penthos moniker, self-assigned, as Ariel reported it, during Woby's psychotic episode, Aris droned in response. "Ah, of course, that is a good sign, not only the meaning..."

"It means grief, or sorrow." Ariel parroted Nancy's definition. Nancy this time squirmed while wincing, she found this physically more comfortable than the other way.

"Yes, Greek, as I am sure you know," Aris droned on, "Superb! Yet while the meaning is certainly good news..."

Nancy stopped wincing to consider why calling Woby "sorrow" would be good news, let alone "superb" news. The man lived up to Ariel's impersonations.

"...better still," Aris went on, "is the matching of semasiology with onomasiology at such an early stage of recondite entelechy. Adumbration, via aleuromancy? Or enoptromantic?" Aris asked, his voice dropping lower in tone, almost moaning.

Nancy continued to wince. She really, she decided, hated him.

Yet poor, poor Ariel had to answer, so Nancy prepared her eyebrows and stomach for a good, productive cringe. Ariel's voice rose in pitch, "Yes, I think I get it, you mean he said this intentionally?"

No, Nancy thought, *that is not what those awful words mean, you poor girl*...and she waited for a snooty correction from the word-murdering professor.

But "Yes!" Aris said, happily. "Yes, exactly! You are a natural, a wonder, a thrill and mountain-mover! You are unbolting wisdom's door! This is definitely going places. Mind-omnific! As Wordsworth famously said..."

Samuel Taylor Coleridge said that, Nancy thought, *and it made sense when he did, unlike this. What the hell is this all about?*

Aris continued. "This could be the first breakthrough on Freudian Screen Memories in many decades. Such equipoise! Keep going, Ariel. And, as I am sure you now realize, you need to, surreptitiously, watch Applemon. This is key. Keep an eye on him. But he must not know."

Nancy peeked around the hallway corner to see Ariel nodding into her cell phone and writing tempestuously. Realizing a pause however, Ariel spoke. "Yes, of course, I was thinking that. Because," she answered as if in an oral exam, "he is the lead psyche, the primary mover, the source."

"Precisely!"

"Really?" Ariel didn't mean to say.

"Inexorably!" Aris boomed. "The waggishly hapless Punklett-"

"Plunkett" Ariel corrected quietly.

"—and the haplessly waggish Wobly—"

"Woby," Ariel mouthed.

"—are derivative consciousnesses of the big consciousness. Ah, Ariel," Aris' hum softened, "this will be a degree, if not much, much more; a triumph, unless I am much, much mistaken, frontiers embowered!"

Nancy frowned tall as Ariel smiled widely.

"That is," the thrum of Aris' voice emphasized, "that is if you can do these next steps correctly, avoid dross and chimeras—and I am much, much confidently of the mind that you can. Go along: Analyze the brothers, but keep an eye, a secret eye, and both ears, on Applemon and his actions. And continue to report to me."

Nancy was much, much pissed off, and vexed, and concerned, and pissed off. Her face and torso were tired from the assault, the torture, of the word *terrorism* and the multi-levelled manipulations of meanings. She knew that Aris was brilliant, everyone knew that, but Nancy now knew that he was also full of larger brown expired beans. And he was up to something. And Ariel was falling for it.

Aris and Ariel said goodbye and goodnight—though of course, not in such simple terms. Aris in fact said, "Oh, but for superannuated diurnals, my dear! But keep to the whetstone and goad, mind your charges, though they be impalpable as minor chords—soon you will see through!"

How predicable, thought Nancy.

"Goodnight, Aris," Ariel said.

"Keep me apprised," said Aris.

The call over, Nancy entered the common room. Ariel did not look up from her desk but asked her roommate whether all of Aris' words were actually words and how some were spelled.

Nancy assisted, saying "Unlike some of yours, they are real, or they are when by themselves. But shoved together the way he does they are like mustard on a silk hat."

"Oh stop. Anyway, thanks, but I need more help." Energized, Ariel's bright eyes relentlessly beseeched Nancy, flashing rich and greyish brown like the tea within her mug—only warmer, clearer, and more inviting.

"No. Stop. That's enough. Come into town with us," Nancy replied as she walked away, away from the imploring eyes.

"I can't, this is too big. If you help, I can cover more ground, and really get into it, and—"

It was Ariel's growing grin that made Nancy interrupt. "Wait" Nancy said with an only partly mocking seriousness. "Are you enjoying this?" Nancy explained her fears: getting too close to her subjects, too comfortable with using them to achieve a man's attention, which is something that should be low on any serious student's list.

There was the chance of Ariel being hurt, again, and more of the disruption and ruin of potential, and lots of chocolate and sad, screechy songs on repeat. And in the meantime, Ariel had, in Nancy's estimation, one leg stuck in the university's social ladder and was dangling upside down with unkempt hair.

Ariel was heads-down in her notes.

"Assure me, please," Nancy bent between Ariel and her lamp-light, "that this isn't fun for you in place of real fun like drinks tonight in town with me in serious dance mode."

"Only in a scientist-on-a-new-discovery kind of way," Ariel assured, raising her face to Nancy's. "I promise. Please don't worry—unless it is about my patients. I'm fine. But there is danger here for Woby and Plunkett. Seriously, they are at the edge of an emotional precipice, and I should help them."

Nancy backed off, but something in Ariel's voice, though her words were meant to ease Nancy's concerns, rose them up with two hands and held them up high. From across the room, Nancy looked at her friend, keeping her in a telescopic gaze for a full minute. Ariel's face moved in tight circles but submitted quietly to Nancy's own analysis.

Nancy spoke. "If that is true, Ariel, then they need *professional* help. *Not* you." Nancy did not care if this insulted her roommate and said so. "If this is as serious as you are saying, then you can't analyze them yourself. Don't." This was something Nancy had read on Ariel's notepad, her desire to get the boys on "the couch".

Nancy's gaze held for a few more seconds, then relented, switched off like a prepaid phone card whose time had run out. And in that spirit, she offered, one more time, "Please come out with us tonight? We can talk more about it, and shake out a week of study at the same time with postgraduate-level hippety-hop disco moves." Seeing Ariel waver, Nancy cooed, "I won't help you unless you do," and "Come with me and I'll help you…ooo ooo ooo?" Nancy sang and teased and danced until Ariel laughed.

"No. But thanks," Ariel said. "Okay, I see what you're saying. I'll sleep on it, see what tomorrow brings."

"Yes, get some rest then. Don't do anything. Talk to Professor Barfield about it too." Nancy switched to a sufficiently low Aris-voice. "Monday your two waggishly hapless patients will still be hap-wagging with ineluctable modality! And they will still be here, and still in the present."

Nancy was soon heading out the door. "A belt!" she said and chuckled dryly. "Why not suspenders?"

Ariel returned a laugh, one whose purpose was only that Nancy should hear it.

Then she made black coffee, stuffed laptop and notes into her bag, and went back to Plunkett's dorm room.

CHAPTER SIX

Late Friday night. In which Ariel eavesdrops on text messages while awaiting Woby and Plunkett's return back, backward, to the time and place the cosmos originally assigned to them.

Plunkett is thin and yet shaggy. Woby is shaped like a capital R, or sometimes like a lowercase r.

Ariel had long ago finished the large tar-black coffee she brought to Plunkett's—and Applemon's—college dormitory room. The place was still and boy-less. She had cleared herself a work area at the kitchen counter and tinkered with her ideas for over an hour, fighting the urge to clean, and then instead fighting the urge to even look toward certain areas—corners where things generic had accumulated, under plates that might be covering life and death, inside the refrigerator. She was not into biology anymore. She forced herself to only look down at her papers or forward into the personalized themes of her laptop screen.

She was now realizing that she was too tired for quality work and that her notes, like her latest comparing her subjects to subsets of the alphabet, were getting silly.

She was too anxious to go back to her own rooms, however. She decided to stay here, perhaps sleep, and remain until Woby and Plunkett returned.

But she could not sleep.

And the thought of looking for them, around campus or in the town, troubled her, probably because of the lingering words and looks from Nancy, her friend's worry, and her friend's warnings.

Am I getting too involved in their lives? Do I really want to find what they did on Friday nights? And be seen with them, socially? Lord knows where they might be...

Ariel shut her laptop and sat in the hueless semi-darkness, listening to the intermittent energetic rumbling of footsteps in the hall and the onrush of percussive music that also vibrated the walls—and she thought about the workings of the human mind, and of her particular lab rats. Why time travel? What should she ask them when she got them on the couch? Did she have enough background? *Might I do more harm than good?*

Thoughts eddied and formed mental pools as her head slowly moved down to rest on the cool of the laptop cover, her arms enclosing all, when the noises came.

At once, a jarring and distinct rattling came from the kitchen area in front of her as musical tones flowed out from her bag and then were met by thrashing noisy chords—all sounds battling now in the air and settling over the whole dorm room.

She realized that these were awakening cell phones—hers playing piano and feminine vocals denoting that text messages were arriving, and another, as she could see now, from atop a dirty pot on the kitchen counter, bashing heavy metal guitar while also vibrating.

She checked her own as she clicked to settle the other to quiet.

Woby had texted her; it was a series of questions:

> If you see P, can u tell him to spend nu years eve home...from now on?

And:

> they don't no bout you here so can u help us?

And of course:

> How do u light a fire? from scratch

And then:

> Where do u think you might live after graduation?

And finally:

> do u think Im fat?

Ariel stared now at the other phone, Plunkett's, which was security locked. With a quick look toward the ceiling at nothing and a small demeaning chuckle, she attained his password from her mental folder of feminine instincts and then read the messages. The new ones to Plunkett were also from Woby.

> Where r u? Its cold

And:

> do u have ur phone?

And then:

> do u have ur phone?

And:

> Check this big button out

And then one more:

> do u have ur phone? if u don't then hurry and get it

But before Ariel had time to wonder about the depths of Woby's blankness or consider the first steps toward changing majors and becoming a dentist instead, there were more noises—coming from the hall, outside the door, and along the walls that led to it. Two people were coming in a clamorous panic. From the sound it might have been more than two, perhaps eleven, and might not have even been people, but three-legged large-headed zebras. Yet Ariel knew it was two and knew it was people because she knew which two people.

The boys came in through the door.

They ignored Ariel. They were shivering, their faces were wet and bluish with cold, their hair wet, their clothes had, perhaps, snow on them. Ariel returned to her stool and swerved in it to watch as Plunkett went to his room and emerged wearing a bulky sweatshirt, the hood on, rubbing his arms with his arms.

Woby went to one couch and submerged everything but his nostrils under two blankets like an overheated hippo taking to water.

Plunkett joined his brother on the couch opposite and said, "That was so confusing...." His voice was jittery, and his lungs puffed, and he rubbed his hands out in front of his body and near the flames of a comforting fire that was not there.

"Yeah," Woby answered, "but see? It is better coming in from the hall."

"Wicked weather, next time we go in June." Saying this, Plunkett looked around, searching for his pen and notebook, and only now it registered that Ariel was present, though quiet. The girl rose and walked over, light-footed, like she wanted to trade trinkets and pelts with newly met savages. She didn't speak but held out Plunkett's unlocked phone to him.

"How did you get on my phone? You know my password?" Plunkett said to her, coming back to the present time and place and his usual, itch-just-out-of-reach persona.

Ariel ignored his words in favor of poking at him with two fingers—he was icy to the touch. She withdrew her hand. Plunkett squinted at her, then enjoyed it, then squinted again.

"We got your messages, Woby," were Ariel's first words.

Plunkett said, "I told you not to use your phone. My bill is going to be ridiculous."

Woby answered, his voice muffled under inches of puffy blanket. "They went through? Cool...doesn't that make you think?"

He shivered as he spoke.

"All of a sudden," Plunkett said dejectedly, "everything makes him think."

Woby was blowing like a bellows to increase the trapped warmth of his breath. He was also wriggling, the large round lumps mass shifting and rolling like a floating dock—until an arm rose from that quilted sea and held a bright cell phone screen aloft to show Ariel the messages sent.

Ariel did not look at it for long, certainly not long enough to read the dates that the messages were sent, which was Woby's intent. She was more focused on the frost on his shirtsleeve.

Plunkett read his own messages as he rose from the couch again with a look of reddening annoyance. He approached and fiddled with the thermostat protruding from a stained part of the kitchen wall.

Ariel asked where they had been. She took out a pen and notepad.

"The future, mostly, but it was more wobbly than usual," Woby said, his face and shoulders emerging like a periscope.

Plunkett quickly turned to tell his brother to "Shut, shut, shut up." He plopped back on the couch and worked his temples with his hands the way army cadets in basic training are taught to scrub floors. "I need to think!" he blurted. "And so do you, Woby."

Ariel began to play a character she had dreamt of many times: wizened, honored, insightful clinical psychologist. She sat among the newspaper and paper plates on the cruddy end table between the couches and spoke to Woby calmly and patronizingly, the way Woby liked.

"How was it?" she asked, trying to contain her excitement, trying not to picture Aris telling her how superbly this was going.

"Confusing," Woby answered. "Like Plunkett said. We jumped around a lot. And that girl. She kept slipping in and out."

"Everything was slipping in and out, including my stomach walls," Plunkett added.

"Yeah…but the girl, the same one? How?" Woby asked.

"Couldn't be the same girl, from the hospital you mean?" Plunkett spoke. "That was centuries before. Maybe a great-great-whatever granddaughter. What did she say to you? I couldn't hear, I was holding those furry things to my ears. They bit me, the little bastards." Plunkett picked coagulated red ice from his temple and earlobes.

Ariel wrote on her pad, her glee kept in her throat for now but beating to get out.

"Yeah, that was her, in and out," Woby answered, "about ten times, here and there. You didn't notice? And she said, 'Penthos, how are you following me'. I think…what does it mean?"

Ariel looked up to rub her palms and tired hands, but Plunkett held up his own tired hand and spoke before Ariel could. "Don't worry," he said, "you don't want to know."

"Okay, good," Woby said.

Plunkett gave Ariel a *we-all-agree-this-is-best-so-just-go-along* look. She nodded.

"'Why are you following me' is something you guys hear a lot, I would think," Ariel said but did not mean it cruelly, only clinically, factually. She returned to her riotous notetaking.

"The girl said 'how' not 'why,'" Woby said quietly.

"Uh huh…" Ariel said with understanding and an evenness that hid the emotional bungee-jumping that was going on in her chest and head.

"Mind blowing. I need to think…" Plunkett seemed to add, but the words came meekly and from some deep place where thoughts were cornered, outnumbered, and perhaps frightened. He rubbed his head and ears.

And perhaps because of Plunkett's current confused and weakened state, Ariel was able to keep Woby talking, trancelike, explaining what their night had been like.

Ariel took notes which, eventually, read as follows:

What Woby and Plunkett saw of the future was confusing to both young men, as has already been admitted. It was cold and snowing hard, the wet air freezing on their skin and into their hair and clothes (this was verified tactilely). They wandered about, and people would appear suddenly and zombie-like, emerging from the whiteness and groping at them with paunchy, mittened hands and pale faces. The two ran from these encounters and tried to keep warm and find shelter. All was icy pavement and tall metal posts rising from the ground at street intersections—to their left and right were ploughed snow mounds lining the avenues, and barely perceptible buildings hidden by the storm whistled their presence in the changing gusts of wind.

The snow-people seemed especially intent on poking their giant insulated thumbs at the time machine belt.

All about was unnervingly patterned and ordered, and, they claim, seemed to "wobble" in and out of clear existence/reality. The landscape repeated the same shapes—buildings, vehicles, signs all looked to be spherical, globular, or button-shaped and shone in bright, primary colors. The whole escapade grew hard to accept, harder to comprehend, hardest to explain later.

The boys separated at an intersection, quite accidentally. Plunkett was pulled into a mass of people who wore drab clothes and moaned a lot but otherwise gave way.

Woby then found himself alone and behind a rounded, thick hedge—the only plant life they were to see until they returned back to the dorm and to the time appointed to them by the gods (as he nervously expressed it). The hedge was large and round and reminded him of himself somehow. Woby ran.

Dodging crowds, wind, and storm led them both separately but ultimately to shoveled steps that ran up to an important looking structure, shiny and sleek it rose among the snowflakes and an air that was thickened with flurries.

At their sides rose statues that looked familiar—they were peripheral to their vision as well as to their memories. A vague dread overcame the boys. This was like déjà vu within a dream within a daydream while looking at old childhood drawings that Mom had saved.

At the top of the steps was a wide circle, Druid like, walled in and like a temple and, given the storm and the darkening gray, seemed to be among the clouds. There was a large monument, a broad cylindrical shiny marble flattened giant hockey-puck of a monument, at the center. It glowed a ghastly ghostly green.

Woby and Plunkett looked at each other, held hands, held the time-machine in their others, and Woby pressed its yellow button with his nose to return home.

The rest was mere detail.

Through Woby's story, Ariel was able to keep within her character, that of an elder, knowing, probably bespectacled and definitely renowned psychoanalyst, and to merely reply with encouraging simplicities, like "I see" and "yes, go on." With Woby now finished and sitting up, and with Plunkett also erect with his head back staring at the ceiling in mesmerized thought, she mumbled to herself:

"It's worse than I thought. Correction: It's better than I thought."

The boys rose to stretch but did so silently. The room was tired, the time late, the dorm quiet, the night subdued.

Ariel gathered her things with easy movements. "You guys need to rest, okay? I'll get you help. We'll talk in the morning."

She gave them one last look, hoping to get a nod. Woby was looking upward, like a duck, and pacing, but Plunkett's form was downward, and sitting, like a spiritual follower. Both seemed to be praying—and, perhaps, thinking about the future.

"Don't do anything else without me," Ariel said. She left the dorm.

CHAPTER SEVEN

Late Friday night. In which Plunkett sends Woby to the family home to rest and aggressively admonishes him not to use the time travel belt.

Whenever Ariel's proper, proportionate, precise and pretty presence left the drab and disheveled dorm room it left a tangible hole, like a large, brimming vase of spring orchids removed to make room for some junk from the basement.

Plunkett came out of his trance and realized that she was gone. Then he realized that she had been there.

"Oh no—we told her too much. Correction: *You* told her too much!" he said, pointing a now-sweaty finger at his brother the penitent. "And she will be back. She will keep coming until she ruins things for us. And I bet Nancy will be nosing around soon also, and, worse, Ariel's psych-major cronies. And we can't keep the belt lying around. Bring it home with you."

Woby nodded and was removing layers now—sweatshirts, blankets—as the room had swung too warm. "I think we need her help, Plunkett. The future was very confusing. I told you we shouldn't go there."

"I admit it was hasty. And your girl-chasing is no more helpful or dignified when it happens across eternity than in normal time. But I think I have a handle on things now." Plunkett indicated his head, poked at it, tapped on it, wherein, he implicated, sat a large, underappreciated brain.

"Oh yeah?" Woby said, with a large fat and humid smirk.

Plunkett ignored the expression on Woby's face but answered. "Yeah. The problem is that, apparently, the future, or futures, are as wild, chaotic, and unplanned as we've been. The time you saw, with the ploughing, and the one we just saw, with the button-obsessed ice-savages, are a direct result of our current lack of belt sophistication and savvy. If things stay the way they are now, and since we are newbies at time travel—you are especially bad at it—then the logical conclusion is that we are creating such a future, and it is the one we will inherit. But…" Plunkett was pacing the room, and removing clothes, and he was now down to boxer shorts and a T-shirt and had also started brushing his teeth at the kitchen sink. "…but, once I make things cozy for us in the present day, by cashing in from the past, the future will play out the way we want."

"Did you decide what we want? Because I think I—" Woby began.

"Yes," Plunkett assured.

"Good, because I think I know—" Woby tried.

"Doesn't matter."

Woby yawned and started to make himself comfortable on the couch again, commencing a progression of small movements that showed his readiness, willingness, and ability to embark on a good night's sleep.

Plunkett came over to him and undid each of Woby's steps in reverse order and continued to speak. Soon Woby was fully dressed and standing at the door, the time machine belt stuffed unevenly under his shirt.

"I'll make a plan and take a trip tomorrow and do it right. This all shouldn't be so Wobing hard." Plunkett enjoyed this new adverb, so did Woby. Plunkett went on. "But for now, you are going home, and you are taking the belt with you—hide it and keep it from Ariel. And Nancy, Applemon, and any other potential detractors. I am not ready to deal with Apple. And you know Ariel will be back here first thing in the morning if not tonight. She can't get enough of me."

"Yeah," Woby yawned, his reality mixing and melting with the puffy warmth of oncoming sleep.

"I will get us some real money. I just need to sleep on it," Plunkett said.

Woby said, "Me, too."

Yet Plunkett had more to say. At this point, neither of the two young men were reminded of the scene from *Hamlet*, Act I Scene 3, when Polonius gave his son Laertes lots of direct and fatherly advice with unintentional humor—because Plunkett was aggressively admonishing Woby *not to use the belt* but to just get some sleep and not attempt anything more complex than that so as to avoid a *real* tragedy.

Woby nodded and promised all the while; he yawned and re-nodded until they were at the door to the hallway.

Plunkett opened the door and shoved Woby out into the hall.

Then he pulled him back in by his sweatshirt pockets and closed the door.

He wanted to see conscious acknowledgment in Woby's eyes. "Don't use it!" Plunkett commanded once more. He wanted it committed to Woby's muscle memory, since his brother's graymatter memory was not so reliable. He wanted to see whether any "*unless*"es or "*but what if*"s or "*but I was thinking that maybe*"s were still possible, were still lingering in the corners of Woby's squishy mind. Especially not any "*I had a great idea; I thought I would also tell everyone we know about this, and then do everything else you said not to*"s.

"You have seen how risky this is," Plunkett spoke directly to his brother's subconscious and instinct, since he could never tell who was really in control of the large body, stubby fingers, and droopy, fleshy ears. "If you use it, who knows what harm might come to the belt. And whether it will come back safe at all. Remember all the people grabbing at it before in the future? Don't risk it. Don't."

"Okay."

Plunkett added, "And you might get hurt, too." Woby nodded with his neck and eyelids and was soon on his way down the hall.

A boomeranging thought buffeted Plunkett in the back of the brain, prompting one last instruction: "Woby! Don't sleep on it! Especially figuratively!"

CHAPTER EIGHT

Saturday morning. In which Woby
explains what he did instead of
sleeping. He looks noticeably older.

t seemed to Plunkett that Woby had just left when he burst back in
through the dorm room door. This time there was nothing unnatural or inexplicable: through normal everyday cause and effect,
and time passing at one-second-per-second, Woby had returned.
It was early Saturday morning; Plunkett had fallen asleep on the
couch with his notebook on his chest and his pen still wedged
between his fingers.

Plunkett jumped up at the surprise and the noise and saw a tall
but doughy figure come through the door.

It was Woby.

It *was* Woby.

Wasn't it?

His younger brother's normal blobby and R-shaped outline was
there in the door frame, and now moving toward the couch. The
form in motion jiggled in a familiar way, and still looked ready for
someone to keep long-stemmed flowers in; and it all still swished
as if carrying more than enough water for any emergency.

But this person had short hair, and it was neatly parted to the
side. And this person was dressed in pleated khaki pants and a golf
shirt and had been carrying a suitcase, which now remained near
the door. He had papers under his arm, an umbrella in hand. And
this person's face was mature, creased, and with fewer blemishes,

and these in brown and not jelly-pink. He looked the age of a young college professor.

This person had a moustache. A moustache.!

!

Through it, came: "Okay, well that was interesting."

Since it still walked like a Woby and talked like a Woby, Plunkett knew it was his shortly-lost brother. His mind was getting used to *not* ruling out the impossible, and caught on quickly.

"You used it!" he yelled.

"I couldn't sleep," Woby-man replied. "I think."

"You think?"

"It was a while ago."

"Why are you so old?" Plunkett said, body and temper rising like a pissed off dawn. "Why is this so Wobing hard?" he said to the ceiling and any Lord who might be on the roof or even higher above it.

Woby wondered what his much younger older brother meant, and then didn't wonder. "I missed you," Woby said.

Plunkett tried to blink away flakes of remaining dreams as he stared at the other's clean-shaven chin, less-angled still-chubby form, and even chubbier, even Wobier neck.

"Tell me everything that happened," he said.

"I will. I can't wait to tell you. There's so much—"

Plunkett held up his hand rudely, not struggling with whether to treat his elders with respect in this instance. "Tell me only about time travel and what will help me do what we want, and whether the world is still okay. Big things. Not about your career in accounting, or whatever you did."

"Ah, yes, that stuff. Don't worry, you can still do your thing. But there are people I want you to meet. In fact, I met—"

Plunkett's hand went back up, as did a yawn. "Tell me only what I ask. First: When you left here last night and went home, what happened then?"

"I couldn't sleep…yes…I remembered to want to say that to you."

"So you time-traveled instead of reading a book or something?"

Plunkett yawned as aggressively as possible. "Did anyone see?"

"No—Langston and those guys didn't think I was serious, of course."

"Langston?" Plunkett yawned, fighting awakeness, and struggling with Woby's response. At first this name rang only a dim bell from across a wide hillside. He searched and soon had it. "You mean those middle-school warts you hang with? You told them? How long ago...what?" Plunkett was getting ahead of the data.

"Last night, *your time*," Woby answered. "*Our time* now, I should say. It is good to be *now*. AUNT, right? Remember that? Ha. Anyway, I missed you. How's things?"

"You told those mental-hobbits about this?" Plunkett had moved to the kitchen to grab some fresh orange juice that he knew would not be there, squinting his sore eyes at the rays of a bright sunrise that also wasn't there and not warming the kitchen with long golden arms. He opened and sipped from a fizzing Diet Coke can.

"I emailed them, actually, I kept a printout so I could tell you. But I lost it. That night, I just asked them something like '*What would you do if*, you know, something about a time machine. That started a whole bunch of...stuff."

"The Ariel thing didn't teach you anything? She's on our trail now."

"Ariel! Oh yeah! How is she doing? That's a hell of a long trail at this point." Woby fought to remember, visibly straining, his face a mirror of vague recall. "Looking back...hm...I couldn't sleep. It got late. I was bored."

"But Langston the half-a-Siamese-pimple was awake, of course. Don't those bit-head meta-mutants go to bed? Don't any morons sleep at night? Is it a conceptual challenge or something? Geez..."

"They were up hacking. Their idea was that we should send a robot to do the time traveling. What do you think?"

"Of what?" The Diet Coke was finished, the can crushed and crashed on the kitchen counter.

"That idea. This is the stuff you want to hear, right, for your big plans? I hope you can find what I found and be happy. Me and—"

Plunkett's stop sign hand went up, flashing red. He was befuddled but awake now and secure in the knowledge that he should be vein-popping mad. He did not answer at first.

Instead, for now, here is a list of things:

- *Guys next to a pickup with dirty baseball caps drinking canned beer;*

- *Road rage;*

- *Delayed airline flights;*

- *Josef Stalin or Benito Mussolini;*

- *A dog peeing on a nice carpet;*

Plunkett addressed his brother via a chorus of questions. "Just tell me exactly what you did that might help or hurt my plans, or the belt itself. The trips you made. Did you make any money? Did you screw anything up? Tempt any paradoxes of the cosmos? Does the world still exist in a few days? You are older—are you rich yet? You don't look it."

Plunkett burped and calmed a bit, unhappy with his breakfast Coke and disappointed in himself as much as with Woby. He had not been a good master, and his brother—this middle-aged man, as Plunkett experienced him—needed mastering. "Why is this so Wobing hard?" he said again, weaker. "Why can't you just ever do what I say?"

As Plunkett searched for food in an attempt to restart himself and give a second chance to a day that so far had broken its promise, Woby settled upright on the couch and took out a pair of eyeglasses. He was ready to tell his tale and answer Plunkett's many questions. And whenever it seemed Woby beamed with bigger, or personal, news, his brother raised his hand to thwart their expression.

In this way Plunkett learned that, since Woby could not sleep that fateful night—last night—he used the time travel belt to just wander around, back in time, following his own curiosity and interests. Doing mostly "kids' stuff" as he phrased it. This included wanting to know when and where the first baseball hat was worn backward, what Led Zeppelin sounded like playing in a small bar, testing whether watching *The Wizard of Oz* for the 'first time again' worked to recapture the magic—it didn't—and from there Woby followed a thread of related thoughts: He wondered about how things begin, whatever things popped into his roomy head. And he knew that he had the power to find out; he was wearing that power around his waist. He became a sort of groupie hanging around the starts of things.

With those gaps of his intellect filled—Woby's was not exactly the Grand Canyon of curiosity—he next sought more meaning, as people do as they march past the lessons of young adulthood and into a real and waiting world. Woby chose a path dedicated to saving lives, starting with animals. Those doomed to be hit by cars he attempted to steer away beforehand. This proved dangerous. He changed method and tried to steer the vehicle drivers away beforehand. This proved dangerous.

Deciding not to argue with a God that created both raccoons and combustion engines, he took his fight instead directly to the Grim Reaper. He visited children's hospitals in an effort to, hopefully, use his special skills—time travel and lack of philosophical training—to thwart death itself, in certain instances. He failed in this.

But Woby found a rare silver lining, the first in all of his misadventures since leaving the dorm room with the belt: his time at hospitals led to the best thing that ever happened to him, he declared, because it was there that—

Plunkett's hand was raised, and Woby stopped.

"Wait—Zeppelin? Hats?" Plunkett broke in eventually. "And Zeppelin never played around here, how did you see them?"

"I got around a little, though it wasn't easy in those early days, my son—"

"Don't call me that," Plunkett advised.

Woby smiled. "Not easy at all, in those days…" He trailed off, brightening at something he saw in the newspaper, nodding in fond rememberance, gazing over full-rimmed eyeglass frames, crossing his legs, and turning into C. S. Lewis cell by cell.

Plunkett's head whirled in a death spiral, the propeller engines of his mind shot with the permutations of things to either ask Woby or try to learn himself. Butter from a hastily arranged bagel breakfast was smeared on his lips and cheeks and it all shined.

Woby got up to walk—apparently he had weakening hips and a shoulder injury and needed to move around, could not sit for long stretches.

Plunkett watched. His head was aflame, descending rapidly into the vast expanse of an ocean of inscrutability. He was silent and greasy and just stared at his brother.

Woby took Plunkett's silence as doubt in his story. "I can prove it to you. I'll play some Zeppelin on my phone…here, perfect, 'Stairway to Heaven'…"

Plunkett stared as Woby mouthed the words to the all-time great classic rock song as the mystically minor chords of "Stairway to Heaven"'s intro filled the room. It sounded a little different somehow, but Plunkett didn't let that ruin a good, intense stare. He wiped the greasy shine from his mouth.

They listened up to the part where the band sang: *If there's a Plunkett in your hedgerow, don't be alarmed now…*"

Or something that sounded like that. Awfully like that.

Horribly like that.

The lyrics made about as much sense to its audience as it ever did, but still…

"Oh my god." Plunkett said. He needed a minute. It was granted. He spent his minute in the bathroom. The sound of water running, verbal self-abuse, and face slapping was heard. Plunkett returned more like his normal self.

"Okay. Slow down," he admonished aggressively. "Start from the beginning. Tell me what else happened last night."

"I ironed my dress pants, getting ready for the trip. I took my fiber, kissed my—"

Plunkett's hand changed from amber to red. "Stop being so self-centered; I meant *my* last night, not yours. The night you left here. Remember? Yesterday? AUNT?"

Woby paced around in thought. "Let me think. It was like fifteen years ago…"

"Focus. While you were out roaming the past, you probably made things much worse for me here today." He paused, looked around, then continued but with a new face. "Though I don't see anything different, things seem the same. Are they? I still have to work tomorrow, as far as I know. And Ariel is still hounding us, and I am still poor. Right?"

They both looked around and agreed that Plunkett was still poor. His life had not changed much.

"Looks the same. No harm done," Woby said, smiling. "Now can I tell you my big news?"

"No. I will check for harm later, but that was a huge risk, Wobe— Mr. Wobe, or whatever. I don't understand you. Your first trips were all disasters, you were afraid of getting killed, or going to jail, but you took this big chance anyway. Now you wasted your life, and there is no progress, and you will probably still end up getting killed or going to jail. Stop screwing with the belt. You wouldn't like jail, Wobe, they would treat you like a hotdog bun."

Woby considered this for longer than it deserved. After its passage, Woby began a strange-looking exercise, ostensibly to stretch out his shoulders and hips.

"Where is the belt?" Plunkett asked the back of his own hand, raised and poised as it was.

"Ah…" Woby walked back toward his suitcase near the front door and opened it, producing the not-in-new-condition time-machine belt with its little box. "Here," he handed it to Plunkett. The belt had a peace sign on it, and a sticker reading: If found return to…and listed Plunkett and their home address.

"I lost it in 1978," Woby said, "and found it later in 1971, but just a few days ago, right after I was coming here anyway to find it later beforehand."

This made no sense and of course perfect sense at the same time, and Plunkett therefore did not respond beyond a polite request for Woby not to tell him anymore.

Woby stretched and yawned and asked if he could lie down and take a nap. "I need to rest. When you're ready, we need to talk. For one thing, you need to meet my—"

Hand raised, Plunkett walked Woby to the bedroom. He settled and tucked his brother into the outstretched arms of all the pillows and blankets that could be found, and did so surprisingly lovingly. To the nineteen-year-old Plunkett, his big little older younger brother was now hoary and decrepit, in the way that the middle-aged can seem to peaking young men. And, although he could not be said to have "missed" him—since Woby's long, slow aging only took a few hours of Plunkett-time—Plunkett did not like to see Woby require a daytime nap, nor to think of him having one foot in retirement-savings-anxiety land, if not the grave, as it must surely be. The thought provided a soft landing for Plunkett's prior rage.

And things could have been much worse. "Sure," Plunkett responded to Woby's continued gratitude, "at your age you need rest, you know. Have three more pillows."

After a gaping half-minute-long yawn, Woby replied "I'm only thirty-t—" but the closing bedroom door cut him off.

CHAPTER NINE

> Saturday afternoon. Plunkett has
> sanity-checked and wardrobe-adjusted
> Woby's recent travels, and in which
> some minor and thoroughly ancillary
> if not downright apocryphal time
> travelers are met.

*P*lunkett resembles a lower case "i" from any standard and decently sized font.

It is Saturday afternoon, and Plunkett has already returned from his weekly, ritualized college-boy trip home to Mom and Dad's house, to exchange laundry for sureties, trade small news for sundries, give smiles for some petty cash, swap eased minds for Tupperware containers snapped shut with homey foodstuffs to last until, probably, Wednesday, which heralded the return to mac and cheese, fast food, and watered down syrup.

Plunkett craftily explained to his folks that Woby wanted to stay the weekend on the university campus, and that he was fine and acting his age—if anything, he was acting quite mature, in fact—so there was no problem there.

Plunkett returned to the dorm with a cardboard box that was earmarked for the big green neighborhood receptacles collecting items for those in need. It was filled with old clothes, most of which belonged to his poor old grandfather who had passed away a few months prior; and now Woby was in need, as Plunkett judged.

Unpacking the box Plunkett smelled a dignified but musty

musk, felt thick dust in his fingers and throat, and traveled back in time—the less problematic way, using only memories.

The clothes seemed to hold hard onto every scent of every place Grandpa would go—on his walks, unsmoked cigar in hand, to the park; to the veteran's hall and its free meals of turkey and pancakes; to the bowling alley; to visit his friend "Jerry Blues" at the old folks' home in town. Plunkett felt warm with memories. Grandpa roomed in their house for his declining years of TV, sweaters, and contrary points of view. Plunkett and Woby enjoyed the old guy to the fullest, in awe of his aged affability and a freshly free-spirited style that countered their parents' unending, bourgeois life-formulas, a style that also made young Woby laugh himself silly. Grandpa taught them how to spit, for example, and also put all the curse words into context for proper use when the occasions arose. And he was there with updated expertise as the years went on, as the boys grew up, as the world shrunk, and as they became young men.

And it only took twenty-four hours or so in possession of a magical, wondrous, miracle-enabling, prayer-answering time machine for Plunkett to think of a worthwhile use for it: to visit loved ones who are inaccessible through the normal flow of time, to go tell Grandpa thank you.

Yet soon enough that very thought was Plunkettized: "Well, not yet," Plunkett said aloud, "first we need a large cash booty. *Then* we can go get Grandpa and put him in charge of parks and casino nights at the swankiest VA hall in the world." Yea, verily, with both hands was it Plunkettized.

Before all this, and while Old Wobe napped—he had risen briefly only to tell a story about some squirrels he remembered watching once, but soon went back to bed—Plunkett made sure the world was still okay to live in, checking the internet for major differences to the way things were yesterday, AUNT: were there any major geopolitical shifts? The appearance of new sports, animals playing important roles in transportation? Anything that might have been changed with Woby clumsily tripping over the complex interconnecting webs of history.

All seemed fine except that Led Zeppelin's fourth album had only sold 118 copies.

So: The world remained close enough to normal for Plunkett to continue planning.

In the dorm, Mr. Woby finally awoke, drifting into the common area like fog into a junky boatyard on a still morning. He was holding the time travel belt and proceeding to the couch where his face and shoulders were struck with flying clothes from Plunkett's hand: a sweater and suspenders that Plunkett thought suitable given Woby's instantaneously advanced age.

"Suspenders? That's funny because it reminds me of the justice of the peace that—"

"Shh—these were Grandpa's." Plunkett said with a modicum of reverence. He felt a strange and sad distance grow between himself and Woby as the latter, with a tilting head and squinting gaze at the sweater, appeared to have to work to recall any memory of their grandfather.

Woby put the worn and aromatic items to the side, rested the time-belt across his stomach, and reached for the television remote, asking, "Can I watch TV while I wait for someone? If she doesn't come here, I am going to have to borrow the—"

"Fine," Plunkett interrupted, thinking it improbable that any newly biographical, extraneous information from Woby could be valuable. "Just sit there. Resist the urge to knit or send complaint emails or go to the bank or invite people over for gin rummy."

"You are a strange one, Plunkett, but you always were." Woby said and surfed only the lower numbered TV channels. "What are you up to today, my son?"

"Never call me that. I think I know our next move," Plunkett said, assuming Woby was still his playmate. This was a big assumption; Plunkett stared at his brother's thick, bristling moustache. Was Woby now supposed to return to high school? Or direct to factory work? Plunkett made a mental note to figure out Woby's life later—but, of course, once they were supremely rich it would not matter. Does Woby even have much time left? How old is he? This was hard to gauge since anyone over twenty-five seemed fully spent to Plunkett; and since judging his brother's unnatural aging was especially tricky and deceiving; and since Plunkett really, really did not care.

"We have to deal with Ariel first," Plunkett continued.

"Yes," Woby said to the refreshed familiarity of the girl's name, "Ariel. Lovely girl."

"Stop speaking. We need to deal with Ariel, put her in her place. But soon we'll cash in. You are near retirement age, and—"

"Ha! Not quite, but my plan was to buy a little place near the—" Woby tried.

"Stop. I understand that you want to grouse about your missing forty years or so of life, but save it until I can come up with a better one, okay? For you, also. Maybe it isn't too late. But I'm in a hurry now. I'm young and need funds, and to stay ahead of Ariel. You wasted a bunch of trips already."

"Well, it isn't like wishes from a genie, you get more than three."

"Stop speaking on your own. You took too many risks. Did you even try to make money?"

"No, I did much better. At first I waited for you, but then started to live, and then found life. You know, time passes swiftly when you—"

"Zip it, lemming. Or in your case suspender it."

Eyes still on the TV news, Woby twisted in odd looking bends in order to dig his hands into both his front trouser pockets. Each hand produced wads of folded cash. "All I have is this, a few thousand. We don't care about money, in fact—"

"This is good! Is that it?" Plunkett gathered the money and slinkied back and forth in his greedy hands as Woby nodded. "How?" Plunkett asked.

"Career choices. I-"

"Don't tell me anymore." Plunkett increased the pace of his pacing. "But I appreciate this. Geez, a few days ago if I had a few thousand dollars I would have been in Hawaii cloning myself! And now it's just the beginning, like some 'seed money.' And it definitely takes some pressure off; I have had to do everything myself. Still—at your rate we wouldn't be billionaires until the year twenty-thousand, and forty...uh...something."

Woby watched television, patient and amused at his brother's never-say-poverty propellent.

"Woby with a job..." Plunkett mumbled, "even with a time machine you settled into lower-middle class." He spoke in earnest dejection, shaking his head like a god who was disappointed in his human handiwork and considering taking free will back to give to lizards instead.

A complex of feelings swooshed; Plunkett paced and gave mutterance to all of them: a profound, self-centered greed, the rapid changes to his life, the pressure of an impending Ariel assault, his loosening grip on what seemed like simple plans and small asks, and the inevitable reckoning to the great Applemon: The coming retribution for his bites of the forbidden fruit pushed Plunkett's need to make the most of his short time in Eden.

And now what help would Woby be? Plunkett thought.

A moustache? he thought as well.

Woby was on the couch, smiling at the TV like an imbecile, enjoying his whole other life. A life he had without Plunkett! And for that split second Plunkett felt that ants were crawling his face, and he realized that this twitchy feeling was jealousy, ant-sized but swarming and cooperating and tunneling deep.

Woby had shared much of his life with others.

He then pinched the mental ants between his mental fingers and killed them, replacing that feeling with a mock rage, barraging his brother.

"I guess I've lost my partner. You are useless as an old man!"

Woby turned his head and raised his own hand, Plunkett-style.

"This has been fun," he began, "but I really need to tell you—"

"Yes. But now I am going to have to take all the risks," Plunkett ran on, "all that time travel, all those years spent with a belt of miracles, and you learned nothing and profited one dollar-per-hour and with no supermodels. All this *wasted* time! *Ironically!*"

Vehemence in his words, the heat was rising to Plunkett's ears and eyebrows. Here is a list:

- *A mouse going back and forth in the easy part of a maze;*

- *Someone with hiccups in an elevator;*

- *A knobbly, coiling snake;*

- *A rusty, rotting, corroding car battery with seeping, orange, leprosy-like growths;*

Woby turned to the TV and its commercial break. "Okay, you aren't ready yet, I see, still struggling. You need a drink? I make a mean Slow Gin Fizz." He rose to relieve his hips and knees, and, scratching his upper lip, reconsidered the suspenders and moved to the kitchen.

Plunkett moved to the couch and sat with his new best, closest friends: notebook and pen. The world was quiet, except for the nondescript drone of television news, intermittently louder commercials, and an occasional hum from Woby to indicate that he understood well what the newspeople were getting at. Plunkett accepted this background radiation into his personal universe and was able to calm down, to cool, and to expand.

Soon enough his mind grew keen, and plans came into focus. How to deal with Ariel, how to delay Applemon, how to align Woby, how to increase cash and information flow. Life on Saturday was good again. The news show ended, and Woby clicked off the TV and lay back, ice clinking in a glass, the unlovely time belt and brown suspenders on his chest. Quiet was winning the day, and soon the world and all its Saturdays would be at the command of Plunkett and Woby, Plunkett thought. That is, while Woby lasted.

Everything would now go according to plan. Plunkett's plan.

"Want to hear it?" Plunkett asked Woby, who was reclining and tapping and twiddling his fingers on the time machine's leather and raised plastic buttons. But Plunkett did not wait for an answer. "It's perfect. Nothing can go wrong, everything is predictable, I can see the future, I can be the future, we can own the future. Nothing happens in our world that isn't in my notebook. Nothing can go wrong. Look!"

Plunkett held up the notebook with a noisy flourish. And the world did not shake or wobble or anything.

Woby turned around to see it, his hands slipping on, then regripping, the belt. The time-machine belt.

And *that* is when the world shook and wobbled and everything.

Plunkett's vision rushed at his eyes and his perception of the room focused in and out, his vision pushed and pulled toward and away from him and in waves. Light from the room rolled and swirled before reaching him. Sound warped and fed back on itself. He sat up and grabbed tight to the cushions of the couch.

Watching Woby, Plunkett saw his brother's appearance flicker like an ancient movie reel, his clothes and position changed, and features popped in and out of the scene, in and out of existence: Woby's hair grew, then shortened, skin changed color, arms and legs jerked around without any continuity of motion. Moustaches came and went.

Stunned, baffled, afraid, Plunkett was afraid to look down at his own body. Gazing around the room he watched the objects fight with the ability, normally easy, to stay put and stay the same and obey Newton's physical laws. Lights flickered on and off. Streaks and stains rose up and down walls, windows opened and closed. Items appeared and then disappeared.

Plunkett closed his eyes. Was it for a few seconds? Or did he wait until Eternity Eve? Time and space were expensive items that his mind could not pay for at the moment.

There was a harsh mix of sounds, frightening, even with a crusty pillow wrapped over one's ears. Plunkett heard Woby's voice, and it spoke English words, but they formed random phrases. Other sounds were also familiar, in pieces, but not when joined into such strange combinations. Growing above the hellish auditory whirlwind was the sound of a cavernous and cruel animal's growl.

It all stopped—except the growling—when the door flew open with a crashing bang, physical and terrible.

Plunkett eyes jolted open to the spot, when into the dorm came a mountainously large black Rottweiler dog. It leapt at Woby, and at the time machine belt that Woby still held. The dog's paws thundered heavily onto Woby's chest; the belt was tossed but snatched in midair within massive yellow teeth. Thick saliva streamed out of a red mouth and flew in jerky directions as the dog locked its fearsome jaws on the belt and shook it violently, trying to kill it presumably, so it seemed to those with the nerve to watch. The belt lashed around the dog's massive head and huge neck, whipping the chunky muscled coat with each tear and twist, and this served to make the beast madder. Presumably.

Woby—an older version, skin now pale, and without a moustache—stood behind the couch, in fear. "He chased me!" he said, pointing a cowardly finger, then pulling it back in.

"Why? From where?" Plunkett asked with trembling voice.

"I didn't stay long enough to find out."

"Is this who—what—you were waiting for?" Plunkett asked.

"Of course not!" Woby cowered. The neat part in his hair was gone.

Plunkett asked, and trembled, more. "Is this what you wanted to tell me, that you adopted a dog from the Atomic Energy Commission? Is this the 'she' you keep blabbering about?"

"No!" Woby said while thinking that he would willingly give his life to save a car from being run over by the giant dog thing they were staring at. "No…" he repeated meekly, noticing that their new guest did not like that word being shouted.

The walls and door were being splattered with sticky silvery spit.

The growling was awful, vigorous, loud, and real, but it was all welcome *because* it was real. The room had stopped flashing and challenging its observers, physics settled down, and time politely ticked away at one second per second.

After a particularly energetic head shake, the belt crashed against the wall. The Rotty sniffed in its direction, but stayed where he stood, in the doorway, satisfied that the belt was not moving. He sniffed out toward the hall, then sniffed in toward the kitchen, then tilted his nose upward and outward toward the brothers.

Toward them the animal came with a conquering confidence, his huge-padded paws thumping the floor. Plunkett cowered and scrunched behind his ear-pillow, but, peeking out, was relieved to see the dog head toward the other couch, Woby's. It leapt up onto the cushions, stood and shook his whole body, sniffed the fabric, sneezed, made two revolutions, and lay down.

Good boy.

There was something vaguely science-fantastical about the animal. He emitted a strange backing light, a ghostly electric blue that shone from the couch cushions beneath him. Projecting a dangerous intelligence, he moved precisely and sharply, as if he was a leader, a commander, at home, in his own normal time. He was futuristic, certainly, but for now he was at rest and staying at rest. Which seemed good.

Once it was clear that the cinder-block-headed dog was not going to destroy them, Woby and Plunkett moved—respectfully, and with the animal's permission—to the kitchen.

Plunkett knows many creative variants of the standard curse words, and he peppered his next few sentences with just about all of them. In summary, he asked Woby: "What was all that about?"

Woby had to work in between his brother's many interruptions, those creative variants of the standard curse words, to answer as best he could, and when he could, trying to explain his theory of events. It was not easy, but in summary he said: "I think I must have hit the button."

Plunkett's new anger awakened the demonic Rottweiler within him. He marched to the front door to retrieve the belt—with one eye on their canine guest who was cleaning himself on the couch with black tongue and black paws in fluid, semi-circular motions.

Woby removed the time travel little box accessory from a pocket and tossed it to Plunkett.

Woby sighed. He watched his brother with concern, and Plunkett watched back with exasperation.

Woby spoke slowly. "I'm concerned."

"I would think you would be. This is getting—"

"No, not about the dog being here, but about *why* he's here." Woby said.

"Listen, if you're going to interrupt me, you can at least make sens—"

"You don't understand. The girl was with me, and then…where's Applemon?"

"You did it again. What are you talking about?"

"I saw Applemon, just now, in the future."

Plunkett mulled this, and it would have added fuel to his combustible-engine of anger if it wasn't already flooded. "Even when you say something sensible, it makes no sense. How and where did you see him? I haven't seen him around anywhere, not in a while, if that is what you're asking.?"

"I don't know," Woby replied, deep in thought. "There was another guy there who looked familiar, that guy with the bowtie, you know who I mean?"

"No."

"He's part of this somehow," Woby said.

"I don't know who you mean, but it doesn't matter. When we see Applemon we can ask him. For now this is getting out of control." Seeing no change in the sad countenance of his brother, Plunkett went on. "Okay, well don't worry about it, but we can't have these mistakes."

"I *am* worried. Not about Applemon, but the girl. She was there, then gone, then the dog came and chased me."

"Again—no sense. What do you—"

"It happens sometimes, but only when she…and she usually just…well, comes right back, but there is always someone replaced… and she comes back."

The dog growled. Plunkett growled. "Woby—Mr. Woby—stop."

Woby came back to the present. "Okay, yes, you're right, it's probably nothing."

"I *am* right." Plunkett said, trying to calm himself and failing. "You need to leave everything to me. Enough is enough. You should not touch this belt ever again, and it better still work. Keep your dog and your other problems on your side of our lives. I am executing my plan. NOW."

And as Woby said, "I know," and as Plunkett squinted back at him in confusion, he was gone. He had pressed the green button.

Woby tilted his head and watched the space where Plunkett had stood as it vacated: an odd sight or, rather, an odd feeling. The vacuum left behind at the doorway filled invisibly with small, rippling typhoons of motes of being, those destined to fill the new space with existence. Woby sensed it.

"Voooop!" Woby said now, to the dog on the couch, to the TV. "Kids' stuff…but I hope Trice is okay". The dog growled, and it lit the couch blue.

Instinctively and knowingly, Woby waited zero seconds and looked toward the still-open front door where, sure as spacetime, Plunkett emerged.

Plunkett looked madder than ever, but tired and resigned. Woby noticed no other differences, he was the same size, was wearing the same grungy shirt and jeans, had the same thatch of hair. He was wearing the belt but otherwise seemed the same age, personality, height, weight, IQ, as earlier, AUNT.

And odor: the dog stayed quiet.

When Plunkett entered the kitchen Woby noticed a small, subtle difference; not in his brother, but in what followed him through the door: a six-foot tall, four-foot-wide, gleaming metal robot. It banged against the wall as it jostled toward them, in Plunkett's time-wake as it were, pivoting spastically on two rolling, rubber, track chasses. Its dull gray gears and electronics whirred and beeped forlornly.

As the Rottweiler growled, Plunkett said, by way of introduction, "That's a lesson to you," and motioned back over his shoulder with a point of his own stubbly chin. "A gift from your idiot nerdy friends." Plunkett shook his head and bent into the fridge.

Woby asked, "Are you rich?"

"Shut up, 49er." Plunkett replied. Truth be told—which wasn't—Plunkett was in debt a few thousand dollars to someone who hopefully had forgotten it by now.

Woby the man said, "kids' stuff," and laughed quietly to himself.

The robot screeched and buzzed as it tried, as if driven by some kind of time-invariant instinct, to traverse to the couch. The noises it made indicated its extreme difficulty with the terrain, and the handling of many, many, many errors coming from its various processing and sensory units. About its head and shoulders were several miniature radio dishes that spun like so many pathetic pinwheel hats.

It also seemed to bang into just about every obstacle that it presumably was programmed to avoid.

"What do you expect?" Plunkett scoffed. "Its mother are geeks."

At each stiff crash into a table, counter, chair, desk, or speck of dust, the thing bent and twisted at its midmost point, its circular clamp-handed arms waving about, its block of a head tilting that made one wonder whether it was under the control of a madman or a blind man or a bad comedian. When it twisted, at its navel—where protruded a giant metal screw—numerous lights lit up frenetically and seemed to express frustration and growing ulcerous dyspepsia.

Woby laughed and laughed, but only when he believed he had permission from his dog. Plunkett winced and whined.

Eventually the ugly trek was completed, and the robot arrived at the couch, where the dog had stopped growling and started sniffing, head askew and golden-brown eyes opened wide like an eclipsed sun.

The robot sat, then doubled over, holding its, well, stomach. The Rotty growled a little, more of a question then a firm statement, but soon plopped his own heavy head down and then was quiet, its blue light extinguished.

Woby laughed again—until something occurred to him. "Wait a minute," he asked his brother, "when did you see Langston and those guys with this robot thing?"

"A few years ago. Why? Who cares?"

"Impossible! How could they have made it then?"

"Is anything impossible with the damage you have done, the mistakes you have made? You tell me when you told them our plans, wasn't it in the present, but then you went all over the time so who knows you might have leaked it to them when they were younger and even uglier and who cares anyway? Leave me alone. I'm tired and need to re-re-plan." Punctuation be damned.

But Woby would not relent until Plunkett supplied the specifics of what happened, where the robot came from, and whether there was a girl involved.

There was.

CHAPTER TEN

Saturday mid-afternoon, AUNT. In which
the robot's appearance is explained,
to Woby's dismay, more guests come—
including Ariel—and wherein Woby
tells Plunkett his Big News.

Woby was deep in thought and deep in the couch with the others. His sighs of preoccupied lament were sometimes loud enough to make the Rottweiler next to him growl. And when *that* happened, a small red light on the mystery robot would blink, a small radio dish of a sensor would spin noisily for a few revolutions, and then all would go quiet again.

It was enough to make Plunkett go angry. At each sigh/growl/ spin cycle, he was disturbed from his own deep thinking and instead observed the Couch of Unholy Anachronisms, trying to improve on its name each time, while also suspicious of all three of them. He feared the dog, despised the robot, and shook his head at his aging brother.

The massive animal—meaning the dog—still seemed to glow from behind with a blue electricity, like small, constant lightning was coming from its butt, which thankfully had stopped thundering earlier. There was something about it that reminded Plunkett of the future, him having been there, of course. But the dog was otherwise just a normal tank-shaped killer beast from the crooked depths of God's confounding Book of Life, perhaps in an Epilogue.

W.W MARPLOT

Carefully daring to approach, Plunkett saw that wrapped on the dog's stunted bolt of a tail was an electronic device, perhaps a tracker; it was impressively arrayed with tiny signaling lights and minuscule electronics. Certainly this dog was not from the same temporal direction as Frisbees and Moustaches.

Plunkett went back to his notebook and made a list of people, places, and things he hated.

His previous belt-trip to the past landed him only in a warpy time wave, or something. There he ran into Woby's younger middle-school friends, geeky goofs for sure, but quite smart, as all knew. The wavy part was that certain scenes kept repeating themselves, though not perfectly: He saw Langston and the other kids as a few years younger, then older, then younger again, and with a girl. That alone was enough to make Plunkett rub the disbelief from his eyes.

But he soon saw plainly that it was she who was the source of the wavy time-warpiness. Plunkett approached them furtively so as to eavesdrop, and their talk was of Woby and "Wobots" and worse. And they were actually awaiting Plunkett's arrival. Just as Plunkett determined to retrace his steps unseen, a robot indeed appeared, instantaneously, in the place of the girl, who was gone. Plunkett gasped. The warps of reality stopped. Nausea took its place.

He was discovered and chased but outran the younger kids, escaping to seek the lotto numbers and stick with his perfect, impenetrable plan. This called for a trip a little back further in time but came with a new concern: Since whenever Plunkett would travel it would be the same place, the same location as where he stood now. So that his rascally pursuers and their robot would be there also—since, Plunkett assumed, Woby had already trodden all this temporal ground and his friends probably knew Plunkett's every move.

Woby meant well, maybe, but Plunkett despised any more meddling and certainly did not want to have to slice his trillions into more pieces than necessary once the time came to collect the inheritance that the dead and useless cosmos owed him.

He instead made an attempt at a trip to the receding past, trying to outrun, outsmart, or outlive-in-reverse his astigmatic pursuers. But soon his stomach tightened, and space wobbled as before, and the same girl appeared, seemingly out of thin air, grabbing his elbow from behind to spin Plunkett around.

She then recoiled. "You aren't Penthos!" she said, her other hand snapping to her mouth in surprise, her eyes bouncing with confusion.

"Thank you," Plunkett answered, recalling the name and its meaning, then steadying himself as his knees weakened, reality hiccupped, and the girl spun away, as if pursued, and was gone as she had come. But in her place the robot appeared, close, next to him, and also clutched Plunkett's slender, sinewy arm. It braced a second clampy metal hand on the belt, forging a connection among the electronics of the two machines. In a stomach-flipping flash Plunkett found himself back on campus, in the hallway, as usual; in fact it had become a sort of landing pad.

Such was the story Plunkett told to Woby, and which made Woby the moaning, sighing wreck he now was.

Plunkett raised both hands in ongoing apathy to anything related to Woby's new life, so the latter joined the dog and the robot on the couch—with permission, which took some time and smiles and nonthreatening body language—and snapped the news back on the TV to help him think.

Breaking Plunkett's hate-list-making reveries, his cell phone rang its heavy metal music blare. Each of the three on the couch awoke and looked or sensed around according to the manner of their kind. Ariel was calling.

Plunkett did not answer but waited for the message-signaling buzz, and indeed after a few seconds the vibrations came, and he listened. Ariel's voice—energized, almost panicky—told the room that she was coming. It was time for her to "interview" Woby, she said, over and over as if obsessed with such a simple idea. And if they played along, she would keep it all a secret. She repeated that. Then babbled something about patient-doctor confidentiality, mental health regulatory compliance, ethics, trust, and H. G. Wells, and hung up.

Plunkett wondered where he might find normalcy, as those on the couch were, all three, now trying to get at the belt. Woby to protect it, the canine to do what he did best with it, and the robot out of inadvertent physical entanglement, as it appeared.

Now they were each clutching the belt (hand, clampy claw, and jaw).

And now they were tussling with the belt.

Plunkett grabbed hold of the kitchen sink to prepare himself for a shaking of the universe, like that which occurred earlier when their new death-puppy arrived. He wondered where he would put the biblical characters or moon-men or extinct animals that might soon be in the hall.

But nothing happened other than the Rotty winning the tug of war, and the robot resuming his bent-forward position with both its hand-things over the middle metal of its, well, abdomen. It seemed to moan. Plunkett could see that the dog's grip was on one end of the belt, puncturing it, but its teeth, now showing all the way to their fiery red gums, were far from the buttons and therefore all were safe from another episode in unreality.

The undercarriage of the dog glowed neon blue like a with-in-budget movie effect.

Plunkett looked to his brother for advice. Woby answered with a look of his own that made clear that he had no direct experience extracting time machines from evil drooling death-maws.

"Maybe," Woby offered, pointing to the refrigerator, "replace it with steak?"

"We don't have steak. Replace it with the robot's head," Plunkett countered.

"Dogs don't eat metal."

"Maybe in the future they do." Plunkett said and realized that what he said was quite stupid. "Well, do something! Ariel is going to be here soon, we don't have time to play with the dog like this!" Plunkett said, and realized that what he said was quite smart.

Plunkett thought for two moments, eyeing the belt and half-hoping there *would* be an accident that would save him from new moments that would require even more thinking.

Did it matter if Ariel came here? he thought.

Yes. It did. Does.

"She can't come here!" he shouted to Woby, "not with these guys on the couch! And hide that belt!"

Plunkett went to the fridge and retrieved the first edible thing he saw, a smushed half-tube of cookie dough. He tossed it to Woby, who then negotiated with a dark shadow-beast that certainly had a leg up, four in fact, and every other advantage. Plunkett could have sworn the dog was laughing, but eventually the exchange was made.

Plunkett hurriedly called Ariel and told her that Woby would go to her dorm for the "interview" or whatever she wanted, but she could not come here.

"She agreed, but on the condition that Woby bring the belt-thing along. Or else she "would tell"!" So much for professional ethics.

"That's fine," Woby said, "I might want her advice anyway."

"Good, discuss your used-up life with her, she will like that, but don't discuss anything in the century after your seventeenth birthday. No specifics. Pretend it's all pretend. And! You need to shave and mess your hair, and put on a hat!"

Woby nodded to all Plunkett's advice just like old times, but the nostalgia was lost on Plunkett. "Put on some of my clothes, you need to look like you did when she last saw you all these years ago yesterday. There's baby powder in the bathroom. Yes, okay, this isn't too bad. You go to Ariel. I'll stay here and mind the couch. Every time we hit those stupid buttons without a proper plan things go haywire!"

"That's because you're still playing around, doing kids' stuff. But there are more important things, especially now," Woby said. Woby's tone alarmed Plunkett, as did Woby's index finger as it stroked the front dials of the belt.

"Don't! Are you mentally decayed? Give it back!" Plunkett said as calmly as he could, which meant screaming it from his chest to his arms while kicking wildly with each leg.

"I just need to check something. Be right back."

And before Plunkett could shout "No, don't, you crazy moronic insane imbecile doddering decrepit sweaty crazy moron!" Woby had earned all those names on Plunkett's updated list by pressing the belt's red button.

A small Asian woman came in through the front door, unannounced, uninvited, unchaperoned but not unexpected given the range of possibilities; Plunkett in fact considered her punctual.

She was quite old and, using hundreds of steps, and nine or so low bows to the brothers, trekked to the couch and sat between the others who growled and beeped at her rudely. She was wearing a tight kimono made of metal pieces that hung down and lay like roof shingles. It all flapped in pleasant, trilling clicks as she moved.

She said, barely audible through a voice that seemed to still originate from the deep past, "Lost out of time."

She didn't say it in English, and in fact it took help from the robot to translate. This information sent Woby into a tizzy, and Plunkett surreptitiously shoved a dilapidated sneaker into the cavity where the robot's sounds came from since the thing kept trying to elaborate.

Woby paced the room. "This can't be a coincidence. What does this mean?"

Plunkett said, "Nothing. Look at her." Plunkett rudely pointed at the elderly woman, who grunted her displeasure. "Do you recognize her?" Plunkett went on. "Of course not. It has nothing to do with us."

"I don't like it," Woby said.

"You think I do? What do you think I've been screaming about? It's because of a lack of planning. Listen, you can spend the last few Saturdays of your life any way you want, but I need to get on with mine. Keep Ariel off my back for a few hours, and everything will be fine. Help me. And I will help you, once I can afford it."

Woby spoke soberly. "I need to tell you the whole—"

"Not now, you don't. Ariel will show up if you don't leave right away. You heard her, she's crazed. Please." Plunkett was proud of how reserved he was, of his self-control: He hardly screamed at all, and his legs had mostly stopped kicking. "I just need some time."

Woby gave in, but his head sank. They removed to Plunkett's bedroom to find clothes with which old Woby could dress the part of a younger Woby in the hope of fooling Ariel.

Soon enough Woby—pale with powder but otherwise buried under plaid clothes and a brown, well-worn baseball cap—eventually joined his brother in the kitchen where both stood silent and tired. Woby had the partially chewed time-travel belt in his hands. It was still able to buckle despite the years and the whipsawing and biting from the black brute of the couch.

After a moment and a half Plunkett spoke to his brother without removing his eyes from their new Far East guest who sat on the far west couch. "Okay, go now, Wobe. But don't use the belt, please, and don't worry, and I'll help you soon, and don't tell Ariel anything about me or my plans. Tell her it's a joke, or a hallucination, or that you are crazy, that she was seeing things, etc. Nothing specific or true. Okay?"

"I can handle it. I am good with women." Woby spoke from a dream-like distance.

Plunkett could not help but laugh, and a certain percent of it was *with* his brother, as opposed to *at* him. "Since when?"

"There's a lot you don't know. I keep trying to tell you, but—"

"Okay, don't tell me any more, we'll clear it all up soon." Plunkett escorted Woby to the door gently, then shoved him ungently out into the hall.

"I think I have to—"

Plunkett, one hand up, his other shoving Woby over the threshold, said, "Just get out there."

"I'm in love," Woby said.

"Get in here!" Plunkett ended, his hand down.

CHAPTER ELEVEN

Throughout Time, with peeks at
Eternity. In which it is learned why
Woby is so tired, and so old, and of
his switches from joy to despondency.
Also of "the girl", Trice, and her
uncontrollable escapism.

Woby wandered another hospital floor, much like the previous one, during what had become his favorite time and place to live: London in the late 1960s.

He thought he would try this one more time: to find a terminally ill child, whose physicians had lost hope, to discover the cause of the malady, then time-travel enough to fix things.

There ahead of him was she, the girl; Trice was her name. It surprised him. Though he had seen her many times during his travels, until today it was always the same pattern: She always saw him first, she always said something cryptic, she always appeared in a hurry, and she always soon left him. Like many, many, many other examples of experiences during his time traveling—it had been years, filled first with "kids' stuff" and now with more serious endeavors—he accepted Trice's lack of rationality, chalked it up to weirdness of the spacetime continuum, assumed there was some explanation that was beyond his understanding and that only men like Applemon, with some symbols that looked like small knives fighting large insects, could understand.

And that maybe it had something to do with Plunkett's plans, or their failed travels, and that perhaps someday it would be explained. Or not.

But this time, at this hospital, it was different. He was able to sneak up on her, as it were. No one was allowed in this part of the facility, its worst part, without being nearest of kin to the young patients, so Woby was already sneaking. He approached the next destination on his hopelessly hopeful itinerary, room 1834.

The girl did not hear him, though not due to any skill of Woby's, but because she was deep in concentration, and in fact was blinking. Not her eyes, her eyes were not blinking, her whole body, was blinking, flickering like a silent movie. She appeared, then didn't, a few times a second. Woby found that by blinking himself—with his eyes—he could either make her invisible or in fact stationary. In this way he got a good look at her.

Young in face, slight in shape, with short, looping hair that bounced with every twitch and dart of her head, she stood otherwise sturdy, a thick-stemmed flower stubborn and defiant against unseen winds that would twist and harm lesser blooms. She was dressed in something between a middle-aged woman's dress and a Middle Ages woman's gown or tunic, many layered, each billowy, downy, constrained with no belt, though Woby thought he caught a rough skin of blue jeans underneath.

Her deep, indomitable eyes ruled all. They surveyed and searched and pivoted and pierced and were dark clouds of knowing. They caught Woby more than once, and each glance made his thoughts surrender.

Wow, is what Woby thought most.

Then the Buddhists came, dressed in purple, bald, harmonious, and unathletic. They hummed as they trotted nearer, their own robes held in hand, their loose belts disheveled.

Trice stopped blinking, grabbed Woby, saying "Oh, *you're* here. That's why. We have to go."

Her voice was deep, unexpectedly deep, and clear, belying

her small size and a presence that somehow seemed tentative, her existence itself insecure.

Trice fiddled with Woby's time-belt dials. Her eyes never stopped moving, her fingers moved swiftly, and so did they: soon both were in the past, on a wide plain with giant flowers—some looked like Ox-eye daisies though could be sat upon—and meaty birds that did not fly, all within a hot, steamy atmosphere. Before Woby could mention his nausea Trice acted again and in a one-eyed blink they returned to the same London hospital, appearing on its roof. Breathless, Woby leaned over its short wall, sucked cool air and enjoyed the view of eclectic architectures about the wide, brown river and its pretty, stately bridge.

Safe—from the Buddhists—Trice spoke in rapid bursts. "You're confusing the children. I've tried to fix it…so they don't hate you… but they're very afraid when you come."

Woby remained indisposed.

"They have enough to worry about… without the bogeyman coming," she added.

"Me?" Woby squeaked in disbelief. It made Trice chuckle, her bass tones rippling forth comfortably, her eyes wide with a hint of light within their round shadows. She reversed quickly, however, putting hand to mouth. "I was trying to help them," Woby explained. "Save them. Because I can…well, you know, I have special skills."

Trice observed the belt, its dials and poor construction, and though her eyes dimmed with suspicion, she said under her breath, "This does explain it, I guess."

Louder, she explained that whenever she followed Woby—which she could do easily—she was pursued.

"The guy in the bowtie?" Woby asked.

"Yes. You know him?"

"I think he knows my brother Applemon." Woby realized immediately that she saw this as a threat. "But no! He wouldn't mean any harm! Or at least, my brother wouldn't, he's a good guy, unless you are stupid. He doesn't like that."

Trice's telling eyes squinted.

"But, you know," Woby went on, at last refreshed and taking in sun and breeze and view, "I don't know the other guy, so run if you have to. Do what you want. I'll help you. I used to run from my brothers sometimes." Woby stretched his long limbs, whimper-moaning like a puppy.

Looking Woby over, searching his face and its guileless simplicity, Trice admitted it hard to believe Woby was a conspiratorial threat.

"Or at least," she said, "I want to believe that." She smiled, her eyes flashing for a moment, a deep nature's green, though quickly fading back to black.

Woby stopped in mid-stretch. "Is that why you were at the hospital? Helping me not help them?"

With a laugh, Trice's eyes opened wide, then shut and she turned away. "Yes, I was fixing things when the Madhyamakas came. They are the hardest to escape. You're giving the young ones false hope. Don't worry, I did the same thing…but now I know."

"Oh. But wait, I never came here before, I never saw that boy—"

"You would have," Trice said, her words and voice both deep as oceans.

"Oh." Woby understood.

"You are Penthos?" she asked.

"No, Woby."

"Same thing," she said, then waved her hands wildly for him to forget it, explaining at the same time that instead of waving, if he wanted, she could go back and change things to ensure that he forgot because it would never happen, but it takes a lot of energy, and she asked which he preferred.

"You can just wave," Woby said, breathless just listening to Trice's manner of speaking.

"Ok thank you," she spoke rapidly. "I am sorry. Sorry. I am Trice." There was a quick flash of forest green eye, then dark.

"Yes," Woby answered, smiling, red, red and smiling.

He didn't know what to say next, and neither did she.

A door slammed. Trice disappeared. It caused Woby to trip and fall, off the roof—his senses told him so in the ensuing, intense milliseconds, and indeed a very complicated life passed before his eyes, then stopped.

He woke in a grove—tropical, hot and humid, balmy, the smell of salt in the air, sharp, long leaves all around, a few rough husks around like giant almonds.

Trice was near, her dark eyes surveying quickly everywhere for a time before returning to Woby.

"Who are you?" he asked, just as she did, syllable for syllable; and they laughed. And again they laughed as the simultaneously spoke again, Trice saying "I thought I was the only one who…" and Woby saying "I guess a lot of people can…"

"Time travel," they finished. Trice lifted the folds of her clothes, searched for a dry patch of ground, and plopped to a sit.

"Until recently…" the girl began. She seemed unused to speaking in regular conversation, uncomfortable with it. She admitted as much, and explained her life, her intense, restless eyes split between Woby and every other thing in their wild surroundings. "Until recently, I mean, because now there are people after me."

"The monks? What's with them? Why do—"

"Oh—the Buddhists? They say they are Madhyamakas, that type." Trice spoke at a hyper pace. "They are nice, but…I don't know…sometimes I'm not in the mood. They think I am a spirit, a 'sunyata dakhini' they call it, I think. I don't think I am…but it's hard to argue since I don't really know how it works."

"So wait," Woby understandably had many questions. He felt like he had walked into the middle of a movie, and wondered whether, for people who can time travel, it was usual storytelling. "How did it start? I don't see a belt or anything—are you saying you can go anywhere, to any time, I mean? How? And what about—"

Trice interrupted. The best that she could answer was to say that, from what she had been told, she was "enlightened" as "they" called it, though she didn't say who "they" were. But they said she was unguided and would be unable to live a normal life regardless of the era.

She also told how she lost her family when very young and could not remember where or when they lived.

Woby felt sad, with an adopted empathy. Trice had nobody she could be with, as she said, an unavoidable correlate, seemingly, with her uniqueness.

Or so she assumed until recently, she explained with her usual word whirlwind. "The only people who seemed to understand me," she said, "were the mystical ones and out of those the only ones that last through time were the Buddhists ones. But of course the ones that come to me are different Buddhists every time since they don't time travel but get old and die and then to the next "bardo" or whatever they call it. Each generation knows about me and has a lot of questions that I don't know the answers to, and they try to find me, it is in their traditions to. But I don't want to be their spirit angel since I'm not."

"Oh," Woby nodded, understanding none of it. "I think—"

"But I did want to help people, so when—"

"You keep interrupting me," Woby said, with a smile, since he meant it kindly. It reminded him of home and made him feel safe: as long as someone else was talking he felt things would be good. He certainly wasn't insulted, but Trice stood rigid and looked ashamed.

"I'm really sorry."

"It's—"

"I am not used to talking to people," Trice went on, as if able to speak on inhale of breath as well as out. "And I'm not sure of the timing of when to stop and start, you know?"

"It's fine, I don't—"

"So anyway, since I was a child I thought I could save children," Trice went on as Woby beamed happily, "the ones who were dying, since I could see what happened to them, and I could go back and warn them. Like you tried to do, right?"

"Yes, exactly!" Woby answered, glad for the connection.

"But I failed. Over and over. That is when the monks became *really* interested in me. Anyway, I got used to getting along, being whenever I wanted, and I met a lot of people and asked questions until they asked questions back and I learned to stay out of trouble, not draw attention to myself, and I saw how other people lived, and tried myself. I tried school, at different times, and fitting in here or there. I learned to control my travels, mostly."

"Mostly? Well, that's pretty good, I can hardly do anything with it, and my brother—my other brother, Plunkett—and I have mostly screwed up using this thing." Woby held up the belt, it shone in the sun, its abject man-madeness quite distinct from their abjectly natural surroundings.

"It must be nice to have brothers," Trice said. Woby nodded. "The only time I can't control it," she continued, "is when I can't control myself, like when I get scared, or am upset too much. I then go to a place…it's very strange…I don't really know what it is."

"What do you mean?"

Trice had never tried to speak of this, or even resolve this part of her existence in her own mind, let alone transfer the notion to someone else's. She seemed happy to try, so Woby listened.

"I go to a still place," she said, "it's quiet, in my mind I mean, and I can see and feel a lot of things at once, but it is all very still, like I am in one place and many times, or stuck in one time but almost everywhere at once. But either way it is calm because I am sort of outside myself, but inside is calm. And is still me. You know."

Woby didn't try to speak, he couldn't have done so in time anyway since she was speaking so fast, but his nodding, though disingenuous, could match the tempo. So he nodded.

Trice went on. "And I learned that when it happens, it's bad because someone else, some other soul from who knows where or when, switches to my place, where I was in space and in time when I was frightened and went to the still place-time."

"I noticed that," Woby said as fast as he could. Indeed he had started when Trice said "switches" and ended perfectly in sync.

"Yes, sorry! I learned it the hard way." Trice paused.

"Oh, don't get me started on that!" Woby said. He then promised to go next, to tell her all about him, but he had more questions about the "still place" where she goes to, and how she gets back.

"It's like a dream," she said, her eyes still everywhere, her notions also coming from many directions. "But it's still me. And it's like having a whole song in your head at once. And I see things all at once, like plants in a stream from seed to flower and the bees then are like a needle and thread."

Woby let that sink in as fast as he could.

Trice went on. "The Madhyamaka Buddhists called it emptiness, a science guy told me it is eternity and maybe only in my mind or maybe it's just a math thing as someone else said. But I can't control it, it sometimes feels like the instant of time travel, that infinitely small time it takes to go sometime else, but it is like that all the time there. It's very calm."

"I get it," Woby said, getting none of it. He was still on the bee-and-thread thing,

"I didn't explain it well…but I am still me," Trice said sadly. Woby looked as lost as he was.

"How do you get back?" He sat up straight and asked. To Woby it all sounded like somewhere to be rescued from.

"When I calm down, I guess, I don't do anything on purpose…I just find myself somewhere else eventually…that part is the scariest, but if I breathe and sort of concentrate it isn't bad and I come back."

After some silence broken only by the wind fighting through the stiff, exotic leaves of the dense bushes nearby, Woby perked up violently. "I have one more question! You said people were after you—who? You don't seem worried."

"Oh yeah, until recently, as I said, I was the only one who would do this, jump through time. Now there is you, and the others. There is one guy especially who scares me. But I'm faster, better—I'm hard to catch. And he isn't good at it, he has some weird electronic thing he uses, he doesn't pray or think. He doesn't wear the thing, he holds it. I guess this is when it is finally invented, when time travel is invented by scientists. I have been far in the future, and far in the past, and never saw it invented, but I guess that's how it works…right? And it's now?"

"Yes," Woby wanted to say, and did say, in resignation; his honest answer would have taken much longer.

"It scared me, the man in the bowtie guy coming to the roof, that was the first time anyone came after me like that."

"The first time?" Woby asked "But I saw them all following you before, and didn't you say—"

"That," Trice replied, "was in the future, so the other was actually the first time. It's your *now* but it hadn't happened yet for me, sort of, though I remember it."

"Should I remember it, or is that wrong?" Woby tried to hang in there.

"Well," Trice explained, "there are two types of memory, one of things that happened in the past, and another one of that given in the present of the past, like the light from a distant star. It's complicated. Words are useless, when I explain it to myself I avoid words. I can try apophatically, maybe?"

"What's that?"

"When you describe something by saying everything that it isn't."

"It sounds like it takes a long time," Woby observed.

"It does," Trice said. Woby felt something missing in her response; it was that she hadn't laughed at his response.

"I can try that, if you think that would help…?"

It didn't help, and eventually Trice handed Woby some aspirin she had taken from the hospital.

They walked to a stream for a drink and looked around for a time. The rivulet dropped over successive falls, crashing among slick, large, rounded stones that were bluish in color, the sun dazzling on the rippled water. The overloaded branches of trees—their fruit was massive and light in color—formed natural umbrellas, with drying, flat, blues tones beneath a natural patio. Woby looked nearby for a natural chair to bring the lady, heard growling, and returned with nothing but a dead flower. It was large, orange, and complexly petalled and dwarfed Trice's hand.

"I've learned a lot of things, Penthos, and a lot of things I still have to learn. I will tell you about them, I still have a lot to tell you. But we have a lot of time! Do you want to come with me?" Trice asked, "Where next?" By the time Woby stopped smiling they had indeed already started traveling, and traveling adventurously.

Having temporarily put aside the pressure of ultimate meanings, and the confusion of their improbable, paradoxical uniqueness, the two spent their young lives, spent wonderful, rich, full time…and of course doing in so in a way that was beyond all other human experience, certainly since Adam and Eve, as they joked.

Their time was not Plunkett's time, or even Applemon's, whose minutes of piqued greed or stimulated intellectual vainglory passed while nestled in the security and gravity of their own track across seconds and days and sequential moments, their AUNT, sequential moments of planning and theorizing, of cause and effect, of stone-kicking pain, of sunrises, and other assurances.

No. Woby and Trice sped through years, not yoked by one month per month perception or living, or the non-overlapping flows of individual points of view and of time. The two flew, it can be said, as unnaturally as a rhino jumping from a cliff and rising to gore the clouds above it.

Soon enough, their adventures took a certain form. For example, if Trice was an expert snowboarder, and Woby was just beginning on the slopes, she would have saved him from numerous embarrassments from dressing improperly, the stickiness of the getting off the lift and into traffic, and the pain of many falls without first knowing basic skills and mountain etiquette.

But since they were not snowboarding, she instead saved Woby from his own past, and various police, two armies, two phone companies, the IRS, and on a technicality liberated him from an impending trial for cruelty to animalcules.

From his future, there were rescues from the Global Alliance for the Prevention of the Spread of Horrible Disease, the Anti-Button League, and the Society of All Equals. There was a close call, a misunderstanding really, where Trice freed Plunkett from lengthy prison time after he accidentally sat on King Zonkendigit's personal Squeemzonk 4000, tried to hide it, and was accused of theft. But it ended in a banquet that overflowed with joy and gray and black fruit.

And more stuff like that.

Woby, of course, learned much: about himself, about time travel, and becoming a man, about Trice, and about general quirks and specific existence.

They avoided any pursuit, quite easily in fact.

Very importantly, and before and above all else, Trice warned him never to time travel in order go see himself. To emphasize, this was why Trice never sought her parents. Trice was unable to explain it fully, not through lack of word power but because of the swell and choke of slow tears.

It occurred to Woby that this was never part of Plunkett's plan, to revisit themselves.

"Well, he sounds smart," Trice said to this.

"He is, but nothing compared to Applemon, who is older, and smarter—I told you about his fame and degrees, and his belt. Remind me to thank him for it."

They aged a little bit, together. The laughter was worth it.

Woby gave Trice confidence, and removed her fear, mostly, and when together they were not bothered by the man in the bowtie, or by shadows, or ghosts; and in fact she hardly ever flickered off to the "still place" with Woby as her companion. When she did, it was brief; Woby would make new friends and await her return.

Eventually, after many eternities that were all too brief, Woby said to Trice that he had to go back.

"To where, Woby?" Trice asked.

"To AUNT."

"Oh," Trice misunderstood, turning wistfully away, eyes darkening.

"It stands for 'Agreed Upon Normal Time,'" Woby said.

Trice visually bristled at the word *normal*; it took more explaining.

"It just means," Woby said, "the time when Plunkett and I started using the time machine belt, that part of my life. That point of view, back at the dorm on the weekend."

Trice visually unbristled. "Yes! Yes!" she said. "I understand that! I have questions!"

Woby couldn't answer any of her questions. They were all about whether Woby's agreed upon normal life with his brother was like her "other place," which of course it was not. But Woby enjoyed his ignorance since Trice seemed very, very happy. He did explain that he had a plan: for them both, and for Plunkett, for the three of them, and for Applemon, for the four of them, and for everyone.

Woby wanted to go back to his brothers, to explain to them as well, and then they could all meet again, soon. Instantly, perhaps, if he did it right.

"Oh! Great!" Trice said, and laughed, eyes green, her usual constant motion rejoicing as dance. "Aha! I can think of things I would like to do also, while you do that."

They kissed and agreed to meet at a time and place where their time together could begin again.

CHAPTER TWELVE

> Late Saturday afternoon. Aris explains
> the significance of this "girl"—as a
> figment—to Ariel, as they await Woby
> and his first couch session.

Ariel's nervousness was palpable. She hoped it didn't transmit so clearly on her video call with Aris, but every time the professor spoke she panicked to find—in notes, on the internet—what in fact he might be talking about. She was sure of 10 percent, could guess well on 40 percent, could fake 30 percent, but 20 percent of the conversation was obfuscation or mystery.

Aris was pushing a new thrust for her research: to go deeper into the delusions of her psychological subject and to now focus on Woby. In fact, they were awaiting his arrival for analysis, her first attempt at any such interview, and her first move beyond the purely academic and theoretic.

There were many forms for Woby to sign that would limit Ariel's responsibility from, well, everything.

"But he can't sign, he's not an adult," Ariel said. Did Aris actually laugh? Ariel looked up from her usual breakneck notetaking to check her laptop screen.

"We shall worry about that some other time," Aris said, and, yes, did laugh, though his face didn't change much.

Nancy, increasingly intrigued—no, not intrigued, she said, but curiously sickened—by her roommate's project-slash-obsession, looked on, out of sight of the laptop camera, and shrugged her shoulders.

Aris described the new ideas he had for Ariel.

"Correct me if I am wrong…" Aris began.

"Okay," Ariel said, regretting it more than words can convey, but Aris went on.

"But I believe you are onto something significant with respect to this girl character that Woby sees popping in and out of time, as it were, the time in his psyche. If we are correct, we need to be on the alert for archetypes like this one, this girl figment of his imagination."

"Oh, yes," Ariel said and watched as Aris paced off-screen. His words came fainter, she had to bend an ear to keep up with her notes.

"One of us," Aris said, "mentioned the other day—was it you or me? Regardless, that the archetype of the free-spirited girl may be germane, one who has special powers over natural forces. Hm, let me look something up…" Aris trailed off but only for a second and a half. "…well!" he exclaimed, "of all the black beans of Abyssinia! How Olympian! Yes: in this case, of the subject claiming time travel, the girl he would fantasize about, that he would project from his unconscious loneliness, would be one whose powers were over time itself. Sweet epicurean dews of Isis! How providential! This may be—and if it is, we would have cause to celebrate, along with the rest of the psychology establishment, mind—this may be the case with this girl of Woby's. This mysterious, ephemeral female who calls her male Penthos. Why, it's clearly drawn from the difference, the serious difference, between Sopdet and Sothis, is it not?"

Nancy muttered her pain over the man's confusion between and conflation of Egypt and Greece.

Ariel nodded, however, as Aris had returned to the screen. His large navy-blue bowtie was now crooked.

"What a breakthrough, if it were." He spoke. "Superb and excellent. The lodes we could mine toward curing multitudinous typological psychoses, neuroses, and the like if we indeed have found a concrete reanimation of this type-archetype in our subject. Like the Etesian wind over the Memphian reed-groves."

"Oh, my God." Nancy said, over and over, while vowing "to look that one up."

"Makes sense," Ariel said. Nancy snorted a laugh, apologized for it, but repeated it so that Ariel had to mute her laptop microphone and, while laughing herself, scold her roommate harshly, mentioning how much respect a man of Aris' stature had earned. Nancy, while bent over in hysterics, agreed to take this seriously and swore to do her part to help the seriousness along.

"There is a goddess of temporal creationism," Aris was saying, "among the Meso-American sheep herder clans named *Lamtayle* that serves as a perfect example. Though there are others. The Portuguese Stone-age Manxmen worshipped a Queen 'Atoi' who could reverse the growth of plants and certain white birds. Some sub-Saharan tribes during their most devastating Ice Age would summon 'Oo-ooloo,' a female spirit of doing things rapidly and without interruption."

Nancy slapped a twenty-dollar bill on the tallest of Ariel's textbook piles and said, "It's yours if he's not making this up." She then retrieved the loose coins that had noisily escaped her pocket and rolled over desk and floor.

"Yet: all those deities of humanity's subconscious," Aris continued, no longer on the screen since he had paced away once more, "are derivative of the one, a one called Trice, one of legend whose appearance in cultures across the globe is well documented. Different names, different forms, but always Trice: she who has power over time. And note the name, a classic epigenetic subconscious clue, yes?"

"Yes, of course, I was just going to say that," Ariel said as Nancy helpfully wrote on a pink Post-it note, "Trice means: a short period of time," to which Ariel bowed her thanks.

"So in extreme mental distress," Aris droned on, "there may be such a character living within poor Woby. It may be Trice herself, or some manifestation close to it. When you find it, it could represent a case of Freudian Screen Memory that would provide new paths of insights for years—nay, decades—to come."

"Gosh," Ariel unmuted her microphone to say. "That's exactly what you and I discussed last time, the Screen Memory angle to all this."

"My thoughts precisely. We need to pursue it. During analysis, bring your subject, this Woby, to pursue this figment, this girl. See where it leads. This is very advanced, are you up to it?" The professor asked.

Nancy was waving her arms vigorously in the negative as Ariel answered lamely in the affirmative.

"And Woby's health, his sanity depends on it," Aris continued, "depends on capturing this creature, this illusion, this Trice. Where and whether she abides—within his mind, of course—is very powerful, very dangerous. But this accomplishment would help all the Wobies of the world, and indeed create a new branch of research. A trunk perhaps."

Ariel was catching up on notes and didn't answer.

Aris added, "a trunk with your name on it, Ariel."

Nancy made a fist, shook her head, and spun around, but didn't speak.

"Thank you, Professor. Aris. Thank you, Aris," Ariel answered. There was silence and smiling over the internet connection.

"So then! What are we waiting for? Where is your subject?"

"He should have been here by now. He's at Plunkett's dorm and—"

"Go there! Carl Jung never waited on his patients! Nothing stands in the way of learning, of research! Go get him, and analyze!"

"Okay! Yes, good idea!" Ariel answered, and began to pack her laptop bag immediately, on camera, and with a flourish.

"Good. And one more thing, Ariel," the professor purred, straight and centered on camera and adjusting his bowtie, "while you're at the dorm room, take the flash drive out of Applemon's laptop and bring it back with you. Okay. Bye."

This was so abrupt that Ariel and Nancy both stiffened with the absence of reaction.

At length Nancy's expression turned grave, and Ariel asked Aris, at the risk of sounding unsure and overly ethical and moral, why.

As the professor reached toward his screen to shut the call, he said in haste, "It has his backup, his notes and work, his time travel research, experiments, and theories that will be relevant here. We need it. If you're up to it, that is. Recall that Plunkett, and especially Woby, are getting these notions from their brother, as we have discussed. The former is a case of *volo ergo sum* and the latter *visum aliter deo*. Names are everything! Do it. We need to see the raw source. Knowledge without action is death! Get Woby and get the data. You can do it."

"But…" Ariel said, as Nancy's head shook determinedly.

Aris had gone.

"Don't do it!" Nancy said sternly. "He's nuts. He's right about Plunkett and Woby, he summed them up in Latin," this was in answer to the Ariel's pause in notetaking, stuck on the "volo" part, "but this isn't right, you can't just take from other people whatever Aris wants."

"No, of course not."

Ariel wrote and wrote.

CHAPTER THIRTEEN

Saturday 5:00-ish, AUNT. In which Ariel comes back to the dorm looking like a garden, to collect Woby, and to see Apple's Mac.

"Why are you trying to ruin my life? Because yours is over? Then stop being in love." Plunkett shaped his hand as a gun and aimed it at his own temple to sum up his theory of the allegory of love in thirteenth century literature. "I was going to take care of you, you know, I have a plan. Everything I need is on Applemon's laptop. I think. Where he keeps all his research."

"Man plans, and God laughs, and Plunkett finally reads the manual," Woby said dryly. "Anyway, I tried to tell you about Trice."

Plunkett raised his trigger finger to a safe height. "That's what—who this is about? That's all in the recent past. Leave it there."

"I can't. there's something wrong, I think," Woby said.

"Okay underbrain, then what do we do now? I don't want to double-date, if that is what you're thinking. Just because you're happy with *your* life—"

"I am, though I'm getting worried." Woby interrupted and explained while his brother paced the apartment to eventually settle on the kitchen counter, his arms around his knees searching the ceiling and alternately gazing out the browning window over the full sink—each move calculated to show his lack of fascination in what Woby had to say.

"Trice wanted to meet you and Applemon and explain her abilities," Woby said. "Then she and I were going to meet at her favorite time—which is twenty years in the future from AUNT, isn't that interesting?—to prep for our lives together. That was MY plan. But the dog, and this lady, have me worried because it means she is worried, or scared, of something. That's what happens, she switches with someone when she gets nervous, she can't control it, she goes to a quiet place."

Plunkett's obligatory nodding gave way to a look of concern and understanding, of loving brotherly empathy, and he said, "Save it for Ariel."

"What?" Woby asked.

"It's crazy, so it's perfect. It'll distract her, and give her a lot of psychotic stuff to dig into. Keep time travel out of it, focus on the unrequited love stuff. Keep her guessing." Plunkett believed that, until he was secure in his riches, Ariel could still screw things up terribly and counterclockwise. The future(s) they had seen were proof of that. They were the result of bad planning, and of Woby driving.

Plunkett's next look out the window led to an energetic dismount from the counter, a two-handed clutch of Woby's shirt, and a curse.

"Shit!" Plunkett exclaimed. "She's outside! She can't come in here!" Plunkett waved his arms toward the couch where their three guests—the result of Trice's nervous time-twitching as he just learned—sat, the ultimate conversation starters.

Plunkett said to Woby, "Call Ariel. Steer her to come in the back way before she doesn't. Then get her to leave, go with her. I need to get on Apple's Mac in private. I can't fail now, I'm so close! Get her in here then out of here. Okay?"

Woby obeyed, though with some sciatic nerve pain. He opened the back door that led to a drab, cement hallway with exposed pipes and electric wires. That led to a stairwell of similar make. Spider webs, dust, dampness, an emergency exit sign, and a stray yellow construction worker's hat kept him company as he awaited Ariel.

Plunkett searched Applemon's room for the laptop and then for any clue as to what the password might be. He overheard Woby welcome Ariel through the thick emergency entrance, then through the back dormitory door.

"Hi Woby—you look terrible!" Ariel said. "You sick?"

Plunkett had a control-freaky revelation and ran to the hall to oversee this conversation by miming hints in the background to Woby's face and Ariel's back, her wildly colorful, flowery dress contrasting with the raincloud-colored walls.

"Not really, just some joint stiffness." Woby answered.

Plunkett waved his arms in an X shape to indicate that this was a bad thing to say.

"I thought you were coming to see me," Ariel said.

"I'm ready, I was on my way."

Plunkett approved this with two thumbs up.

"There's nothing to worry about. I see you have the belt." Ariel smiled.

Plunkett mimicked reading from a clipboard, that Woby should stick to the script.

"Yes. But I want to talk about a girl. I have girl problems."

Plunkett clasped his hands and rocked them high in the air to show his triumphant pleasure.

"Superb!" Ariel said, her voice slightly deeper. "And very excellent. But first…" she spun on a heel so quickly that Plunkett was caught with his hands still clasped. He lowered them slowly then ran to Applemon's room.

"Hi, Plunkett," Ariel said, coming directly behind.

Just as Plunkett hid the laptop under a pillow, she-who-would-not-be-denied came blossoming into the room, dress and work bag exploding in yellow and pink. If something could be both florid and tempestuous, she was it.

Plunkett explained that he had been cleaning the front door, so people had to come through the back. Ha-ha. Heh. Heh?

"I don't care," Ariel said. If a thunderclap could sprinkle flowers, she was what it would be like. "I want to see Applemon's laptop."

Shit, Plunkett thought. Why was every moment of his life a worst-case scenario? Why did each succeeding moment belie the previous worstness, and top it?

"It's not here." Plunkett said to the verdant wikka, but as he did, a medium-sized droplet of insecure sweat formed on the young man's prickly heated forehead, just enough to be perceptible and to tell Ariel many things.

She twirled gracefully and headed directly to Applemon's bedroom, her skirt spinning to life a hilly landscape worthy of an impressionist painting, pinks-and-purple poesies a-popping.

The laptop was soon on her lap, with Plunkett watching from his usual resigned, second-row position and Woby having to "have a sit" which he did on Applemon's made bed.

"You can't get on it, I tried," Plunkett said, meaning the laptop, as Ariel typed into the screen's login box and the laptop's background picture of a grey, billowing mushroom cloud became visible.

"How did you know his password?" Plunkett asked with unencrypted annoyance.

"I know men."

"What's my password then?"

"I said 'men,'" Ariel replied, mean as a garden snake.

"You admit I am beyond mere manhood now?" was Plunkett's witty comeback. "You admit you can't figure me out? I am inscrutable, unpredictable."

Surprisingly, Ariel took the bait and the challenge and played this game. Woby smiled in anticipation. Secretly he even hoped Plunkett would win.

"Go ahead, what's my password?" Plunkett served.

Ariel hissed a first guess, mean as a snake that eats other snakes. "Is it my name?"

"Don't flatter yourself."

"A curse then?" Ariel volleyed.

"Maybe."

Ariel tilted her head, closed her eyes, and thought. Her rose barrette seemed to grow and bloom. After a few seconds she turned and leaned and whispered into Plunkett's ear.

Plunkett's face dropped. "I'll change it to your name," he said quietly. Ariel laughed sardonically and returned to her business.

Woby felt left out. "You'll never guess mine. I've changed it, like, six times. Ten years ago." He was defending Plunkett.

Ariel said, "Password7" while typing and maneuvering among the windows on Applemon's computer in a serious temper.

"Nope," Woby said.

Ariel answered again, "Woby7." And kept typing and mousing.

Woby said to Plunkett, "She's amazing," and he tipped his cap.

Ariel continued her activity on Applemon's computer as Plunkett's unease grew like a weed. He was not sure what she was after, and, of course, he could not be sure what she would find. Yet: Plunkett's newest planning required this same tactic, his goal being to find a Time Travel Belting For Dummies book or the equivalent. So he looked on with great interest from over Ariel's shoulder, learning what he could but afraid to raise suspicion, to give Ariel reason to lock him out from view.

She was whizzing along now, sliding windows around on screen, selecting and rejecting document content, Web links, and emails. Plunkett could not keep up nor could slow her; nothing would as it seemed. Next she opened four desk drawers, closed each, sat back for a half-second of thought, then with a squeak of satisfaction she overturned a Styrofoam coffee cup porcupined with capless pens and picked up the lone inch-long flash drive that spilled among the pens and paperclips.

She plugged it into the laptop, thought better of that—having scanned the others' eyes upon her—and dropped it into her daisy-decorated bag instead. She snapped it shut.

Plunkett reacted first. "You can't do this. You shouldn't. He won't like it. Stealing from Applemon?"

Ariel may have had a pang of conscience shoot through her

chest, buried under all that budding embroidery, because every body part paused, whereas each had been in nonstop motion since she arrived. She hugged her bag tightly as if to show that neither they nor Nancy nor anyone really understood.

It couldn't be, of course, that Plunkett was, um, what's the word, that condition that he is usually not in…um…'correct'? Couldn't be….

Ethical dilemmas were not Plunkett's specialty, so although he was not sure what Ariel was mumbling about he was glad of the delay, and repeated what he thought Applemon would think.

"Him, either." Ariel said with resurrected confidence, ending any debate, internal or otherwise. "I've seen enough anyway."

Plunkett objected one more time, got Woby to nod, but Ariel smiled her way through a blowout victory. "Knowledge dies without action you know."

She spun her dress into another moving meadow and headed to the back door, flowers bouncing as if bullied by April winds. "Come, Woby. Now. Follow." So saying, she exited, her colors gone.

"Yes, I'll be right there." Woby said.

Plunkett shrugged. Since Ariel had not completely closed the laptop he was able to get a thumb under the cover and stop it from locking. He was very impressed with himself.

"She was always very alive and pretty." Woby yawned and rubbed his neck and stretched his back and scratched his head.

"Shush. It's time for you to go, old man." Plunkett was on a roll now. "She's diseased and awful, but she's gone, and I am in. My plan starts now. I will travel in the morning, after I get a good look at Applemon's notes. Soon you will be rich, Woby! Remember me in your will!"

"You, too!" Woby said. He was glad that Plunkett was glad.

"Only nineteen, and I will be a billionaire. Me, you, my date, or dates—like *that* girl," Plunkett pointed without looking at the memorized direction of a poster on the common room wall of a girl drinking a beer but who otherwise must be uncomfortably cold. "*And* whoever is on the cover of *Women's Fitness Journal* that month…No! *each* month…and whatever old bag you want to bring can help me spill champagne on a French beach. All by this time tomorrow night, Agreed Upon Normal Time." Plunkett was smiling and reveling.

Woby was smiling that Plunkett was smiling; Woby didn't revel simply for money and champagne. But he soon turned, with a new face, to his own life, his own happiness, both of which awaited Trice's return, and she, the girl of many times, was late.

"Well, Plunkett, I wish you luck, and now, my lad, I have to—"

"Never call me that, or else…ah, forget it. Even your on-time senility can't bring me down. Champagne! Billions! Nineteen! *Women's Fitness*! Master of the Present! Me!"

Woby left.

Applemon came.

CHAPTER FOURTEEN

Saturday 5:25-ish, AUNT. In which Applemon comes, explains much that includes danger, and vows a solution.

"Well, you're involved…" Applemon said as he entered the dorm, straightened his clothes, and tucked in his crisp, white, collared shirt.

"Why did you come in through the back? Why the bushes?" Plunkett asked his legend of an older brother after he made the obligatory introductions to the dog, the lady, and the robot—during which Applemon only said "facile" and only to himself at that. Then came the unnecessary explanation as to why Ariel and Woby used the backdoor to leave, after which Applemon had popped, scratched and annoyed, from the unkept and thick hedge off the back stairwell.

"To avoid Ariel," Applemon answered.

"And Woby?" Plunkett asked.

"No—"

"It's the opposite for me, usually," Plunkett said.

"Funny. Ariel and I aren't talking. Yelling, but not talking. I have bigger fish to fry at the moment. I wouldn't jump into a bush to avoid Woby. In fact I have been seeing a lot of him, though he hasn't seen me."

"Yeah, I know what you mean…what?"

"Listen, you mental thumb-puppet," Applemon said, "I know about everything you guys have been doing—and don't interrupt, and don't deny anything. I am not Woby or Ariel. But now you're involved in my own plans, so you need to listen to me and shut up."

Applemon took off his watch and placed it on the kitchen counter. Plunkett, already shutted up, waited for Apple to explain. Applemon, annoyed, slid the watch across the counter toward his brother's hand. Plunkett sat up straight. Applemon, annoyed, picked the watch up and held it two inches from an unflinching Plunkett's eyes.

"Oh!" Plunkett said. The watch was a smaller, slicker, more excellent version of the time travel belt that Woby and he had used to fall in love and not get rich.

"The one I let you and Woby play with was a prototype, but I'll start from the beginning. Have a Coke."

Plunkett dutifully sat and listened while his impeccably credentialed and appropriately arrogant older brother told of the brief history of time travel, of the belt and other devices, of Applemon's own plans and those of his adversary Professor Aris, of nicknames, of the girl Trice, and of what they needed to do now that they—Plunkett and Woby—had almost "bonkerized" things.

Plunkett of course had many questions. Most were answered with versions of the following:

- *Would you shut up and just listen?*

- *Stop asking about lottery numbers, jackass.*

- *Calm down, because if I can control this you'll be able to sleep on my couch and trust me it'll be the richest couch on earth.*

- *You're wearing that shirt again?*

- *You were good on analogies on the SAT, so please realize: as you are to Woby, I am to you.*

- *Dopey. Just listen.*

Others were received better, even simple ones, like, "Why a belt?"

Applemon answered, "I should have made time-travel-shaving-cream or clean underwear so you would not have used it."

"Who is Professor Aris? What department? Physics?" Plunkett asked next.

"Professor Chatterton. He is a polymath, specializes in Physics but dabbles everywhere and anywhere his latest stupid ideas take him. 'Stupid' compared to mine, I mean, not yours. Aris is just a nickname, like mine, yours, Woby's, Trice's—"

"Trice? Woby's girl?" Plunkett said.

"Yes. The name denotes a small span of time, but Aris' name is much more lame. When he was a kid and a philosophy major at Berlin Polytechnic, rumor has it he began wearing bowties and blowing people away in debates though he had to stand on a platform to reach the lectern; so they called him 'Aristoddler,' part Aristotle, part toddler. Forget it."

Plunkett forgot it. He asked next whether Aris could time travel as well. "Can all you people?"

"Your betters, you mean? No, not all we people. Aris borrowed—you know, stole—a lot of my team's research, and from the beginning we disagreed on a lot. My device is better at navigating within one universe, his has trouble in multiverse schemes. Mine is a two-seater, can take two people for whatever that's worth. I tested it with a cat who is now a god somewhere."

"The belt can take two people, too, if it fits around them. I dragged Woby to the future in it with me."

"Yes, I know. And were those good results, genius? It's not good to push the prototype too far."

"It was confusing..." Plunkett began.

"And cold, and with monuments to time machines within time machines? And jittery like video through a bad internet connection?"

"Yeah, but I thought—" Plunkett began.

"Don't think. Mine is better, trust me. And my work is better than Aris', in general."

"Yours is flame retardant," Plunkett said.

"You noticed, great." Applemon rolled his eyes beneath his glasses. "Was your plan to be famous for being idiotic?"

"No. To outlive anyone who knew," Plunkett said evenly.

"Ha! *That* I can respect. Good one." Applemon laughed, then went on. "Anyway, the belt was a successful test. It adjusts for Newtonian projections, for the movement of the earth, for example. It is also designed to limit temporal feedback looping, and to isolate the subject. You might have noticed people staring at you, they can sense a difference in conscious time perception, and are confounded as to whether what they are seeing is a memory or projection. It helped prove one of my theories."

"Well, yes, professor," Plunkett said in the appropriate faux-fawning voice, "I do believe your theory is correct. But why do they stare all the rest of the time?"

"Stop being stupid. Listen, the point wasn't for you two human placebos to screw around, but to move science and human knowledge forward. In fact, the original idea, and the whole design—and more importantly what was approved by those who paid for it all—was to get the answer to any question we might have in the present. To skip years ahead in the pursuit of truth. And to also control such advancements, I don't mind telling you. But along the way, we found some interesting half-truths, like this girl Trice."

"How can you," Plunkett asked, pulling from something very near his heart, "get information using it? I'm dying, and Woby practically already died, to know."

"Yes, your bravery is well documented. And so is the proposed method, but I don't have the three years it would take to explain it to you."

"Okay, smarty-trousers, what did you all learn then?"

"Well, things took a weird turn. We discovered the girl, Trice, and that she can time travel naturally. It put Aris onto a completely new track, from what I can tell, his device reflects this change in research direction, his focus is on controlling cross-time normalization, when the equations collapse toward solutions on the imaginary plane, or as they approach the perceived void of the QOV. Aris thinks there is great undiscovered energy and power there."

"Of course that's what he wants. And you want control of knowledge, and no one wants to get rich," Plunkett said.

"All reductionist atheists aren't the same you know, academic glory is good enough for me, but not Aris. The only thing he and I have in common is the need for secrecy. In that way, you and Woby now pose a danger, but all this can't be hidden for much longer—not in the normal course of time at least. As for Aris, I get the feeling he wants to use this girl to understand the QOV and harness it once he can further his technology. Ethics aren't his thing. I prefer to study her, to make time travel better, more efficient, to get what we want."

"You keep saying Q-O-V, what is that? A void? A black hole?" Plunkett asked. It didn't sound like it was a hoppin' place of the kind he had in mind to visit, plunder, and perhaps be king of. In that case, Applemon and his nemesis could fight all they wanted over it.

"QOV is the qualiomniumvelt, an extra dimension that is still a theory, but if Trice can do what Aris thinks she can do, it might prove to be the greatest discovery of theoretical physics since quantum mechanics, and in fact would have many more ramifications. So it is dangerous stuff, and needs to be studied."

"An extra dimension, a fourth you mean?"

"No. In this theory we treat the three dimensions of space as one, and time as another. QOV is a third, at a right angle to both."

For this part of his lecture, Applemon produced from his front pocket a diagram in pen on a single sheet of old-style graph paper with its many tiny, blue-lined boxes. The professor pointed at it pointedly, or alternately held its face to Plunkett's face.

The page was titled "Longitudinal Unpack"—in Applemon's stringy handwriting—and showed a simple graph—in Applemon's sticklike hand-doodling—made of many doubly-arrowed lines. They all had the same forty-five-degree slant but were displaced on the page as if a single arrow had broken into pieces that slipped away, either straight up or straight down. The y-axis was labeled "her time," the x-axis "her place." A legend of sorts at the top of the page indicated that dotted lines meant "observer (probable)." A squiggly curlicue was drawn at the origin, its terminal arrow gave the illusion of a third dimension attempting escape from the flat page to shoot into the reader's space. This was labeled "orthogonal omnium" and must have been important to the conversation because Applemon poked at this part the most.

Plunkett ingested Applemon's word banquet, converted what pictures and syllables he could into simpler, more digestible tidbits—*arrows, got it; 3D, sure, okay; power and danger, yes, yum-yum*—and puked back the rest, secretly thanking his parents for making him so different from his brother.

"We," Applemon went on, "myself and my team here at the university, were looking at new forces, using new particles, and we stumbled on this other dimension through complex Galois symmetries. We were years away from making real discoveries, or we were until we found Trice, through the legends of the buddhists in fact. She seems to experience these forces, she carries its spin and charge like a large human particle. She used vibrations in time, as opposed to in space or energy. While I need to know based on observation and measurement, she understands the QOV in terms of perception, experience, memory and emotion."

"Um, yeah, and she loves Woby."

"That's a flaw," Applemon joked as he folded the arrow diagram and slid it to his jeans pocket. "But the rest is fascinating. Following Trice, I was the first to realize that the QOV, to her, is pure point of view, you might say. In fact, that might be all it is. Imagine, locating the thing we all take for granted in the universe, your individual experience of existence, your consciousness, pure observation, pure perception. In its own dimension, like space or time. A fundamental so fundamental that it defines what it is to be. Trice might be a new type of life, or even a new type of matter, or force. Who knows?"

"And she loves Woby," Plunkett repeated.

Applemon smiled and shook his head. "This has all happened very fast and has become exponentially complicated thanks to you two. And yet, maybe it helped thwart Aris in some ways. I have spent my time fixing your mistakes, repairing your rejected futures. We have a council that decides these things, but I had to take personal responsibility."

Plunkett was interested in this QOV place, though perhaps not for the same reasons as his brothers or Professor Aris or the various councils and sponsors of useless research. He wondered if it had any practical uses, like the ability to combine big metropolitan penthouse apartment living with being on the beach. *Two points of view, right?* he thought.

"How does time and eternity fit in?" he asked.

Applemon tried to explain further, first saying that time was like reading a book, but eternity was re-reading it, or was the author itself. Then, no, he thought it better to say that time was like explaining a concept like time, but eternity was how the concept was understood once it was understood. Applemon then asked Plunkett to forget that, and to think of an algorithm, like a computer program. It runs in time, but..."okay, sorry, go back to the first one, keeping in mind that one's eyes are not *in* the book, one's body is in the book, but one's understanding, one's mind, is outside the reading, outside time. That's eternity."

"And you are a teacher?" Plunkett asked afterwards.

"My students are smart," Applemon said.

"What does this have to do with the QOV, Trice, Woby and, most importantly—"

"You? Well, with Aris trying to master the QOV, he will need to study Trice, and this isn't a man that measures costs in a way that maximizes everyone's happiness, if you know what I mean. And that impacts Woby, and you are his brother."

"So?" Plunkett said, "He's pretty old now, I hardly know him."

"So I hereby determine now that you need to help and not be a selfish imbecile. It will probably mean doing nothing, so hopefully that is within your abilities. QOV is not for you to play with. Trice escapes there when she is threatened. She can't control it, thankfully, or else it would be easier for Aris to understand. The QOV is time-free when experienced at a certain angle, so she can in fact 'rest' there, there is space also, and head-space you might say—which all has to do with consciousness, and this is the part that bothers me and all physicists, this is the part that allows the mystics and whackos a way into science where they don't belong. Some believe that the third dimension that QOV is denotes the origin subjec-tivity. Its name—I didn't name it—takes this into account, because we only know space and time, any third 'direction' must be one's experience of both, their qualitative umwelt of the universe, of everything. Umwelt is one's life experience, what it's like to be a bat, for example, as the philosopher once said, or a kitten, or a college slouch. So: Quali-Omnium-Velt, Q-O-V. Another nickname."

"Damn!" Plunkett said, impressed.

"Yep. Time has a beginning, but space and this new dimension do not have limits. They form a plane that is like a stream that is its own source and is an eternal creation of reality. This is all theory of course, but Trice's transport to QOV is caused by wave equation transpositional drag—like a sonic boom—so the research papers call it an 'Omnic Boom,' or 'Tidal Wave Equation,' or 'Tsunomni.'"

"You guys need help naming things, I observe." Plunkett observed.

"No doubt." Applemon laughed. "Some of my colleagues say it is home to a fifth force, a fourth color, the Z prime or leptoquark with third generation mass. I don't agree with the physical inter-pretations, but I am afraid of the consciousness ones. Aris isn't."

"Trice goes there, so why not just ask her?" Plunkett asked.

"She definitely does not know. I have observed her a little bit. It is not easy; my device is no match for her instincts. She escapes—sometimes from me—to the QOV but not purposely. It obviously helps her and is tied to her abilities, which we now understand must be mental, subjective, to cut across time. So thereby it is tied so some notion of eternity. Yet there is some conservation of… well, I don't know what, but when she does disappear to the QOV, another person, another conscious point of view takes her place. You saw that, I think, and Woby is rightly worried about these new guests you have—yes, I already knew about the dog and the lady and robot. These in fact help me track her, sometimes, though the replacement is stochastic—that means random—from what I can tell. One time when I snuck up on her, I was left with a big, white llama. I had to bring it back here. Luckily it was during one of your parties so the smell and noise and muddy hooves went unnoticed until I could find it a home nearby, but in the sixteenth century."

Plunkett laughed. Plunkett continued to laugh. In fact he was soon doubled over with an outpouring of joyful relief, his pent up frustrations and thwarted plans, mixed with unreal excitement and danger and stress, and also fun, was something he now realized was good to have shared. Applemon was soon hysterical also—they are brothers after all.

After the opening of two more Cokes the snorting died down and Plunkett asked, "What's next, then?"

"Well," Applemon said, "Aris is pursuing Trice, but I am not too worried about her keeping herself safe. I will help her if I can, but the real issue is stopping Aris. He has his own device and can really make a mess. I think Trice should be studied, but properly, and with the agreement and consent of the scientific community."

"And Woby's consent?" Plunkett asked.

To this Applemon laughed through a curt response. "There's a lot riding on this, for humankind, for science, for knowledge itself, and for me."

Plunkett began to speak, but didn't, other than to ask again what the plan was.

"Here is what I am going to do…." Applemon said.

He explained that he expected Aris to take advantage of the unpredictability of the wavy spacetime mess that Plunkett and

Woby had caused. For one thing Trice could not navigate as easily with the resulting shocks of energy; it would be like surfing an ocean typhoon waterspout sideways.

"And Woby is his usual anchor, of course," Applemon said. Plunkett said nothing, and his brother went on.

"I'll try to fix it. Aris and I have been furtively, tentatively, gauging each other for some time now, but it is all accelerating to a critical point. I can't wait for council approval, and will do what I can. We'll win. Woby and Trice have been together for some time now, their time, and it weakens her position, but there isn't much Aris can do yet by himself either, unless I'm mistaken."

Plunkett raised his hand and asked, "Why don't you and Aris just keep manipulating/changing the future and past, and fight it out that way?"

"Like you tried to do?" Applemon laughed. "Well, how can I explain…that would be to battle on our own distinct timeline, distinct from this 'AUNT'—I like that, by the way—and so it would be distinct from the world Aris and I want to succeed in. There's a risk in being successful but changing the world so much that is a pyrrhic victory, fruitless, worthless. When you and Woby were seeking selfish goals you were impacting futures that are distinct from AUNT, and so they were only theoretical and, as I have proved, reparable. My devices are made to account for that, as I explained."

"How much does Ariel know of all this?" Plunkett had raised his hand again. "I tried to keep it from her, but Woby…you know. And she wouldn't…you know. I told Woby to tell her it was all in his head."

"That's perfect. With her new all-out-on-fire for all-things psychology mentality she won't see it as anything else even if you brought her backward a million years and put her atop a dinosaur. She's very single-minded. No, I don't see how she could know anything of my serious work. She is smart but very silly, it's a jealous-girl sideshow-thing, don't worry about it. But maybe, who knows, this will lead even to great psychological insights. And that will actually help keep this contained somewhat until I can figure out how—"

Plunkett interrupted to tell of the theft of the flash drive from the pen-holding coffee cup.

Applemon stopped in mid-final-Coke-swallow, the can vertical, his eyes to the kitchen ceiling. He lowered the can slowly and wiped soda suds from the sides of his mouth. The only sounds were the subdued, ragged snoring of the Rottweiler and the electronic heartbeat of the robot, one beep every ten seconds. After five beeps, Applemon crushed his Coke can and threw it away, saying "That's not a great development, but if Ariel doesn't know that I know, then that's fine. The laptop info doesn't matter. Why did she take the flash drive, did she say?"

"No, she was just being nosey, searching everywhere. What's on it?"

"Nothing she could decipher and use, not without a few advanced degrees in physics and five years of special research in quantum engineering. It did have the remote-control operating codes for the belt prototype, but they're created using some very advanced mathematics and are secure."

"You could control it! Is that what that means? Control us! Then why…"

"I couldn't. The remote codes can set the destination time—and even adjust location to somewhere within a few hundred miles, which is a nice feature—"

"Yes, that would definitely be nice to have," Plunkett understated.

"—but it all requires some very precise calculations of the motion of the Earth relative to, well, everything else in the universe. You need the belt, and one of the little control boxes, and the codes to work together, and I've been busy. Your useless adventures are only given a small slice of my time."

Plunkett rolled his eyes and crushed his own emptied can of Coke dramatically.

"And I still am busy," Applemon went on at a quicker pace. "You know enough now. I am disappointed in Ariel, and there is other sensitive material on the drive she took that I am more worried about than the tech stuff." Applemon looked at his time-travel watch, but simply to learn the current time, within the current place, and at the current time. "And it's all the more reason for me to get out of here, quietly, and quickly." Applemon exited to his bedroom, Plunkett followed for the last of the instruction.

"I'm curious," the younger brother asked, "what your password is?"

"Yeah, right. And then I would like to also buy land in your future Plunklandia Kingdom." Applemon shook his head, his eyeglasses falling down his sharp nose, the sarcasm as crisp as his tightly trimmed hair. "The fertility of your dullness continues to astonish me and the scientific brotherhood."

"No, I mean just the Mac in your room that Ariel got on. She guessed your password, so I'm just curious—"

"Don't be. But you can use the laptop, there is not much on it that you haven't already learned by direct experience. The password is 'heartmachine.'"

"Gross," Plunkett gagged, though Applemon had already begun a hearty laugh. "I won't screw anything up," Plunkett went on, "and I'll try to get the flash drive back. But the whole thing is a waste of an easy way to—"

"Don't worry, little brother, your awful greed and misguided goals will be rewarded! Once I get this under my control, that is, and don't trouble yourself about the flash drive, I don't think it will matter much, and unless I am mistaken you will soon be very busy here."

Plunkett looked askance at this, but did so to Applemon's back as the brilliant professor disappeared again to the vagaries of the world of time.

CHAPTER FIFTEEN-A

> Saturday early evening. With Woby on
> Ariel's literal and figurative couch,
> and as Plunkett minds his own couch as
> it fills with new guests, Aris purports
> to help Ariel by her purporting to help
> Woby help Trice, but—well, what do you
> know?—things get worse.

Woby worried.

As he crossed the campus through the windy twilight the coming dusk filled the spaces among the squat, ugly brick buildings that sat at awkward angles and asked not to be stared at. Lights were coming on in their hazy windows and in lampposts above the cement walkways. The sun was behind clouds but was bowing its goodnight wishes anyway.

It reminded him of Trice; most things did, as he wondered what this latest escape to her "still place" might mean. He longed to go to her to help her, tempted to skip Ariel's assistance, set the belt, and go….

The thought was sliced by a voice, Ariel's, coming from her second-story window, her beaming, audible enthusiasm blending with the night air as if it were another source of light.

He pictured her even as he saw her above him. Ariel waved and called again. Woby shone happy. He always liked Ariel, and he realized now, with relief, it was filial, platonic, fraternal, as a sister—and now he could continue to like her as a little sister. She was exciting and fun and intense. And helpful?

Woby merged his worry with growing hope that speaking to Ariel was a good idea.

He waved and quickened his pace, hip pain and all. As Plunkett once described it: when Woby was encouraged, he wagged his tail.

He wore his weathered baseball hat down low and was dressed in borrowed but age-appropriate clothes. The ensemble was too small, too slender, and fit him tightly, uncomfortably. It was not too comfortable for the clothes either, and they gave way at the edges, allowing Woby's historically corpulent parts to seep where they would.

He entered the dorm of roommates Ariel and Nancy, where neither Woby, nor Plunkett, despite his claims to the contrary, had ever been. It smelled of fresh flowers and hairspray. The room looked like an advertisement for affordable candles and indoor plants of the type that might help one to contemplate.

Ariel had changed from her bright garden dress to a navy-blue two-piece women's business suit. She looked sharp and distinct, each angle of apparel stiff with propriety and perfectionism, her shoulders square, her knees and ankles in line, her hips straight and causing no curvy trouble. Every bit seemed to anticipate each disciplined movement with a coordinating intelligence. Her hair was collected tight to her head and from there hung straight down her back; the lengths were at her command to remain and not to sway or swish unnecessarily. There was really just no time for that.

She was wearing glasses and looked like a psychologist: pad and pen held *just so* and in sturdy readiness.

Ariel led Woby. He kept his face downturned as they walked to a corner of the main room that was politely spot lit with a free-standing, antique-looking stained glass lamp whose pull-chains were hanging nobly in strings of tiny gold beads. Beneath its cup-cake- yellow glow was a long, richly comfortable and richly purple chaise lounge.

"Couch" was just an expression, she explained, seeing his nervous state.

"And Woby," Ariel blew her words to him, to calm him, each syllable floated in its own bubble and popped with a *boop* near Woby's ear, "everything is all right. I just want to talk. Like friends. About your..." Ariel checked her notes for the word she carefully selected to describe this crazy person's fantastic whacko psychotic batshit delusions.

"...adventures," she finished.

"Me, too," Woby said.

CHAPTER FIFTEEN-B

| **In which Plunkett is alone.**

With Woby gone from the room, and Applemon off again to who-knows-when, Plunkett replaced his own frustration with anger, an anger that came as naturally as the return of low tide, and with all that seaweed and millions of those little crabs.

Plunkett placed a thin, bumpy, knuckled finger on the hole that was leaking a mixed stream of other emotions. No one else cared about his plans, he felt, only their own professional ambitions or silly, improbable love stories. He almost felt alone, nearly betrayed, on the edge of abandoned, borderline disappointed—and the source of all these tributaries was the ever-beige peak of Mount Woby, its snows melting under the heat of the ex-slacker's new importance. Woby had lived, spent his time on trifles like helping others, had found a girl he loved, and even maintained a few friends—like that unholy nerd-alliance. He had even, in the blink of an eye, grown old *and* obsolete. *All without Plunkett.*

Poor, deserving Plunkett.

And now Woby and Trice and Applemon and Ariel were busy. Busy with distractions—all of it interfering with Plunkett's fatefully inexorable destined fate of providentially kismetic greatness.

Plunkett removed his metaphorical finger from the leaky hole as a new thought spurted like a fountain: None of this was really Woby's fault. To be fair, he was born useless and grew uselesser as time went on. As time went on. And then back, and then forward, and then back, then staying awhile, and then forward and on again.

To be fair, Woby had only done what Plunkett asked.

But Plunkett did not want to be fair, he wanted to stay mad. So he did. It helped him think.

He revisited his plans, plopping onto the vacant couch, eyeing his guests who were receding into the brown and blotchy cushions of the other. They were quiet. The woman and the dog—shoulders of one touching the hips of the other—had their eyes closed and ignored Plunkett's movements. The robot was bent over forward, square head down, nothing lit, nothing beeping, not even its annoying, artificial heartbeat.

Plunkett's pen made doodles of dollar signs as he mulled over previous plans for the assurance of riches, and updated them with a new first step, to get on Apple's Mac and learn what he could, then decide: should he help Applemon help Woby, by doing apparently nothing? Or should he re-figure how to avoid the Aris-Apple tragicomedy and live for himself?

He calmed and ebbed.

Obviously, he thought, *I can do both.*

Lastly, he wondered how Woby and the belt, both in Ariel's clutches, were doing.

The devilish dog growled in its sleep.

CHAPTER FIFTEEN-C

| In which Ariel analyzes Woby very
professionally.

"The last two times I saw you, Woby, you were telling me some interesting things that you, um, were doing." Ariel, seated upright and in a small plain dark wooden chair facing the chaise lounge, was reciting from her notepad.

"Ariel?" Woby asked calmly.

"Yes?"

"Can we talk about something else?"

"Sure, but I was just curious because yesterday you—"

"That was a long time ago. I am not sure if I'm going to remember whatever you're going to ask me."

"Oh!" Ariel chirped, having since to someone who believed they were a time traveler, like her patient, this might in fact be, or seem, true. She wrote that down.

Ariel decided that she enjoyed being a therapist and wrote that, too.

She searched Woby's reclining body and haggard face for any sign of deceit, treachery, duplicitousness, subterfuge, disingenuousness, dissembling, insincerity, chicanery, facetiousness, or falsehood—but found, as she expected, just a dejected form of honesty. "Of course, Woby," she answered, "whatever you want. How about your girl trouble? That?"

"Yes." Woby was stiff and visually nerve-racked, his hands jumpy as he spoke. The belt-device he was no longer wearing, having found as he walked that it scraped the fatty overflow from his waist and back, but it lay on his lap, and he tapped it tellingly.

"Okay. I didn't know you had a girlfriend, so we might need to start at the beginning. How long have you known her?"

"Geez…" Woby pondered on his fingers, "I don't know—fifteen years? It depends on how you look at it."

"Oh, wow! That's cute. When did you meet her, in kindergarten or something?"

"No. I saw her a lot here and there, and then saw her when she was pretending to work at the hospital helping children. That was yesterday."

"What? Does this also have to do with time travel, Woby?"

"No," Woby said, doing various calculations in his head, like lies-times-distance-plus-more-lies, divided by time, equals something exponential. It took time, but he decided to say, "Oh, well, it's just that she is very hyper, and our relationship has moved fast, that's all. Not really time travel, just seems like it. Heh."

Ariel's wrist already hurt as she tried to capture every word, movement, twitch, and facial expression of her patient. And her face pained from the smile cemented there and stretching her skin.

"Oh, I see, I get it, that's okay. Describe it any way you want to. What's the trouble?"

Woby calculated for a time, trying to code his troubles into normal-human English, that he was afraid his buddhist dakini-angel girlfriend was forced to escape time-traveling enemies by going to her eternity-dream-escape land in exchange for a luminous hellhound, an elderly woman, and a robot too many times.

"Well, suppose peanut butter represents minutes and days, and the bread is people who don't understand you, and the knife is fear…" he tried.

"What? Why?" Ariel said. "Can you just tell me? It's okay, Woby, I believe you, and you are safe here, and we are friends also. Can you just tell me?"

Woby gave up. Woby just told her.

"So I'm worried about her now," he concluded, a few minutes and an almost-full yellow-pad of Ariel scrawl later. "She should have been here to meet everyone, that was our plan. And I know she must have been in trouble three times at least."

"See?" Ariel said, "this isn't so hard." On her pad's last page she wrote "*OMG, he is banana-nut crackers,*" and excused herself.

Ariel returned with two icepacks and while finishing a sentence. "This is superb, I mean like superbly superb."

"Why?" Woby turned his head to ask.

"Oh—just because you have really opened up. I can help you. This will help. Talking to me. Like you are." She removed the ice from her head and wrist. "Let me just catch up on notes."

Woby looked at the ceiling, which seemed far away, but clean. The room itself, Nancy and Ariel's dorm, seemed big compared to that of Plunkett and Applemon. A look around explained why: the lack of mess, of clutter, of evidence, of tell-tale anything. There were no stories to be read from the few items visible, rectangles and squares of furniture, with square stacks and rectangle piles of papers, books and folders on top, a grid of floor below. The square sink was empty, the faucet aligning directly outward from center. Not even time moved as straight as this dorm room did.

Ariel let out a loud exhale and cracked her knuckles. "Okay!" she enthused, "so you believe you were traveling through time. Like what you and Plunkett were telling me yesterday."

"Yes," Woby said, "I was time traveling. Yes. Those were the first few trips you saw, if I remember right. but there have been a lot more since then. A lot more."

"Well, I want to ask about those first trips first, okay?"

Woby perked up. "I don't know, right now I really need help with—"

"We'll get to that, I promise. It will all be okay, but listen." Woby reclined again, slowly, as Ariel went on. "When I saw you doing time travel, you said—to refresh your memory—you said you were 'confused.' Both you and Plunkett used that one word, that the trip was 'confusing.' Why? What happened?"

"You know how," Woby replied, "a deer in the road will just stare at a car coming right at it?"

"Yeah?"

"And you know how a squirrel will go back and forth across the road and you never know which way it's going to go?"

"Yeah?"

The rest was silence. Ariel waited patiently, as she knew she ought. Woby just stared upward at square ceiling tiles. Then he opened his mouth. Then he closed it again. Ariel crossed one leg onto her other thigh. Silence. Ariel waited. She began to bounce her raised foot up and down to provide some count of time.

Woby sighed. But that was it. Apparently no more was coming.

Just as Ariel was going to offer some encouragement and begin her pre-planned interrogatory on experiential time travel—*Is it like a dream? Is it loud? Are there voices? Tunnels of prismatic light?*—she noticed that her patient was starting to jitter, his face twitching nervously. Then his hands moved in a jerk down to the belt and fiddled with it.

Ariel looked down to jot a note on her pad but was presently very unsure of herself.

CHAPTER FIFTEEN-D

| In which...back to Plunkett.

The quiet of Plunkett's couch was disturbed by a noise in the hall.

"He can't be that stupid." Plunkett theorized aloud, thinking of Woby. He quickly concluded that Woby was easily that stupid.

And that he may have, even in front of Ariel, used the belt.

The robot's body kicked into motion, sensors first, and was soon fully alert and sounding like a 1990s-era fax machine. The small lady opened her eyes and shut them again. The Rottweiler lifted its fire hydrant of a head, a small army of rippling shoulder muscles twitching to attention as it did, its coat sparkling a feathery black. He was the most impressive of the new guests....

...until the bullfighter walked in, asking questions in Spanish. Plunkett had taken two years of Spanish and recognized the upside-down question mark in the man's voice.

Plunkett of course could not be sure at first that the man was a bullfighter, an actual matador. He was sure dressed like one, but so what? Plunkett himself was dressed like a gravedigger and yet he has never touched a shovel. *And you know what they say,* Plunkett thought to himself, but could not come up with an appropriately wizened expression, so instead stared at the Spaniard's tall, shiny, silver boots and their long, winding stairway of gold laces.

Until the new guest made it to the couch, puffed up his chest at the growling monster dog, and said "Toro!" Then the couch lit with lightning strikes of blue flame.

"Ay!" the man then said, with a new respect for his would-be foe.

Ever the good host, Plunkett remembered his middle-school Spanish classes, tests, and minimal efforts at homework. Addressing the large man—and his silly hat, his cool cape, his broad back—Plunkett thought hard, and successfully declared his own name. Then pointed out that *Maria went to the school*, that *the boys play soccer*, that *today was a sunny day*, and that *we eat in the kitchen*.

The bullfighter did not take his eyes off the Rottweiler, however, calling him—indeed *naming* him—"*Torito Azul*." And Torito Azul did not take its cement-mixer growl off the man.

Plunkett wondered, almost worried, about his little adopted brother, but the feeling soon passed.

CHAPTER FIFTEEN-E

In which Ariel's analysis of Woby has a significant breakthrough.

Nancy slammed the door on her way out of the dorm, and for a second Ariel thought this was the reason for the vibrations that were playing a loud game of ping pong between her ears. She knew Nancy was mad, but Nancy did not understand. When Ariel had gone earlier to retrieve the ice packs, Nancy came from her dorm bedroom and confronted Ariel about the presence of the flash drive that she had promised not to take from Applemon, and did so while reading the notepad Ariel had left on the counter next to the kitchen freezer. Nancy had threatened to tell "I don't know, someone…" if Ariel didn't stop messing—probably illegally—with amateur psychiatry and stealing—definitely illegally—what looked like confidential research, and from her ex-boyfriend no less. This was messier than Ariel's handwriting, and she had better stop, Nancy said.

Ariel brushed Nancy away like lint from her shoulders, said she would explain later, and returned to Woby and the couch while saying that Nancy should stay and listen to a sample of this session because it was, as Aris might say, superbly superb.

Woby overheard that, and the questions continued, until Woby's worry got the best of him.

So that Ariel, while still unsure of herself and her ringing ear, considered her patient's nervous twiddling and childish playing with the belt that he held on his lap.

She was then unsure of more than herself. Surety was soon

lacking in her balance, the time of day, and the difference in her patient. She did not like uncertainties, and these piled within her like fluffy pancakes and squished together when the fork of reason tried to cut through them. And there was much syrupy doubt.

Ariel was also unsure why she was suddenly so hungry, and for breakfast. She had just eaten dinner before Woby arrived.

Her hands were still clenched, having gripped her chair with the first ear-ringing noises, and she felt off-center, as if leaning over, and it seemed that shadows passed over her, as if she was in motion, her vision struggling with random dashes of light, her inner ear trying to adjust to new, varied, and strange input. But she was not in motion, she was sitting…*right? Or am I falling?*

Once Ariel steadied with both feet on the floor, and hands easing their grip, she looked at Woby and could have started swearing: She could *have sworn* he had a different hat on a second ago, she could *have sworn* his shirt was not this loose, she could *have sworn* that he now looked very different, she could *have sworn* he had not been in the fetal position.

And Woby's hands were no longer touching the belt but up close to his eyes reading from a piece of paper that Ariel could have sworn was not there previously. It looked like it had been stuck in a folding-unfolding machine for a standard workday. Woby himself was in a ball and turned away from her, so Ariel rose—carefully and using the armrests—in her seat to watch as he spoke.

"I can tell you what happened now," Woby said, reading directly from the paper. "We made a lot of trips, but most of it is not important, it was stupid kid's stuff."

"Okay," Ariel believed she had calmed enough to say.

"It's only Trice I need help with."

Ariel went stiff. "What did you say?" she asked. She asked until she heard her own voice and was sure she had asked.

"My girlfriend, Trice, I told you. I'm worried and now don't know what to do."

"Trice. You said Trice." Ariel's head swam with little fishes of observational excitation and big, big, giant humunga-bunga-whale of a realization that this was *exactly* what Aris had spoken to her about. There was a famous ancient goddess, symbol, archetype, myth or fairy or something named Trice. *Superb.*

"Trice is her name, yes."

"Are you sure?" Ariel's voice cracked far upward with barely contained eagerness.

"Yes, of course." Woby uncurled and looked over at her briefly. "Geez, Ariel, you look like you need dialysis, what's wrong?"

Ariel, flush with sweaty anticipation, had been flipping papers in the air looking for what Aris had said about how important Trice the myth was, and now gathered herself in an attempt to reset her professionalism, fighting the visions of fishing trophy after fishing trophy given for her record-breaking catches.

"No, sorry, just worried that you're worried. You needn't be. This is already a breakthrough. Trice. I can help you with Trice, for sure." Ariel spoke slowly, controlled.

"Really?"

"Yes, definitely. I need to know a little more. Hmm…" Ariel calmly consulted her laptop, Aris notes, and her own research. Her glee she suppressed from her face, but it fairly seeped out of her tapping feet. There was no doubt that Woby had visibly changed, and it was due to the intense delusions he brought to life. There were seriously power-ful mental forces at work here, and they were affecting his body. She could see it—he looked ragged, sickly, stretched, squished, stressed, and strained. He looked bent and thin; his skin was pale, blotchy, and a watery pink. She had studied this phenomenon in class—the ability of the mind to bring about bodily changes was well known in the scientific community. And this backed her theory perfectly. And was fascinating.

And now, perfectly, superbly, Woby was speaking of Trice. Unsolicited. The book would sell in the millions; they would name a disease after her.

Ariel's feet tapped loudly against the leg of her desk.

Woby waited, quite fidgety but visually more relaxed given Ariel's happy assurances.

A noise came from Ariel's bedroom, then one from the kitchen. Woby didn't react, but Ariel's stomach jumped a bit, wondering if she had missed Nancy's return somehow.

"Hold on a second…" she said, and again she went to the kitchen.

There stood Aris.

"I was in the closet in your room."

"Oh my god!" Ariel said, but not from surprise or confusion or contempt. "Did you hear what he said! Trice!"

"Yes, my dear. These penetralium hallucinations are powerful, the immured deliquesces to diaphanousness. Keep him talking! Loquacity! Think! Haruspex, or bibliomancy! Good, good!"

Ariel nodded stupidly, fighting the temptation to write these words on her forearm.

"And please," Aris almost hummed, "don't listen to detractors, those always in the way of greatness."

"Nancy, you mean? You heard?" Ariel asked.

"She is small potatoes, just a root in the dirt. Resist her bathetic need to translate or mistranslate my words to you. In fact for your own sake you had best look them up yourself. Oh, and she was full of threats, wasn't she! Perhaps to tell Applemon about us! How laughable! Perchance also to tell me, about you! Well, whether she is a god or a pig I won't breathe for her. We know how to handle her type, don't worry. How superb and delicious." His humming turned to an acid hiss. "Now go!"

Ariel took a long but silent breath and returned to play the character of trusty, thoughtful doctor. Her patient was now in supine position, laid out flat, and freely speaking.

"I have to tell you more about Trice. It's getting worse. She keeps disappearing. I need to find and protect her." As Woby spoke he adjusted his hat and scratched his head, and it caused Ariel to gasp audibly. Woby's hair was definitely different, shorter and, *could it be? Graying?*

Woby looked at Ariel. Her stare was hot on him and outshone the stained light that fell on her face. He looked as if he felt old. He looked as if he ached in his hips and shoulder. He looked like he wanted to sit up to stretch but had to weigh the benefit versus the effort.

He remained in fetal position and clutched his stomach.

"You're going to help, right?"

"Oh yes. Definitely." Ariel smiled.

CHAPTER FIFTEEN-F

In which Plunkett copes with a hippie.

P lunkett coped with a newly arrived hippie.

CHAPTER FIFTEEN-G

In which Ariel gives Woby's free will no choice.

Ariel had to center herself and blink a few times. She considered her hunger and whether it was making her lightheaded. She raised in her chair again and, again, watched Woby stare at what she could see was four pieces of much-unfolded paper. *He really looks worried*, she thought, *but could that explain these physical changes?*

"I want to hear about Trice, and everything will be okay," she reassured him. "But we can't rush. Take time to calm down. I would rather you go back to the beginning. Again."

"Beginning?" Woby asked with an empty stare.

"Beginning," Ariel reiterated.

"Beginnings! Yes!" Something seemed to fall into place under that strange hat, and Woby began.

"For my first time trips, one thing led to another..." he said, and paused, thinking outward to the wall, away from Ariel, then continued, "oh okay. Sorry. One thing led to another, one idea of when to travel to led to another, like reading Web pages when you hop from link to link. But then I got better organized and wanted to look into the starts of things. Basketball. Led Zeppelin. Expressions like 'what's good?' Babies. The universe. Random things. How they started."

Ariel was done staring with wonder and was instead writing with abandon, flipping pages rapidly since the scribbles grew larger and less controlled in capturing every word Woby spoke, especially that odd list.

"All beginnings?"

"Yeah, how things started, those are things I was wondering about."

Looking over her notes again, Ariel asked, "What was the 'blimp' one?"

"Huh?" Woby started twitching again, his eyes shaking, mouth stretching, spine and legs stiffening into a capital Y.

Ariel rippled her voice to a navy-blue velvet. "I want you to relax, Woby, it's okay, we can talk about all of it, if you want. I am very interested in this. You don't have to worry, I—" Ariel stopped short, there was noise from her room, a knocking, a rapping that had a pattern to it.

Woby hadn't noticed it. "Can we skip this stuff?"

"Excuse me a second…" she said, to return to Aris and his closet.

"Skip this stuff!" he said in a manner Ariel hadn't heard before: curt, colloquial, verbally cropped and unkempt. "My goodness, get back to the girl—he wants to talk to her, and it seems you don't… get on with it!"

"Ok. Sorry," Ariel said as the man harrumphed and muttered his way back among Ariel's hanging clothes and scattered shoes, leaving behind like blown leaves such words as *petard*, *epicedium*, *anacreontic*, and *incarnadine*. Ariel wrote them on her forearm.

Upon her return to the couch, she found Woby as anxious as Aris. "Ariel, I really want to talk about Trice. It's getting worse."

"Great, I was just getting to that, please do, Woby."

Woby settled back into a capital R. "Thank you. You have to understand some things…" he said, and explained Trice's skills and shortcomings, her ability to surf time waves, but sometimes wipe out, if stressed or scared, when a bigger power forced her ashore to await calmer seas.

There was the knocking again, a simple medley this time, and Ariel excused herself. Out of her closet came first a thumb in an upright, approving posture. Following it was the long arm and upper torso of Professor Aris. His full frame only escaped after twisting free from the sleeves of a raincoat and numerous shoebox traps. He handed Ariel a page of his handwriting. "Do this," he said.

Aris was wearing a white hat, and white handkerchief about his neck. He straightened both as Ariel decided whether to ask the man why he had brought a change of clothes and accessories—he had been wearing neither a few minutes earlier.

She decided not to ask.

Aris entered the closet as a gladiator to his ring. Ariel returned to Woby while reading the sheet of notes from Aris.

"Sorry about that, Wobe," Ariel said, still reading as she sat. "I want to explain something to you about free will."

She did. Aris' instructions were very specific: She was to exhort Woby to allow his free will to overcome his fate. That he could *not* leave things to chance.

Like ninety percent of Aris' mentorship, Ariel talked herself into understanding it.

"My free will…" Woby started slowly.

"Yes," Ariel encouraged, "what does it dictate, what does it declare?"

"To be—"

Ariel guided him. "I declare…"

"I declare…" Woby repeated.

"I want to…"

"I want to…" Woby went on, then to Ariel's sustaining hand gestures, he finished boldly, "be with Trice. I want to be with Trice, and will be, and am going to be."

"Good! Now do it!" Ariel raised a fist in solidarity.

"Do what?" Woby asked.

"Go get her! Go be with her! Declare it loudly, and do it!"

Woby slapped a hand on the green button.

He instantly appeared sweaty and disheveled.

Ariel felt nauseous, pale, and bloodless.

She thought the power had gone out, or maybe that thunder had struck, or that vampires had taken the city, since for a second the whole world seemed to blink its eyes, and then the whole world seemed to jump on one foot to get water out of its ears. She adjusted herself on the chair, loosened her grip, and, feeling lifeless and sickly, wondered *Did I faint? Black out? Almost?*

She considered making a cup of tea, or, screwing that idea, having a large black coffee and a large pink cheeseburger.

She returned to her subject and knew not to cut this examination short. Woby had assumed his tightest fetal position yet, seemingly breaking the record from when he first learned the maneuver as a fetus. His jittery hands were up and around his head, holding tight to his hat. This was spotty and dirty, Ariel noticed, and—*what's this?*—the alleged time-travel belt was wrapped around Woby's chest, with one arm through it. *When did he put that on?*

Ariel beseeched herself to pay closer attention to detail. Sigmund Freud would have.

She checked her notes, sat back in her chair, and asked Woby how he was going to "go get her" if he remained looking like a lower case o.

"Oh no," Woby said in response and with growing agitation, "oh no no no! Ariel! It's bad, it's worse!" He sat up.

Ariel didn't answer.

Woby put his head in his hands. "Ariel!" he shouted. "What do I do! She's gone! It's worse!"

His voice imitated out-of-tune piano strings being tightened, tightened taut, stretched, tightened more, and at the point of bursting.

Doctor Ariel remained in her own thoughts and did not fully emerge until there was a loud knocking from inside the dorm.

"Oh!" she jumped. "Oh!" She then read from Aris' note. "Okay— what happened? Are you okay? What did I say that bothered you? What are you thinking? You don't have to go get her right away, we still have a lot to talk about…."

"I tried already."

"You did?" Ariel was confused, but Aris' note had ended.

"And I'm afraid, more now. And Applemon tried to help, and he disappeared also. The bowtie man did it, he was there! He's always after her!"

Ariel did not know how to handle this delusion, and searched mind and material while thinking, *What was that? A bowtie? Did he say that?*

"Okay," she managed, "you're safe here, I know this seems real to you, but we can handle that. Say again what you said. Did you say *bowtie*?"

"Yes, the bowtie guy, as Trice calls him. It was white this time, and he had a white hat and bandana, and now he is after my brother, too. Ariel…" Woby's head returned to his hands.

Wow! Ariel thought, admittedly a bit lost but elated nonetheless.

Woby ignored both Ariel and the rapturous knocking coming from the back bedroom.

CHAPTER FIFTEEN-H

P lunkett was putting out chips, salsa, sliced cookie dough, and bowls of water when he became aware of scarcely audible sounds from the hall. Shushing the hippie, which included a polite request to hold still the many beads he wore, Plunkett heard the heel-to-toe beat of a small and light footfall as the other couch-guests—now spanning both sofas—hushed and perked their ears and ear devices to listen, toward the door, again.

The footsteps stopped and all the guests hushed in a multi-specific anticipation. The silence was followed by a nasally voice making short, sharp vowel sounds mixed with gurgling noises.

"It's this way; come on in," Plunkett called, while placing paper towels as napkins since the bullfighter had overdunked in the salsa and made a spill that the Rottweiler was staring and red-drooling at.

In came someone, someone small. Now, Plunkett did not know about indigenous hunter-gather peoples of the highlands of the Congo, nor their anthropological history, nor the ethnological threat to their way of life during AUNT, given the politics of rain forestation and forced acculturation, nor could he date any individual of such people to the mid nineteenth century in order to offer a proper greeting.

But he did know the word *pygmy* and had seen pictures.

In it came, a small person, popping upward on one leg, then the other, as if on springs, all as vivid as a full-page, oversized, overly stereotyping magazine photo spread.

Plunkett of course could not be sure at first that the little figure was an actual pygmy, ignorant of the precise definition, but Plunkett did agree with himself that it sure dressed, underdressed as it happened, like one. But: so what? Plunkett himself was dressed like a waiter and yet he had never received a tip. *And you know what they say*, Plunkett thought to himself. As before.

The lined, leathery, rich nutbrown skin of the perhaps-pygmy's face and bare legs seemed to magnify the sullen, sunken light of the room. He wore brightly colored beads and wreaths of multitudinous flowers that beamed like rainbowed eyes as their petals flapped and bounced with his precise, prancing movements. From the waist down he was thick and muscular, but each bone of his upper body seemed ready to reach out, to want to touch. The skin of ribs and arms stretched taut like a tribal drum despite the motions of the figure and the vivacious kicks and hops of his legs and feet.

The Asian lady raised her eyebrows; even Satan's pooch seemed surprised.

Plunkett coped with it.

CHAPTER FIFTEEN-I

| In which Ariel, etc.

Ariel was afraid to leave Woby in his current, distraught, folded state even for a minute of counsel with Aris. Aris had anticipated this, however, and left a long note on the kitchen counter.

Before reading it, and after a few rapid, connected thoughts, Ariel calmed Woby and asked him to describe the bowtie guy that he saw harassing Applemon and Trice, and if he was aware of the significance.

He answered the second question first: the significance was that Trice was in trouble, and Applemon was trying to help. Then he described Aris and his bowties to Ariel's satisfaction.

"Do you know who Professor Chatterton is?"

"No."

"You have to be honest with me, Woby. Now, did you see anyone else here? Did you get off the couch and look around?"

"No."

The get-on-with-it rapping came to Ariel's ears.

"What was that?" Woby asked.

"Rats, or birds or something. Big problem. Nothing. Give me a second." In that second, Aris admonished Ariel to read his notes and stop thinking for herself.

"He thinks you were there," she whispered to her mentor, "you were in his hallucination in real-time, somehow."

"Who cares? Stop going off script." Aris, this much less verbose

Aris, pushed Ariel physically back toward the kitchen to return to her patient.

"Isn't that significant?"

"No. The note says what to do next..." Aris said and pushed.

"That was a long second, Ariel," Woby said as she sat again. "What's going on? We have to do something. Is Nancy here, too? Maybe she can help. Someone has to find Applemon and tell Plunkett, and I have to go back."

"Yeah, maybe," Ariel said distractedly, opening the Aris note. "Hold on..."

She read how superb it was that Woby believed Trice to have disappeared, and how rapidly her session was progressing, and that it was not only curative for Woby but good for his therapist's career.

The note read further: "Note that Trice must hate, or be scared of, Woby—in Woby's mind of course, the figment/archetype of Trice that is—or else she would not have reacted so badly to his declaration, his free will wanting to possess her. It sent her away. That's good."

And that she—Ariel—should not be concerned by any physical changes in her or her patient. It was the sign of a good doctor to experience "psychotic semiotic symbiotic Sibylline sympathy—it shows your commitment, intelligence and depth of ability, and ability to handle your future successes, which will be unbounded."

Ariel smiled.

Woby spoke. "Ariel? Please. We need to do something."

"Okay, we will. For sure. Hold on..."

So saying, Ariel kept reading.

And Woby fiddled with the belt.

CHAPTER FIFTEEN-J

| In which Plunkett.

Plunkett made a shopping list and read about robots on the internet.

He had put on the TV for the Rottweiler "Torito," the robot, the eastern Asian woman, the bullfighter, the hippie, and the pygmy to watch. It took some time to find a channel that none of them growled at.

The bullfighter asked the hippie how much he thought the dog's ear weighed, in kilograms, and was told it was "a heavy grok…dig?"

Peace reigned for a short time, though Plunkett always had one of his own, small ears tuned toward the hallway.

Plunkett wondered, almost worried, about his little adopted brother. The feeling lasted a little longer than last time, and included the girl Trice, but faded when the astronaut came.

CHAPTER FIFTEEN-K

| In which Ariel.

Ariel considered Aris' latest advice before expressing it to a fitful Woby. And—at the risk of more closet-knocking from her mentor—she considered other techniques, from her own studies, that might help. For example, word-association; though Woby's limited vocabulary might only lead to food-related dead-ends. Woby seemed to be obsessed with, as he phrased it, "beginnings" so perhaps there was some retrieval inhibition where state-dependent recovered memory therapy would be fruitful…?

Doubtful. Woby seemed to always be an open book.

Should I hypnotize him? she thought next. It would be child's play to hypnotize the young man, he seemed preconfigured for it. *It's surprising that the guy doesn't go into a hypnotic state at every railroad crossing or upon meeting a ceiling fan.* She wrote on a new page: "Maybe he does…pursue this."

But for now she accepted that with Aris listening in she had better do as he suggested.

Aris' note prescribed that Woby should be told to find Trice again—since her disappearances were temporary, and she would come back to him for existential energy, as every good Jungian knew—and Woby should help Trice to relive her own bad memories. This memory-within-a-figment-within-a-hallucination is very powerful, Aris wrote, and he hoped Ariel was up to it. Woby and Trice should go—psychically of course, and via Freudian Screen Memories as he was sure Ariel would agree—to the spacetime locations of the girl's worst fears. So that Trice, and thereby Woby, could get better.

Woby was practically bouncing by the time Ariel expressed all this, and when she finished speaking Ariel, too, felt as if she was bouncing. And shaking, and rattling, and rolling, and sneeze-cough-burping, and puking from the outside in. And she had to pee.

She gripped her chair with every muscle in her slender body waiting for it to pass.

Was this more "psychotic sympathy symbol" something? She didn't like it, and prayed for it to go away, career be damned.

She opened her eyes a sliver to see if Woby was okay.

He was not. Ariel jumped from her chair in concern. Woby was shaking, sitting upright on the chaise. Every crease of his face, head, shoulders, and exposed lower arms was glistening with sweat, or blood, or grime, and who knows what else. When she saw that he was conscious, and breathing and otherwise outwardly okay, she went for a towel, and was handed one by a grinning Aris who was already using one on himself and overflowing with a crazed glee that Ariel assumed was her imagination given her own manic state.

Toweling Woby calmed both doctor and patient, and he was able to tell his story.

"It is so much worse, Ariel, nothing is working."

"I don't understand, Woby, I don't get how it happens so fast, how you think it happens when—"

"It doesn't, it seemed like it took forever. Trice came back to me, but she was very scared and wondering who to trust, afraid of everyone and everywhere and everywhen and it took time to find a time to calm her down in."

Ariel reached to grab her pen and pad without leaving Woby's side, but could not.

"Go on," she said.

"I couldn't get her to talk, to say anything that made sense anyway, and definitely not to answer anything you wanted me to ask. So I told her about my memories instead."

Ariel stood and went to get her pen and pad. *This is too good; it must be dripping with meaning...*she was thinking.

She sat, and Woby went on, but there wasn't much more.

"I tried, Ariel. I tried." Woby sobbed into his towel. "I told her all I could remember, and she disappeared. Why? And she didn't come back this time, I tried everywhere. Why did this happen?" Woby cried. "Why?"

Behind Ariel, Aris stood, his towel around his neck. She turned to look at him.

"I think she is trapped. In her 'still place'—trapped, Ariel." Woby's tears overcame him, and he collapsed, shaking, crying, wailing, calling to the heavens for understanding. "Why, Ariel? Where is she?"

"Yes," Aris said faintly to Ariel though a broad grin, "superb. Trice *is* trapped. And Applemon, too." Aris winked, and it pruned his whole face. Ariel found it ugly.

Ariel's confusion served to calm her. She escorted Aris back to her bedroom, questioning how it could be "superb" that Woby had broken down so completely.

"It's perfect," Aris told her, "Trice is doomed. Exactly what we wanted."

"Oh." Ariel said. She excused herself to use the bathroom.

CHAPTER FIFTEEN-L

In which there has already been a
noise in the hall and all that.

Plunkett placed one foot on the refrigerator door to gain the
leverage needed to pull the astronaut's helmet off as a woman
within piped with discomfort. She was bent over toward him,
and shorter than astronauts appear on TV, Plunkett thought.

Plunkett pulled with both hands, wondering if there was a lever
or something they were forgetting to pull. The person within the
spacesuit did not answer.

On one couch loud growls came from the massive black dog-
head, interspersed at whiles with guttural barks that sent shivers
down the spine of the people and the building and perhaps the
whole town. The noises seem to come directly from a major iron-
works plant in hell.

"Shut up, Torito!" Plunkett barked back at the dog, frustrated
with the stuck helmet and the Wobingly long night this was becoming. He wished his brother would come through the door. He
missed him, and wanted also to kick him.

Separately, Plunkett increasingly did not like the way the bullfighter looked at everyone.

The pygmy, for the second time, started a dance, standing on the
couch cushions and jumping around like an idiot. This shut the dog
up at least; the growls from his fiendish jowls were replaced by the
off-key gurgling of the small, dark mouth of the small, dark person.

It looked like a happy dance this time, at least; the previous one had been more mournful. But still: "Don't you start!" Plunkett yelled. He was still tugging, and screamed as best he could between gritted teeth. Then he gave one last yank with both arms and one thigh…and pop-crash-roll, the helmet came off, and the white astronaut suit opened.

There was another pygmy inside. Who began a dance, stripping off the heavy protective gear and gurgling to the ceiling.

Plunkett sat on the floor and wondered what Woby could possibly be thinking and doing, what kind of world he was single-handedly creating, or evolving, or mythologizing, or whatever—all completely by accident; an underachieving cosmos where he was the inadvertent and out-of-shape godhead banishing his creatures to the dorm room.

"Man is he screwed up!" he said aloud. "History will never be the same! I can't believe we're still alive."

But Plunkett had to laugh, his first all day.

CHAPTER FIFTEEN-M

In which Ariel gives Woby one more
thing to do, and in which there is a
song.

Aris tidied himself in the bathroom as Ariel waited impatiently in her kitchen. Woby was inconsolable, but she had given him a drink and "something to relax him"—a placebo of a mega-vitamin—and told him that the session could go no further until he could focus, and that he shouldn't worry, that she knew what she was doing and had even consulted with a colleague and that this was excellent progress, and, she added in conclusion, blah blah blah.

Her voice reposed him sufficiently, for the present.

Aris had left some of his things—tweed sportscoat, two bowties, white cap, a few papers, wallet, keys—at the small kitchen nook table. Among them was a small electronic device that looked like a miniature headphone set, a small metal box, and an ornate wrist-watch that Ariel considered carefully but could not figure how it could possibly help someone to tell time.

Physicists are weird, she thought, as the professor emerged clean and refreshed and put on his brown bowtie and coat.

"I know you must have questions my dear, but there is no time," he said, "there is more to do."

"Okay, Professor. Aris." Ariel tried to smile, but it had been a long day, which obviously seemed even longer to poor Woby.

"Good. He's fine," Aris added, seeing Ariel's facial landslide, "and this won't take long. Trice is trapped for now—in the boy's mind, of course—and it seems obvious that Woby's memories are the key. Would you agree?"

Ariel's upper body moved sideways a bit, her head caught between a negatory shake and a non-committal, shoulder-support "I have no idea" posture, her eyes declaiming clearly "key to what?" while her lower body sagged with apathetic exhaustion.

Aris took this as a resounding *yes!* and went on. "Superb. I believe we can lock the door, as it were, on Trice forever, lock her into that nether-place she, I mean Woby, described, by cohering the offending memories into a single universal point. Oh!"

Aris had been rising in joyful countenance as he spoke, and he ended with a celebratory hop in the air. Ariel smiled halfway, was too tired to finish, but accepted his behavior as about as normal as anything else from the past hour or so.

As if in answer, Aris actually started to dance and hum a tune, presumably of a traditional melody, but with oddly non-lyrical lyrics, presumably of his own making.

The Ultimate Tidal-Wave-Equation

he sang,

Will seal the young girl's doom,
Scientists: please all man your stations,
Here comes the Tsunom-nic-Boom
Yee hee!

Aris ended, then spun and clicked his heels.

Ariel's cheek was squished in the palm of her hand as it supported her drooping head.

"Wake up, protégé! It is the last mile. You have to continue your session, your historic, earth-quaking interrogatory. Destinies await! Your patient awaits! Woby awaits! Look!"

Woby was indeed sitting up and calling for her.

"I'm coming, Woby, sorry." Ariel answered.

"Go to him. And here is the last throw: Tell him to go get his younger self and bring him to the present. Metaphorically, of course."

"Ok, wow, yes," Ariel perked up enough to say while sipping leftover, cold coffee. It was certainly an interesting thought, and she intuited what the psychological ramifications might be, and how profound such an experience, when combined with the others, could be. Of course, she wished she had had more time to truly understand it—this was supposed to be her own research, after all—and perhaps even to have come up with the idea herself. But Aris was not to be gainsaid, so with new energy she aye-aye'd Aris, and went to Woby.

Aris removed to his position in the closet; on the way he softly sang,

> Trapped in the QOV hyperplane
> We'll remove her spatial dimension
> With her world a mere line,
> Oh, won't that be fine?
> When we can track her exact position…
> Chee chee!

"Wobe, how are you doing?" Ariel asked upon return to her desk. "Lay down and tell me."

"I'm lost, Ariel, I can't get to her. It's worse now. What happened?"

"Well, you have to trust me that this is going to work, and it will be better for you."

"Forget me, what about Trice? She's the one in trouble."

"Well, yes, both of you, of course, if you want to think of it that way."

"What can I do? I've tried everything I can. Can you help me find Applemon and get him to help? I think I upset him, my brother who was trying to help! And he might be in trouble also. Maybe from here you and Plunkett can help, while I—"

"Yes, we will, yes, okay," Ariel said. "I thought of that, so here's what you need to do."

Ariel explained, in psychologically sound terminology compromised within a dialect that Woby could understand, that he needed to concentrate, to think back, to bring to consciousness, to the present, his younger self, the child Woby. To reach back and do that. It might be painful, but it was the last step. "For everyone. Okay?"

"Ariel..." Woby said and sat up.

"Yes, Woby?"

"I did already."

It was then that Ariel noticed that Woby no longer was in possession of his time-travel belt. In its place he handed a small wristwatch that looked awfully familiar and awfully difficult to tell time from.

CHAPTER FIFTEEN-INTERLUDE

What Woby "did already"...

"What are you doing?"

Applemon looked at a version of Woby who looked to have been forgotten at a laundromat and reclaimed many months later. Applemon knew of many of Woby's time travels; that is, he knew the when and where, but lost track of the whys, and it made the great Applemon angry.

"Ariel is helping me." Woby answered. "Trice is in bad trouble. Are you okay?"

"I'm fine," Applemon said, "but you are making a damn mess. I am trying to fix it and help you, and her, but you…" Applemon paused, then reacted to that name he had hoped he hadn't heard. "What do you mean Ariel is helping you? What does she know about any of this? How could she possibly help you?"

Woby, even elder Woby, as Applemon's senior, still was used to that "Wobe, what have you done?" face from his brothers.

"Ariel thinks it is psychological, that this is in my head."

"Oh god. She's an idiot. A smart idiot, and now a dangerous idiot, the silly girl. Well, I'm glad she thinks that, but her latest buffet-intellectual pet-project is unimportant." Applemon looked hard at Woby. "Wait—do you believe this is just in your head?"

"Well…" Woby began, "I go back and forth wanting it to be, then not wanting it to be, but no, I know this is real. Trice is real."

"Yes, real and extremely rare and important for reasons that it took an hour to explain one percent of to Plunkett. So listen, this is important: You can't be here, especially here, this is the most dangerous mistake yet, you can't do it, you're breaking time-travel rule number one."

"Here" was at a park and playground where a child, a five year old, had just fallen off a seesaw.

"Ouch," the older Woby said. "I remember that. It happened a lot."

The child got up and wiped his eyes with his sleeves and cried. He stood and cried, alone. The kid on the other end of the seesaw remained sitting with arms folded. With no one coming to help or caring in any way, the hurt child rubbed his scraped knees, retrieved his eyeglasses, and returned to the seesaw.

"I remember that, too," Woby said.

"You can't help him, and this is dangerous. You can *never* come back and visit yourself at a different time, never engage with yourself. Even Plunkett knows that. And now, with what's happening with Trice, you can't intrude. Madness! You need to get out of here."

Woby muttered, "Now that you mention it, it *is* strange that this was never a part of Plunkett's plans…"

"Because he is not the King of the Imbeciles, just a vast landowner. Let's go, before you make things worse."

Woby wouldn't budge, and looked very sad, overwhelmed, distraught, and clearly needed some action, some answer that would help his younger self.

Applemon wanted to oblige somehow, knowing that he should impose his will on Woby while he was this fragile, yet doing so might break his brother mentally, which wasn't all that difficult to begin with.

But the dangers of crossing one's time-paths, Applemon knew, were long-established and well-known within the equations of hard physics—the energy! The displacement! Dual singularities! The asymmetry! But this was now compounded by that nagging consciousness problem. Nine-tenths of scientists had successfully ignored this aspect until the one-tenth very recently convincingly equated the QOV with individual point-of-view within the existence of sentient living things. It seemed to solve everything and explain everything.

So meeting oneself would also cross-consciousnesses, not only math equations. Who knew what would happen….

Woby nodded to much of this, yet all the while staring longingly at the child Woby.

"Okay," Applemon said, "let me take him somewhere safe, or just remove him before damage is done. We can talk about it later."

"Okay."

"My device can transport two people, safely, easily, without any new apocalypses." Applemon tapped his watch. "He just needs to hold onto me."

"Okay, take him back to the dorm then," Woby said through a deep breath. "I belong to a different time…"

"What? No!" Applemon urged. "That's dangerous, too. And what do you mean? Listen—"

But Woby wasn't listening. He twisted on a swing, deep in thought.

Little Woby was approaching, while a familiar voice far off was yelling for the child to stop, that the swing was dangerous, that he should remember last time…but the child came on.

Applemon swung around at the sound of the voice, but Little Woby was ten yards distant and coming fast. When the boy fell to the ground it bought the professor time to set his time-travel watch. He unfastened it and fiddled with it with both hands.

Applemon's head was down when he felt Woby crash into him. The older Woby.

It knocked Applemon to the ground. The younger Woby came to his older brother and older self, and Applemon screamed.

"No!"

Little Woby spoke happily, "It's okay, I fall all the time. You can get up!"

But in the time it took to say those words, and for Applemon to get to his knees, the elder Woby had snatched Applemon's watch, thrown the time-travel belt around Applemon's neck, and…

Vooooop—both Wobies were gone.

Applemon knew where: The watch was set to Plunkett's dorm room, to AUNT.

Applemon hurried to set the time belt for the same but was stopped by a nightmarish vision and a quickening realization of his own doom.

In his dry throat he felt depths of an irrevocable mistake; Aris stood in front of him.

Applemon saw the flash drive that held the belt-remote-control codes for the belt that he was now wearing.

In a trice Aris set the codes by manipulating the small metal box that Applemon had invented. Applemon panicked to remove the belt, but it was too late.

"Say hello to the year 3000, jerk!" Aris said.

CHAPTER FIFTEEN-N

> In which Plunkett copes but discovers
> what a Uroboros is and how it has very
> few uses (especially on campus).

P lunkett was growing tired, but felt somewhat satisfied that he:
(1) had things under control with respect to the growing couch
population, having arranged two junky lazy-boy armchairs
between the couches to make a sort of rounded one piece sectional of
it all, with the pygmies proving to be sufficient entertainment as they
danced their many duets and helped to sustain a mesmerized peace
so that all Plunkett had to do was cleanup after them all since they
were messy eaters; and (2) was ready to pursue his latest idea, an idea
as ingenious as the invention of time travel itself: to get into Applemon's computer and find out how to properly use the time-travel belt.

Not so Wobing hard after all, now is it? he thought smugly. If
life was a game of checkers, he had just told Mother Nature, "King
Me. Baby."

On his way back to the longitudinal revelry of the common-area
couches, he heard a noise from the hall, and reflexively, like a fancy
restaurant maîtres d' on a busy night, surveyed the capacity of the
remaining couch space. *I can get whoever it is between Chatarra
and Flormeleno that long-haired hippie freak.*

Now these names Plunkett remembered only because his
Spanish was improving, and at the same time the bullfighter was
good at giving nice, memorable sobriquets to the couch guests.
Every creation, someone has to. This was working out well, except

in the case of the large, caped matador himself, who had taken on the moniker Plunketto. This was entirely Plunkett's fault, he admitted, a simple and honest mistake of first-person conjugation, but it could not be undone.

At the moment, however, the large, caped matador was whopping it up too loud, and Plunkett was trying to listen: The noise in the hall was a curious one, and, unlike the others, its maker had not made it to the door within a few seconds.

"Plunketto!" Plunkett yelled to the Spaniard, "Callate! Esta…algo…en el hallway…o."

The pygmies stopped dancing at a sign from beefy Plunketto—a swing of the cape being his *only* sign, it seemed—and the room settled to silence.

Odd sounds were heard by all. One was a man's voice, speaking in a strange, chirpy language, and he sounded panicked and afraid. That voice was overlaid with a distinct hum, then gasps and chokes were heard, then the small crashes as of multiple items dropping to the floor.

Plunkett went to the hall, opened the door and crossed the threshold, only to jump in reverse back into the room again in a bursting, one-legged backward leap.

"Ew!" Plunkett said. Then "Ewwww." Then waved his hands for someone to come in, and someone did come in: a man dressed medieval style with colorful waistcoat, wide puffed-up beret, baggy trousers, pointy leather boots—all with stripes and ballooning out in shiny silken curves. The man had an intelligently clipped beard and bright eyes that flitted their aim around the room. He held numerous items close and secure to his chest.

A mortar, a pestle, and a retort.

"Hey, cool, man!" the hippie said, the first to speak. "A wizard! Man."

"Shut up, Flormeleno," Plunkett said, "and make room."

"Alchemista," the man said, in clarification while pointing to himself with one free finger. He shuffled to the couch as if he was accepting it as his destiny to do so but was also being pulled there by giant magnets, just in case. He paused for a second, holding his equipment tighter.

Plunkett spoke. "No one is going to take your stuff. Just sit."

One of the others "booo"ed the man, but this went unexplained.

Now in through the door, almost unnoticed, slithered a red and grey banded snake, a yard in length and the thickness of a garden hose. It would have gone totally unnoticed if it hadn't wrapped itself around Plunkett's thin leg and causing him to flinch from the knee down. This sent the snake flying across the foyer of the front door, revolving in the air, its sleek ends turning at different speeds like sped-up clock hands. It landed in the box of Grandpa's clothes, silently, without the usual noise a snake makes when it lands in laundry.

Before Plunkett could decide not to approach the thing, it approached him. It rose majestically a foot straight up from the cardboard rim wearing Grandpa's old red and charcoal striped trousers caught within the belt loops. The snake's tongue searched and flicked, the whirring of Chatarra-the-Robot's own data-hungry sensors the only other noise. And then down, in a loop, dove the diamond-shaped head, and its serpent's body followed perfectly, leaving behind the old man pants.

To Plunkett's relief, of its own accord it slithered toward the couch, passing too close for Torito-the-Dog's liking, and the black beast shook with throaty maledictions.

Plunketto-the-Bullfighter was enjoying this, a wide smile on his face as he and Alchemista-the-Alchemist whispered to each other.

"What's funny?" Plunkett asked, his annoyance sliding worm-like across his face.

But as Plunketto removed his black felt montera hat to answer, the snake did a very odd thing: Just before reaching the further couch, it stopped, and formed a circle, head to tail.

Then head proceeded to eat tail.

"Este," the matador said, was what was funny.

The Asian woman stood with an oriental formality, it seemed to the westerners that she was preparing to make a long speech. Opening her eyes wide, she said, or, rather, Plunkett heard, "Long. Yin Yang." And she sat back down.

"Shut up!" Plunkett said.

The snake was now in a tighter circle, six inches of its own length inside its mouth. The self-circumscribed creature then gagged and backed out of itself.

"Ewww," Plunkett said, which the Asian woman repeated to his rising annoyance. "Give her a name," Plunkett called to the matador while pointing at the little lady, "then tell her to shut up." The name given was Flotadora. Flotadora shut her eyes.

Flormeleno, on the other hand, raised his hippie self from a cross-legged, barefoot, ripped-jeaned, beaded, bearded, vested, bare-chested state of far-out wonderment and stood at his place on the couch, afraid of the scaly living rope that was now moving into position next to him.

Once there, the snake, bright red and shiny grey and contrasting starkly and uglily to the drab brown couch, curled into a tight spiral, fantastically. It first reached almost perfectly, vertically up, and then wound tail to head downward in a coordinated, bedazzling corkscrew spin. Its head last and finally at center, it flashed ebony serpent eyes open in an intense gaze straight ahead and at nothing. It stayed that way, stiff and unreal.

Ta da!

This was a Uroboros, as Plunkett was to learn.

The others of the L-shaped, sectional-seating of the damned were *not* as still as waiting snakes, however, since the Uroboros' presence created some gut reaction of familiarity and subconsciously recognizable agitation pulled from human instincts that were millennia old. It was as if a being from folktale legend had joined the party, and then turned into a statue of a being from folktale legend.

Torito growled more of its displeasure, and this time the sound seemed to come up through the floor. It tremored through the whole cluttery dorm room, even sending a vibrating threat directly to two empty Diet Coke cans on the end table that rattled in response. Or maybe they shook in fear.

"Toro!" was yelled.

Flormeleno was still afraid, as whiningly demonstrated by calling everyone "Man," stating that this was not "a blast," was in fact "a drag," and trying to keep his dirty toes away from the new guest's fangs yet still keep his balance high above the couch cushions. He also said that, although he once rode a white swan, he did not like snakes.

Chatarra, offspring of nerds, was upright and shaking with a constant frequency, seemingly in some deep and noisy calculation, a routine that every twenty seconds or so collected new data by spinning its little radio dishes.

Alchemista, Renaissance scientist, and Plunketto, master of romance languages, spoke animatedly, their mellifluous voices seeking places above the din. Flotadora looked on, but with eyes closed.

And for the next hour, at least, the Pygmies did not wholly stop their jiggling jubilations, which seemed to originate and seep from their scrimpy lungs down to power dexterous legs. They jumped up on the cushions regularly and gurgled like giant babies.

Plunkett coped.

CHAPTER FIFTEEN-O

In which, Ariel's session over, Woby is shoved homeward.

Ariel accepted her dizzy spells as a consequence of waxing and waning energy fits. She, tired to begin with, found herself alternately energized and exhausted by Woby's own episodic adventures. She had learned to grip hard to the chair, to reverse-blink—that is, to start and end the blinks with eyes *closed*—and to wait. Then to observe and write it down.

But it was over now, her first Woby-session was completed.

After sighing through the period at the end of his "I already did" declaration—referencing his trip to bring Little Woby to AUNT—Big Woby kept awake only due to Ariel's prodding, and only long enough for her to record a wild debriefing of his fantasies and explanations. As Ariel transcribed the audio, Woby passed out from exhaustion. He lay in Nancy's bedroom.

"Isn't that amazing, Aris? Woby had already done what you asked, and made the mental connection to his younger self, making him 'present' as we say."

"I knew," Aris said "he had made contact, but I wasn't sure if he went all the way with it. I needed to be sure. It didn't happen already when it was going to before later on."

"Oh," Ariel said, and wondered whether Aris was experiencing the "Sybilline-sympathy something-something" thing with her patient as well.

Reviewing her hastily written record of the session, she noted

Woby's "Plunkett-dependence"—which was not surprising—but more substantive was the pattern, in these fantasy time trips, to fantasize others' involvement, manifest them into his own psyche, like with Applemon and Aris. This was notable, even striking, since Woby did not know Aris. It was like someone speaking languages they never learned. And with each interaction, Woby was increasingly convinced that his intervention hurt these people in the real world. In the case of Applemon and Aris, Woby believed he had cancelled out their greatness, throttled it, at its source, and for all future time. And Time also, as personified in Trice.

Interesting…and soon a PhD.

She jotted ideas on what the next sessions should accomplish. Instead of lab mice and lab rats and small monkeys she had Woby's psyche, and she looked forward to more. Nancy would not approve. *Nancy is an English major*, Ariel reminded herself. *This is psychology. The heck with Nancy.*

Lastly, Ariel generalized Woby's "severe psychoneuroimmunologicalsomaticism!" as she expressed it in a notebook's inside cover, a location reserved for summarizing any central observations. She underlined the word using a second pen of a second color, and once written it looked like a growing Pinocchio's nose, practically daring a reader like Nancy to correct it.

And there was the mystical connection, the Buddhism, which Ariel had many questions about….

"Forget that Buddhist crap," Aris finally cut in, having heard enough and having finished washing his soiled, never-to-be-white-again hat and handkerchief in the kitchen sink. "Stick to psychology and what I told you. Or don't—it's your project. I don't need any more sessions, and I don't want to hear anymore. Geez Louise."

Even Nancy, who had returned to do her usual Aris-eavesdropping, recoiled at the complete change in tone and vocabulary of the great man. She preferred it, this more direct rudeness; it seemed less condescending, and it saved herself from having to translate for Ariel. Furthermore, Nancy believed the girl in need of some comeuppance.

Nancy looked up toward the sleeping form, Woby's bigness slouched sideways across her prim made bed and looking like an achy lowercase "y". She thought Ariel's messing to be despicable. The boy was a wreck, he even looked like he had aged under the stress of her meddling. And now she knew that Professor Chatterton was just as culpable.

She listened to the conversation in the kitchen, and peeked a look when she could, like now as Ariel, after Aris' latest cutting, remonstrating dismissal of her ideas, looked at the older man like a heartbroken puppy who just watched the Easter Bunny get run over by a tractor-trailer and who was then kicked by the man with the flat shovel who came to clean it up.

The Ariel-look that had launched a thousand sympathies, it was. Even Aris was moved, and he deigned to explain.

"Okay, I will tell you enough so that you can take it from here. Woby's internal personas have been battling, but it was important for Woby to come out on top, not his other inner voices, of which there are many, even some who are otherwise real, like his brothers. We helped him banish the mythical time-goddess Trice, whom we half-expected to see. I expect she is, in his mind, now very old in fact. He would have thrown her much forward in time. Which is standard with this particular archetype, as you should know. Woby also has kept the imposing shadow of his successful older brother at bay so that he himself can be his own person. He did it by using the same symbols of his illness, the time-travel suspenders or whatever..."

"Belt," Ariel corrected.

"Belt, yes. Note that Woby's fantasies lastly had Applemon wearing the thing, and stuck with it, and was banished to the year 3000." Aris laughed despite himself, but quickly recovered. "The meaning is obvious: 'Bye-bye overachieving elder sibling, and take your silly belt with you.' Which reminds me, we should disabuse the boy of the facile toys he has been sucking on—he actually had a belt, right? And now has a watch and little box?"

"Yes," Ariel said, but had noticed the same items in Aris' possession, so risked asking one of her many, many, many questions. "You have those also, though?"

"Ariel, give me some credit. These are tools you should have been prepared to use with Woby, if needed, if you had done your research. But you did take the flash drive, and that was good work. There's hope for you."

From Nancy's bedroom came the sound of Nancy biting her knuckles in contempt and disappointment.

Aris went on, rubbing his hands vigorously to show conclusion. "Now we just need one more take: to take Woby's pacifying playthings from him. Or he will regress quickly."

Nancy heard this and acted. There would be no more meddling if she could help it, she decided. She at once woke Woby and helped him to leave, little box and odd watch secure in his pockets, out the window and with directions to use the balcony's access to the exit staircase via an internal common room off the dorm. Nancy brought him far enough along by his hand to ensure his escape into a blustery night.

The noise of getting a groggy and distraught Woby—who, in Nancy's experience, on a good day was sluggish and disoriented—out the window brought Aris with Ariel in his wake.

"Damn," Aris said, without even an accusatory glance at Nancy. Indeed, he ignored her completely. "Well, it doesn't matter, he is quite helpless, and I have time."

"Huh?" Ariel said.

"I mean 'we.' Poor Woby should rest now and keep away from any more exertion or trouble. If I were you I would stay out of his life for a while, and don't talk to any of the brothers, either. Let's see where it goes for, say, eight months. See you then."

Aris left humming a tune.

CHAPTER FIFTEEN-P

| In which Plunkett cannot cope.

Although those on the couches and the connecting chairs were quiet—some sleeping at acute angles to one another, some watching TV—Plunkett found it hard to accept and categorize what appeared to be, standing in front of him, only three feet high, but not a pygmy, and leaning to the side in a curled slouch, but not a snake, dark and messy, but not a dog or a hippie or a bullfighter, but a little Woby. He was shaped like the number 3.

The possibilities were infinite and the likelihood zero. But no, Plunkett was *sure*, it was him. It was Woby, as a child.

Plunkett remembered this little guy from fifteen years ago, or so. Playing with him, hiding his toys—which were never found— and knocking him over with ease. Running around together from caper to caper.

The jackass. What had physically-adult Woby done now? Discovered the fountain of youth, to add to his endless spout of stupid? Why send this clumsy little bonehead here? What would come in from the hall next, a toddler Woby? Would a demented stork fly in with a baby Woby? Were they all as ill-starred, ill-fitting, and ill-looking as this kid, and all as unclean? As far back as Plunkett could remember, there was always a vague existential lag and inevitable, measurable zero-ocity to the boy. A lack of fate followed him, his stars were dim and misaligned; he was bland by design, underlinged from birth.

*Perhaps even before that...*Plunkett thought.

The little Woby was giggling at nothing. Plunkett hoped this was the last visitor.

CHAPTER SIXTEEN AT LAST

Saturday Night, AUNT.
In which Plunkett dozes deservedly
but uneasily.

While Woby the Elder slept at an angle on Nancy's bed, Little Woby responded with a lack of response to the odd heterogeneous crowd in Plunkett's dorm, the exception being his instant liking for, and fascination with, Chatarra the Moaning Robot. The feeling was apparently not mutual. The machine took a binary disinterest in the little boy, and, after some initial radar-eyeing and sonar-sniffing, slumped back to its default position: top bent over at a midsection screwbolt in a metallic heap-slouch. Its output was limited to a low electronic moan that sounded like pain. It's heartbeep had stopped hours ago.

Little Woby sat on the dorm room floor in front of the depressed dorkbot, ate two chocolate bars, and rubbed the dull and scratched chrome of his new friend's square head. Plunkett sat next to them, and eventually the sullen peace of the room pushed them all down into sleep: Little Woby muttering, big Plunkett lip-syncing a melody of curse words and their synonyms while trying here and there to rhyme.

When! Then! The world wobbled. And the room seemed to stretch and contract, contorting into recognizable shapes from a graduate-level Topology class, the standard ones: a donut, a pretzel, a cone. And back. And in through the door came the babies, one after another, a long line of them crawling and each covered in a pink baby-powdered dust that pattered a trail into the carpet and also rose up in a cloud like that of a wagon train slowly traversing the Old American West.

They were diapered and each wore dumbfounded faces that were actively drooling while babbling a drippy baby talk, as if responding to a cooing motherese that went unheard. Each looked familiar, and Plunkett felt the reason in his gut.

They were shaped like lower case "e"s.

Entering the room, the line now reached the couches, now surrounded them, and now filled all the room, all the floor, the babies arranging themselves eerily in rows and columns. But still they kept coming, and the baby-blabber din rose to a loud general noise.

So that Plunkett's screaming could not be heard.

But still they kept coming. And now had to form piles, up, on each other, raising three-dimensional pyramids with a perfect swarming cooperation.

It was a Little-Woby army.

Last came, through the door, stepping long and tall like a military general, Plunkett's older brother, the brilliant scientist Applemon in full professorial gown and garb. He looked with conquering satisfaction at the room full of babies, then winked at Plunkett, who returned a gaze that questioned his brother deeply and on many topics. Applemon, in a deep voice that seemed to come from all the corners of the dorm, answered:

"We…Are…All…Wobies…"

Plunkett woke with a convulsive jolt upwards, a crying shout stuck in his dry throat. Above him the robot stirred with a few buzzing clicks, and nearby Torito growled in its own sleep—but there was only one little Woby present.

Plunkett hugged the one.

CHAPTER SEVENTEEN

Saturday night, AUNT. In which Nancy confronts Ariel and tells her to take a shower.

With Aris gone, Nancy noticed for the first time the sub-dued look about her roommate. Nancy had purposed to give Ariel a long, interrogating look, and assess where her friend's head was at, and how far it was still in Plunkett and Woby Wacko-Land, and then really let her have it. But this was cut short and deflected sideways by an unwelcome feeling of sympathy, damn it. Ariel looked pathetic and broken and tired and unattractive.

Nancy moved toward Ariel's desk where a messy pile of pages sat in contradistinctive relief against the otherwise perfectly ordered makeshift clinical examination room, couch and all. Nancy read from the notes.

Ariel allowed it, though only after she noted the breach of ethics and patient privacy to which Nancy pointed out an acceptable loophole: "Oh stop—it's Woby, like a dog." And although Nancy's opinions were no longer relevant, and Ariel's research, along with Woby's psychological travails, had grown importantly big, Ariel wanted her friend's help.

Disappointment crept across Nancy's face as she read, accented by bottom-lip biting. She was not sure how to begin what would be a difficult conversation.

"The word you want here is *diffident*," she began, pointing to a paragraph of red ink. "And call Woby *desultory* here instead, it's less insulting. But I have to tell you, I don't like all this, look at you..." Nancy dropped the pages back to the desk.

"Nancy" Ariel mewed, "you have to listen to me, and I might need your help. I can't lose Aris." Ariel took a second to compose herself. "I don't know why he left, and he can't mean what he said. This has all been amazing and perfect and superb."

"He didn't sound like he felt that way anymore, Ariel," Nancy said, and resented the larger implication that she didn't intend. Ariel looked very hurt.

"I don't see how he could leave," Ariel said. "How he could leave Woby, I mean, after these breakthroughs? It all must be affecting Aris also. That's all."

"Affecting Aris? What about you?" Nancy said fiercely. "Look at yourself, and listen to yourself. I heard that you took the flash drive. I don't know what is worse, doing it or lying to me about it. And that wasn't your only lie. This needs to stop. I'm your friend but can't be if this goes on."

"What about my research? I guess you don't care about that. Fine, you can..." Ariel trailed off, composing herself again, walking to the oval mirror across the room.

Nancy dug in. "Ariel, Woby needs real help, not unprofessional, theoretical help. Making him a side project of yours is irresponsible, and *really* unethical, if he has serious problems—"

"But he..." Ariel tried to interject, attempting a pose and expression that would charm her friend the way she could sometimes do to professors and almost always do to classmates.

But Nancy had her hands up and interrupted to continue her own thoughts, "which I doubt. I agree that Woby and Plunkett are both mental thumb-puppets, adolescent lobotomy waitlisters. But now it looks like Woby really does need help. You've hurt him, you and that arrogantly prolix Aris fool. I don't want to get you in trouble, so please stop."

Ariel slumped onto their couch, her face in her small palms.

Nancy spoke more delicately. "A lot of this is probably in your own head now. You're getting carried away. Let's talk some time, and figure this out, okay?" Nancy came closer and saw that her friend looked like she had spent a week camping without a tent. "It looks like it is affecting you physically. Seriously, you look…"

Ariel, to Nancy's surprise, screeched "Yes!" Nancy recoiled, pushing her own head back into her neck, stunned for the moment. Ariel went on. "But not me, him. Woby. *He* is affected physically. He was talking about time travel, his adventure fantasy episodes, and he was *aging* right *before my eyes*."

Nancy had an abbreviated thought that this was a drug trip that Ariel and Woby both went on tonight. She dismissed it. For now.

Ariel went on.

"We are dealing with severe and superactive meta-exopsycho-neuroimmunologicalsomaticism." Each syllable was attached to a hand movement as Ariel had grabbed a brush and her makeup bag and energetic repairs were underway.

"Easy Ariel, you have every prefix known to Latin in there."

"All apt," Ariel insisted, a hair barrette in her mouth.

"Regardless," Nancy said, "I think you're really reaching, and I think it's because you want this to be more than it is, and I'm sorry about the way Aris left but I think you're exhausted, physically, emotionally, mentally, are all over the place. I think you need a long break and I think we need to…"

"He had a freaking moustache! How else do you explain it? It looked like his hair was thinning! He had crow's feet!"

Nancy tilted her head to support the seriously grave and skeptical frown that her mouth had carved out of granite. "You probably have stressed him into an early grave, Ariel."

Ariel ignored this, heard her laptop ding with an incoming email, read the bad news. Her official advisor, Professor Barfield, had responded to her hasty update direct from the Woby session. Nancy read over Ariel's shoulder.

I saw your notes—are you joking? And why are you
doing PSY with a PHY? I will address this with
Chatterton, but we should meet first thing in the
morning Ariel. I am free at 8:30.

"So what are you going to do?" Nancy asked after a long, quiet pause.

"I need your help."

"Yes, I am glad you said that. I think-"

"I need you to talk to Aris for me, find him and tell him…something. Anything, just get him here. Tell him I had a breakthrough, and Professor Barfield wants to keep all the credit for my work…yeah, like that…"

Nancy told Ariel not to worry, to shower, to get some rest, not to leave the dorm, and not to worry. "I will get him, and come right back. It's a good plan, good thinking."

Ariel nodded.

Nancy went on. "Make sure you don't leave, so you won't miss him when we come back."

Ariel nodded

"Great!" Nancy enthused. "Why not shower and change? Or take a bath! Long, hot, etcetera! And put on that new outfit from the other day. You have looked like Sigmund Freud's uptight granddaughter for too long."

Ariel nodded; Ariel smiled.

Nancy said, "I will be right back."

CHAPTER EIGHTEEN

> Saturday, late night. In which Woby
> comes back to the dorm looking like an
> old tree.

Plunkett cleaned Little Woby—whom Plunkett allowed Plunketto the Bullfighting Linguist to rename merely to Lil' Woby, but nothing more—and put the diminutive, nearsighted imp caringly into a proper bed, in Plunkett's own bedroom in fact. He then pushed the robot on its tough, rubbery, belted wheels next to the bed to help keep away the boy's terror of the night.

Poor little dufus....

Then: "Well look what Schrödinger's Cat dragged in!" Plunkett said in greeting to Proto-Woby as the old man version entered the front door, his feet dragging.

The physics humor was lost on Plunkett's little brother, though Flormeleno the Hippie thought it was *right on* and in the spirit of peace somehow. Flormeleno was told to shut up, that someone who only eats seeds was not allowed an opinion. But the room was astir in response to the senior Woby's entrance.

"Remember these guys? You and your girlfriend can really pick 'em." Plunkett said, arcing an arm toward the arrangement of Woby's living souvenirs. "Yes! This is your life, Woby the Great Explorer, returned from the Galapagos of Time!" Plunkett announced to all like a variety show emcee, picturing his tuxedo, big, black, butterflied bowtie, and everything.

Nobody understood this joke either, except, again, freaky

Flormeleno, who responded with a lost-and-given-up-for-dead reference of his own—"Man, you are like Flip Wilson, man"—as he was told to shut up.

Woby was one-half big, bent smile, and one-half collapsing mudslide. Only now, as the man-boy's face alighted and broadened, then sagged and darkened, did Plunkett notice the signs of further advancing age. Plunkett felt more abandoned than ever, but just for a second; the feeling peaked then fell back into a pit as he remembered Lil' Woby in the other room, and via some calculation that he promised himself to make fully later, Plunkett believed this all balanced out into equal happiness in sum total overall and on average.

Meanwhile, the crowd reacted as if it was a surprise party for a returning local war hero, a tired one who looked to be quite shell-shocked. Yet they all yelled his name, sing-songed it, like European football fanatics, with Plunketto the Philology Matador adding "Flojo de Cielo!" Plunkett learned that this moniker described the moment the two had met, Woby and Bullfighter, and meant, near enough, "*Slacker from Heaven.*" Plunkett did not want to learn this, but Plunkett learned this.

Alchemista shook Woby's hand violently in greeting, the motion soon turning into a complex show of wrist and shoulder gestures. At the end of their necromantic secret handshake, one of them roared in laughter, the other almost fell down.

Flotadora seemed to linger like a cloud around the scene; she bowed and shut her eyes many times. The pygmies relived a dance that they believed Woby could not have forgotten. And Torito the Tank of a Dog wiggled and whined and slobbered so that the others got to see a new side to it. There were no more flashes of his bluish butt beacon.

The Uroboros slid around and through everyone's feet, then returned to the couch to sleep, tail deep in mouth.

Woby apologized for being too tired to think; he repeated it many times, he wanted only to rest and to "wait for her". During the previous few hours he had been through rescues and kidnappings, chases and searches, seen good and evil, confusion and chaos, delivered the world's detritus to the dorm, and had been analyzed the whole time. Then woken, pushed out a window, and made to slug through the dark, leaf-blown night across campus and against the wind to get home, here, AUNT.

There was polite, misfit applause while Plunkett, temporarily ignored, was able to pull the guest of honor aside and predict to him that it gets even better. "I have someone special in the other room." He said.

"Yes, I-" Old Woby tried to say.

Plunkett was not to be denied the finale of his act, however. "I will give you a hint: I gave him some chocolate to shut him up."

"I love chocolate…" Woby sleepily nodded.

"Yes," Plunkett answered, "exactly."

"Exactly." Woby agreed, as he met Lil' Woby again.

"You can't keep him," Plunkett said.

Woby explained to Plunkett why they needed to keep him.

He explained that he himself had brought the little one to the dorm, explaining that he had used Applemon's safe, two-seater device, explaining that he was very confused by all Ariel's help that all made things worse, explaining that he needed to think it all through, and explaining that he could not explain any more without sleep.

He said "I don't know what to do, I don't know…" barely audibly and did not explain that.

"So wait," Plunkett stopped Woby before the latter collapsed, "where's Apple?"

"He's-" Woby started, paused, then went on, "I don't know. He told me not to meet my old, own self, that it broke a time travel rule, but it's fine." Indeed it seemed to be, since the two Wobies were now next to each other on the bed and it was nap time and neither exploded or disintegrated.

"Maybe it's only a problem with consequential people." Plunkett said. "Good night…hey! Give Lil' Woby more room!"

CHAPTER NINETEEN

| In which Nancy goes where she has never gone before.

"It's real??" Nancy said, asked, said, asked, and said over and over. But the proofs were there: at the dorm of Applemon and Plunkett, the Mt. Everest of reputational risk, Plunkett introduced her to one balanced couchful of time-revelers, showed her Applemon's laptop materials and Woby's receding hairline, and it left no doubt. Eventually.

Woby meanwhile spooned with his younger self in the bedroom and there was nothing to report eschatologically. They left intervening buffer-space to be sure.

Nancy had come to see Plunkett after attempting to report Ariel's behavior to her roommate's official mentor and advisor, Professor Barfield who, they all knew, kept late hours as well as early hours and practically lived in the Psychology Department offices. She caught the man outside the building however, he was in a hurry and heading to the Physics buildings. Nancy followed. Sure enough, as she told it, Barfield was heading to confront Chatterton, aka the awful, unctuous Aris.

It turns out, she told, that Aris has his own couch and his own party guests and his office has its own intermittent wobbles. Plunkett explained why this was so.

"I have only heard about him," Plunkett said, meaning Aris. "He's Apple's rival. It's a mess."

"Yes, and there's a lot more mess." Nancy said. "If time travel and all this is real, then…" she looked toward the dorm bedroom to make sure Woby was asleep. Asleep isn't the word, they decided, and she went on. "If this is all real, then the girl Trice is in trouble, and Applemon is trapped in the year 3000. With the belt."

"Because Ariel took the flashdrive with the codes!" Plunkett slammed his fist onto the kitchen counter, disturbing many red plastic cups. "Apple didn't know she was with Aris, or this wouldn't have happened."

They each elaborated on this for a bit, then Nancy finished. "One more thing: I don't know why Aris wanted Woby to go get Lil' Woby, but it can't be good, and since he did, they might be in trouble also."

"Probably because it's supposed to be dangerous, but who knows, it doesn't seem to be. And Woby said he saw Applemon but didn't say any more that made sense, he was hiding something." Plunkett said.

Nancy nodded. "That's why I came here, to tell you that Ariel is losing it, and this was all bad for Woby. I had no idea it was this bad, but I am glad he is back here. How can we help?"

"We need to find Applemon." Plunkett said.

"How?" Nancy asked.

"Those…" Plunkett nosed toward the kitchen counter, where lay Applemon's funny watch and the little box that came with the time travel belt.

"Aris has the same stuff! How do we use it? Can we save Trice? How does it work?"

"I don't know. But I am going to find out."

"How?"

"I am going to read the manual." Plunkett declared majestically and stroked Applemon's laptop as if it was king of the jungle and himself a minor god.

Nancy joined the party.

CHAPTER TWENTY

2:30 AM, Saturday night (for college students)/Sunday morning (for their parents), AUNT. In which Woby and Plunkett leave the party to engage in small conversation.

The dorm room was rockin'.

Despite: the lateness of the hour. Despite: the jet lag of all the guests who had arrived from vastly different time zones. Despite: the language barrier. Despite: numerous pairs of natural enemies in close proximity. And despite: the mental exhaustion of the two hosts, Plunkett and Alpha Woby—who in fact was alternately snoring and scream-waking in Plunkett's bedroom—the festive air continued.

In fact, to any who might drop in—and a few did, the usual undergraduate dorm cronies who can sense a good time in their jawbones—the common room looked no different than the early stages of a rollicking, well-attended costume party.

Groovy.

The pygmies danced and sweated and danced, teaching steps to Flotadora, who was preternaturally light on her feet.

Spanish, large Plunketto was entertaining the group with contests of strength and endurance, for example War Tugging with Torito the Black Beast From The Junkyard Of Hades who now romped and yipped like a shiny new puppy. Alchemista refereed. More than one pillow was destroyed in their roughhousing, stuffing and small brown feathers coating the couches and floor. They say it isn't a party until a matador spears a couch cushion within the jaws of a hellhound held in place by an alchemist.

That wonderful wizard would also engage in deep conversations with others; Flormeleno the Hippie was an especially attentive audience.

Chatarra The Robot tried to wheel himself into the main room but was chased away and threatened by Plunkett who ordered the overgrown iPad to stay in the bedroom to watch over Lil' Woby.

"Get in there!" Plunkett would yell. "You can't party with our little boy sleeping. What if he needs something, or gets scared? What kind of parenting is that?"

And Chatarra would bend over forward, his head to his wiry midsection, hum a dirge, and wheel crookedly back into the bedroom and slam the door.

Nancy flitted about, fascinated.

It seemed a good sign that no new guests had arrived, though Plunkett was planning to interview newcomers for clues as to Trice's or Applemon's location. He planned to find some quiet space and time to work on Apple's mac, to see what could be done.

"You might have to travel ahead until after the party for that!" Nancy joked.

A louder-than-usual scream, accompanied by hair-raising electronic beeping, came from Plunkett's bedroom. Plunkett rushed over, and soon he and Alpha-Woby emerged, having calmed both Chatarra and Lil' Woby back to species-appropriate slumbers. Plunkett took a full eight seconds to close the bedroom door to ensure that it clicked shut very quietly.

Woby greeted Nancy—his retrograde wardrobe now made of jeans, obligatory baseball cap and levels of sweatshirts—then blasted Plunkett. "It's too loud out here, can't you get rid of them? Did anyone else show up? Oh, well, that's good, I guess, or is it? What are we doing? Did Applemon show up? We need to—"

"Yeah, well, while you were bodysurfing gravitational waves,"

Plunkett interrupted, "I have had to think about things like catering to ten *wildly* different tastes, and worry about sleeping arrangements that would keep things together long enough for me to do what I wanted, and get on with my life. Yours is done. But now I can't even do that." Woby began to protest, but Plunkett went on. "Relax, I have a plan. But I have questions first, now that you are awake and present in the present."

Woby explained to Plunkett and Nancy that he, having failed at his own attempts to find Trice, hoped and trusted that Ariel's instructions might still work.

Nancy straightened him out on that; hearing that Aris—in a white bowtie—was directing Ariel's actions the whole time made Woby collapse onto the couch. Space was made for him.

"She," Woby spoke slowly, apprehensive of his own words, "did this to Trice? Why would she hurt us like that? What does Aris want with her? Why would Ariel help?"

"We don't know," Nancy answered, "she might not know that Trice is real, or what Aris was up to, but we don't know. It seems like she was partnering with Aris, but why I have no idea—revenge on Applemon? Doesn't seem like Ariel, but she *did* take the flash drive."

The three exchanged nods and shakes of the head, both.

"There's more." Plunkett said. "Applemon is in the year 3000. Can you explain that? Nancy heard Aris say he was trapped there. And why do you have Applemon's watch device? Where's the belt?"

Woby confessed to what he did, stealing Applemon's watch and leaving him back in childhood-time at the neighborhood park. "But he was fine when I left. Three thousand," Woby mused, saying that he could find no significance in that particular year.

They explained the remote-control codes that Aris would have had from Ariel. Nancy spoke, "and since Applemon then had your belt, Aris could control him. That must be what happened."

"And," Plunkett added, "Apple is probably trapped if Aris disabled the belt, which it sounds like he did. And we only have the year, no location, no way to use the codes."

The others looked grim, Woby hit the couch with both his fists to hold back cries of frustration, anger, and confusion.

Nancy and Plunkett removed Woby from the inter-temporal mardi gras that was growing around them, leaving the common room and kitchen for the back bedroom.

"Woby," Nancy said as they walked, "Plunkett has a plan, and we'll find Applemon and Trice, don't worry. The answers are on Apple's Mac. We can figure something out."

Woby composed himself as Plunkett spoke. "Nancy's right. I have one more important question, though." Plunkett opened the door and led Woby into Plunkett's room. Chattarra the Babysitting Robot sensed and tensed on their entrance, then hibernated again, awaiting a friendly user login that would never come.

"Why did you do this?" Plunkett whispered to Woby Senior, pointing at Woby Beta. His, Beta's, eyes were lined from the oversized, pinching glasses, which Plunkett then removed. "Why?"

The elder tried to think of one reason among hundreds. He settled on a summary reply, and in a wavering whisper said, "I wanted to tell him that it would be okay. But then I remembered that it won't be, so I wanted to help him, bring him here, or put him in the future with you, when you are rich." He stopped, then added "He can't be with me and Trice."

Woby looked down at the other of him, the kid's mouth open, his face stretched in weird turns of expression and his skin lined from the pillow and wet from drool. One eye was cracked open, just a beige slit showing black behind it. He snored lightly. Then, a movement: the boy turned, and his face changed, there was a deep and broad canyon of a smile which stayed for a second until it was buried into the folds of the blanket. "I'm glad I did," Woby said in a meditative voice.

Plunkett agreed in silence and considered the child in his bed. History would have to repeat itself; Plunkett would take care of a small, adopted Woby. No one else would.

"Well," Plunkett said aloud, "you've had worse ideas."

The truth was that Woby was careful on his time travels to avoid the familiar, in the same way that he always avoided the mirror. No—until he had aged with experience, he never considered going to see himself, since, he reasoned, he was himself.

"You don't have to put him back," Plunkett said, "but we still have to deal with it. It's dangerous. Applemon is of course right, and one Woby in the universe at a time is plenty of creation," he said. Nancy gaped since Plunkett spoke and smiled quite tenderly. "His birth was the littlest bang ever."

Nancy spoke flatly. "Gee, I hate to ruin a very strange moment, but I thought Ariel and Aris told you to go 'bring your younger self to the present,' and all that? Isn't that why you did it? So it can't be good."

"Ariel told me to do it after I already did. But you are right that Applemon is right, I probably put everyone in danger now. Again. We need to stop Aris."

"We will," Plunkett said, and, Woby calmed, they went back to the common room. Plunkett explained everything he learned from Applemon about Trice, physics, time travel, the device, the laptop, and Aris the Antagonist. "And now we have the manual and can use the device right. Lil' Woby will be okay. You will be okay."

Plunkett drank a Diet Coke and a beer and made more lists: of women, mostly, and exotic locations, and of all the things he liked. He took informal polls of the others who were partying with increasing gusto. It turned out that they all liked the beach.

After Nancy's prodding, Plunkett explained that this was his way of preparing to help others, to remind himself what was in it for himself.

"Oh, for heaven's sake!" Nancy said, and meant it.

The fun and frolicking went on apace, yet always orbited back to its center—Woby, who in the mathematical field of dynamical systems would be called a "chaotic attractor." All would reminisce, and Woby would listen to stories, even tell a few, the language barrier overcome by the international commonality of the events, the universal appeal of the exploits being relayed, Woby's animated and sincere oratory, and Plunketto the Bullfighter's edifying help.

Plunkett more than once had to quiet the multi-millennial partiers to listen closer to what he thought might be his favorite youngster's cry in the night.

In honor of Woby's time travels, the Uroboros suffered himself to be worn like a belt, which some of the visitors did for fun, the snake forming a loop by clamping his teeth over his own tail, which was getting a little boring frankly.

However surprised by these joys, Woby would soon find himself and his sadness again, as Nancy noticed. She helped him when she could.

At a point of communal contentment came a brief respite in the partying, the group collectively exhaled, and some quiet descended. Plunkett had made a final version of his lists and plans and called his elder younger-older brother over to him at the kitchen counter.

"I'm ready. Since the world hasn't ended yet, I am going to go home to figure the rest out. I can't think here. Take care of everyone." Plunkett was referring to the little Woby, whom Plunkett would not suffer to be disturbed, being quite protective of his much junior older-younger brother. "I am bringing the watch and box and my notes," Plunkett told Nancy, then Woby. "Obviously you need to stay here—Mom and Dad get upset when you go home looking tired, yelling that I keep you up all night. Imagine their reaction to this."

"Hurry, okay?" Woby said, Nancy's arm around his thin, slumping shoulders. "Do you have the password?" Woby pointed at the laptop under Plunkett's arm.

"Yes, Apple told me. I changed it so Ariel can't get back in," Plunkett said.

"To what?" Woby asked.

"Nothing she'll guess, don't worry. I remain one step ahead of her, as you can see."

Nancy whispered in Plunkett's ear, then stood back expectantly.

"Fine," Plunkett said. "I'll change it again when I get home."

CHAPTER TWENTY-ONE

Sunday wee hours, AUNT. In which
Plunkett "reads the freaking manual,"
as software programmers used to say
to each other.

By the time Plunkett settled to sleep—in his old room back within the family home where his parents lay asleep as they usually did in the dead of night—he found that he couldn't.

After peeking at his brother's laptop and seeing document after document and page after page of mathematical physics and very little English, and seeking a way through to some useful answers as to how to control time traveling and perhaps find others stuck in other times and places, his head was pounding.

Applemon said it would take three years to learn, he recalled.

He lay on his bed, on his back, covering his eyes with the crook of his elbow trying to think of nothing. His mind would not cooperate. It would not stop thinking of iced tea, for example.

For another example, the highlights of his time-travel failures—and Woby's, too—marched back and forth from temple to temple loudly.

And especially his solo trip to the past, and all that nerd-begotten robot nonsense. He cursed a non-specific hex, voodoo-like, making sure it covered many groups of mostly innocent people.

Moving backward through AUNT-based time, he next recalled his initial planning—to research the past, and get the lotto numbers, etc., and how naïve and simplistic that seemed now. Stupid Woby.

Curse him. Too.

Then, in correction, he thought, *Just the Big One, not the Little One.*

"Okay! Now! No more delay! Do it! Now!" Plunkett said aloud with conviction and power, "No! Yes! Here we go!" He sat up, focused, grabbed a pen with a flourish, and set about reading again.

For hours, studying as he had never done before, and never would again.

He referred to the watch device many times, welcoming it like a new friend, one he felt he was beginning to understand, one that would help him in the way that the stupid belt failed.

He felt the watch's smooth metal band, opened it to see no moving parts but a wonderful gleam of tiny electronics. He held it in his palm as he concentrated, he rubbed its face genie-lamp style.

In which burned the last of Plunkett's proverbial midnight oil: as eventually, pen in mouth, Plunkett fell into a dreamless sleep.

Plunkett awoke, energized and alert and unafraid and driven. The morning was bright, and its rays filled the room. And, though most of it was lost to his recall, or mixed with hypnopompic visions, the papers around him, and the dead laptop battery, convinced him that he had learned enough and that his new life began a few minutes ago.

He noticed the thousand messages on his phone and replied to the group that "Okay, I'm coming and all is solved."

He showered and dressed, grabbed the laptop and box, wore the watch and winked at himself in the mirror. He grabbed more clean clothes out of habit when leaving home for the dorm, bid an unceremonious goodbye to his parents, answered them that everything and everyone was fine though in fact he hadn't heard what they asked or said, winked at himself in the reflection of the toaster as a warm bagel popped, got in his boxy, old, green Plunkmobile, winked at the rearview mirror, and was soon parking and winking again on campus, with the strengthening sun winking back.

Coming to the dormitory building and the ugly mix of dark

brick and mossy stone, the regular formations of style-less, bare windows that stood as welcoming as an abandoned army barracks, he was faced once again with the broadening intensity of his cares, the unfair pressure to act unselfishly.

He entered his dorm, and took a quick accounting of attendance and found only Woby, Woby, Plunketto, Torito, Chatarra (in a corner of the bedroom, metal head forward against the wall), Flormeleno, Alchemista, Flotadora, one pygmy, one astro-pygmy, *and...wait...oh no...oh shit where is it? Did it get out? Oh damn... oh okay, there! Thank God...*A Uroboros wrapped around the base of a lamp, gagging.

But that was the full tally, just those who were there when he had left the previous night.

They had stopped partying but were in various states of a precarious repose: they had all taken on Woby's mood, sullen, but without the hope and confidence that the Wobies put in their brother Plunkett.

Nancy had kept Big Woby on the bright side, noting that no new travelers had come, and nothing newly bad had happened. But they pressed Plunkett for action. Whatever he had learned and now had planned they had to try now. They were losing time.

Losing time. How ironic.

Yet it was true, and the collective pressure to be the hero was biting at Plunkett's skull and trying to kill him for food. Everyone in the dorm stared at him, and with looks that said it plainly: Plunkett was no Woby. The man hardly even time traveled, he relied on others. And now Woby needed help, and what had Plunkett done?

Why *is everything* my *problem? Always?* he thought.

In fact, here is a list:

* *A dead, bloated whale, skin stretched in the surf and ready to burst;*

* *An exploded pen in a pocket;*

- *The last few seconds of the sun;*

- *4:30 a.m.;*

- *A cat eating a wasp;*

He moved to the bedroom to curse aloud and alone, but was followed by Nancy and soon heard Lil' Woby laughing at "Unkie," and repeating some of the consonant-heavy words learned three seconds ago from Unkie's funny, funny maniacal outburst. Plunkett pulled himself together. He kicked the robot from behind, in a part that might be considered a hamstring and in any case looked weak and vulnerable, while the thing slacked in the corner. It beeped and whirred, but the sounds sputtered, were discontinuous, broken, hurt.

Plunkett felt much, much better. Nancy upbraided him, but Plunkett felt much, much better and tried out his winking on Nancy. She vetoed it.

Focusing, Plunkett patted Lil' Woby head, and looked at that face, those eyes, the wet upper lip, those cheeks, that numeric shape, and thought of how much worse things could be. After all, Plunkett at least was still Plunkett.

He felt much, much, much better.

Elderly, disconsolate Woby entered the room.

Before he could speak, Plunkett said, not unkindly, "Okay, I'm ready. This'll be great."

Nancy and Lil' Woby came near for support as regular Woby nodded. His younger self looked to exchange a mental high-five. Physical touching was out; the first time it was attempted they both felt an instant of non-existence, like a blank sleep, then of waking as if too much time missed. The feeling was—predictably and in the terminology of neutrino isolinear physics—"icky." Or like death, as someone offered. So they only exchanged knowing, very knowing, glances.

"She'll be ok," Lil' Woby said. "Unkie is smart."

"Damn right. This will be great!" Plunkett repeated.

"Explain," Nancy said.

"I shall," Plunkett said overdramatically, and like a magician ready to pluck from his hat he opened Applemon's laptop and showed the onlookers the digital softcopy documentation of time travel via belt and wristwatch, and a section of his own notes.

Chatarra the Woby-gotten Robot spun to artificial life, twisting to "observe"—it also tried spastically to move closer to the bed, but its muscular coordination, having no muscles, was subpar to begin with and now, its breaths of beeps and clicks abnormal and strained as a result of Plunkett's swift analog kick, the thing could barely move laterally other than by falling over and getting back up a few inches further along.

Yet it did so, even though Plunkett told it to be quiet. It came on, until it was bent very close to Plunkett and further bending all its sensors toward the laptop. The thing seemed excited, and then even delivered some output: It spit some paper out of a slit that was placed so that it gave the appearance of, comically, a mouth hole.

Plunkett cursed it, trying to focus.

Nancy read the printout. "Hey! Chatarra seems curious about the laptop. He called it a quadriplegic robot. The bot has personality, huh? Did you know that the word robot means 'drudge'?"

"Nancy, control yourself please," Plunkett said. "I'm ready. And I don't want distractions. Can you get everyone out of here so I can finish?"

"Finish?" Nancy asked.

"Being ready," Plunkett explained, shoved Chatarra away with dexterous human force, then headed to and sat impatiently by his own printer where pages were spewing.

Nancy meanwhile removed the sullen robot, with Old Woby and Lil' Woby following, to the common room. She offered the youngster a cupcake that she could not have known was a muffin that might as well have time traveled there from 1951.

Nancy returned as Plunkett collected the last of his printed pages. He curled them and held them aloft like an unlit torch.

Plunkett spoke. "These are all I need," he declared, "to save everyone. I'm ready."

"Glad you're ready. Glad you said it four times. Now explain," Nancy repeated.

Plunkett summarized how time travel devices were invented as a means to get answers, the answer to any question a physicist might want to ask. "A stupid reason," Plunkett opined.

"Geez," Nancy observed, "really? Impatience is the mother of invention?"

"I guess so. They just wanted information from the future, not to go there or impact it or save the past or whatever. Just to bring information on very specific things, in a very careful and limited way. Always thinking small…."

Plunkett went on to explain that how to use the watch to do this was very complicated. Overly so. Plunkett had re-read these sections many times, last night, and of the many false starts Applemon experienced. It made him feel better about his own failures.

Most documents were full of counterexamples and warnings, many times mentioned the risk to mind and body, and even to nature, to humankind, and to the universe itself, and how the belt could cause trouble or death, or even a couch full of weirdos.

It didn't say that last part, but Plunkett knew this for a fact and thought about adding it to the document.

"Did any of it mention Aris?" Nancy asked.

"Nothing to hint that he was a power-hungry, indefatigable, psychotic, manipulating, unremitting threat. Just another dork."

"Yeah, in person he doesn't have the simple, fossilized dullness I expected. He's horrible. And verbose," Nancy said.

"Does he teach any classes here? Ever heard him lecture?" Plunkett asked.

"I've never heard him do anything else.…not counting some poetry which made you want to root hard for whoever his enemy is. Wasn't there any warning about Aris in Apple's notes?"

"No, but about other things," Plunkett said, elaborating how numerous schematic diagrams did say specifically and in more than one place not to gather too much information on oneself, and certainly never to meet oneself, and the math symbols accompanying these sections looked like evil insects had broken onto the page and spawned. Plunkett blipped over these.

Weary and needing a good stretch, Plunkett's thoughts returned to his own plans. He consulted his notes, updated with his new learning. He was pleased and optimistic at long last.

He laughed. Nancy vetoed it. Plunkett laughed harder, stood and pushed his tired bones and ligatures and nerve endings radially outward as far as he could, and called to Woby and the wee one to rejoin him in the bedroom.

Inward creaked Usual Woby's back and knees, with the gait of a very tired and rickety old man, and him following came Chatarra, who had also aged prematurely under Plunkett's abuse and was just as bent.

Plunkett faked a punch toward the crookedly mobilizing metal monstrosity, and also growled a sudden holler to frighten it, which worked. Chatarra fell over sideways; some printer paper came out of its mouth, blank. Lil' Woby laughed, and Plunkett tucked him in for a nap.

Old Woby sat, and took a long ceremonial time to do it, as Plunkett shook his head. "My hips," the elder Woby started to say, once he landed. "I nodded off on the couch, and…"

"It's probably cancer. Shush. I need to tell you the latest," Plunkett said.

Old Woby answered, "I'm trusting you, Plunkett, and you, Nancy—please make this your best plan," then coughed like a boxing trainer.

"Gross," Plunkett observed. "I have the same plan as always. To get rich, bury you, and then enjoy myself. The order doesn't matter. But seriously, folks, listen: Applemon had a system as to how to use time travel properly. It is too complicated for me to explain it to you," he said, pointing at Old Woby's head, "but I can use it correctly now.

I can rescue him. I think. Then he can explain how to get at Aris and find Trice. There's a lot on here about the differences between Aris's technology and Applemon's. I think Applemon can win, or least these documents say he can, in about fifty-million words. For sure. Don't worry."

Plunkett's eyebrows looked to Nancy's eyebrows for reassurance since they both knew Plunkett was lying. White ones, so Nancy nodded energetically. "That's great!" she said.

Old Woby flashed crow's feet eyes in resignation; it came with a half-smile that Plunkett determined was smile enough.

That settled, Plunkett put on the time travel watch with a flourish, and gathered his papers into a neat rectangle, until startled by a howl. Above the intensifying din of a renewed party, Torito the hound commenced its most hellish, protective barking, a noise that Satan must be bragging about somewhere. Hairs on human forearms raised and tingled.

There was a knock at the door, the front door of the dorm.

It was barely audible above the intensifying noise of a new, budding party, but distinct and familiar, of course, since it heralded someone in the hall.

Both Old Woby and Plunkett, experienced time travelers, looked at Plunkett's wrist and watch, at its fate-plucking dials and buttons.

"I never touched it!" Plunkett claimed, holding his wrist up as if this proved something.

"Oh no..." Woby said downheartedly.

They heard the knock again.

"They usually just come in," Woby said. "Maybe it's only Ariel."

"Well, good. I have a few more things to tell her." Nancy barked and marched out of the bedroom.

"She doesn't knock anymore," Plunkett said while lowering his arm haltingly as if at gunpoint.

At the front door, Alchemista the Alchemist was welcoming a normally dressed older gentleman. Nancy stopped and stared; they all did.

He looked like a professor. Both younger brothers knew the look: Applemon being who he was, there would sometimes—though always with notice and fanfare and prior housecleaning—be visits from fellow academics, the grizzled and hoary kind.

"Probably quantum field theory with some thermodynamics," Plunkett added. He was especially good at recognizing nerds by their chosen geek-topic.

"A physicist," Woby mumbled with a despondency that could have melted Chatarra's titanium heart. "What can this mean?" Woby looked to Plunkett who, flanked by a yawning, newly awakened Lil' Woby, offered reassurances.

But then two strange—stranger, that is—things happened: a heavily decorated and heavily heavy body came through the front door on its own heavy legs, and the professor said to Alchemista that both of them, himself and the heavily purple and quite slow monk following, "were sent." And they went directly to the couch. Chatarra joined the throng and was told by Plunkett to clean up some space for the man.

"A monk…" Woby said with soft worry, "sent…?" he questioned. Nancy pulled him aside to debate this. An arrival, she offered, might mean Trice was doing her thing, and so was fine.

"But she would come here." Woby said.

"You don't know that. Plans change—look at everything that's happened since you left her. You don't know." Nancy put her hand on Old Woby's shoulder as he slumped. "And he says he was sent—that could be Applemon doing *his* thing."

"But he would come here!" Old Woby said.

"Stop—we can't know for sure, but I think this is good news, I really do. So let's let Plunkett do *his* thing also, okay? Sit with me."

"But monks are always after her, too…" Woby said. The large eastern anchorite did not speak and would not explain. In the time it took him to get all the way from the front door to the common room he could have told a long tale, but he remained silent.

Nancy accepted this; Woby would not have, but he assented to Nancy and sat with her.

Plunkett observed how good Nancy was at Woby-sitting, something he himself prided himself on, but it didn't stop him from scooping Lil' Woby up on Old Woby's way down. Plunkett hooked his brother's arm and led back to the bedroom. Plunkett walked slowly, his head shifting from his notes to the watch and back, and said distractedly "Yes, stay here, stay calm, trust us, meet new people...." Plunkett opened the bedroom door widely enough to shove his brother through it.

"Careful of my back!" were Woby's last, pained words before Nancy led him to a clothes-buried chair and pet him on his way into it.

"Sorry. Probably three multicolored tumors. I'll be careful next time. I have to go! I'll do it from here." Plunkett swung closed the door, his last sight that of Chatarra pathetically cleaning crumbs off the end table using a washcloth that was laid over his clamped hand. Plunkett gave the robot a strong flick of his middle finger.

In the bedroom, Plunkett organized for his trip, consulting with Nancy on a few points. Soon enough, he was ready to leave.

The Plunketized version of prayer was to sit and curse at the walls and ceiling for a few minutes, which he did solemnly.

Barking, and front-door rapping as before made Nancy jump, Plunkett cross himself, and Lil' Woby fall from his chair. Peeking out together they saw another lame hat and ridiculous pipe and conservatively patched sweater-elbows. Plunkett muttered "Math. Looks like Advanced Tensor Fields. Dork. Oooh! And another monk! A thin one, but just as silent, and clocking in at one mile per month."

Nancy petted Woby.

Plunkett stood; he was ready. He nodded to Nancy with a rigid, straight seriousness; she nodded back. Plunkett motioned to Lil' Woby, waving him over, and directed big Woby out to the crowd where it was suggested he mingle.

As Lil' Woby stretched and came forward, his head up in an effort not to sneeze, Plunkett adjusted the dials on the time travel watch, grabbed a preselected sweatshirt in case his destination was cold again, and stood before the bed. Lil' Woby was now directly beneath him, looking up like a flowering weed at the sun. As a weed with wet and running nostrils.

A productive sneeze shot out, up, out, like a firework, then arced in many wet parabolas and rained back to earth. Nancy laughed.

"Wait," Plunkett said, "where's the box?"

"The metal thing? For the device?" Nancy asked.

"No, the bigger one. It was in here before…" Plunkett searched.

Child Woby rose a small toward his Unkie, giving the box he had held. It was the one that came with the belt, the one that Plunkett now understood. Unkie opened it and turned it upside down to dump the junk out—apparently the boy had been playing with it, and out plummeted a bottlecap, a miniature toy dinosaur, and a few screws and wires, and eventually down floated some used tissues like parachuting soldiers of snot.

Plunkett patted Wobito on the head.

"Unkie Plunkie…" said the kid, and laughed and sniffed.

"Damn right," Plunkett returned. "Are you ready?"

"For what?" said the boy, and tilted his head, looking ever the nearsighted puppy.

"To make the noise!"

"Yay!"

"And then you have to wash."

"Boo!"

"But now we can make the noise!"

"Yay!" Lil' Woby sparkled again, as his Unkie shook his head at how easy it is to raise a child. Nancy smirked.

"Okay, when I say three…" Plunkett continued, readying himself, steadying himself.

"Vooooooop!" lilted Lil' Woby's voice, prematurely. His cheeks were inverted inward, his mouth crooked and asymmetrically adorable.

"No, little dufus, when I count to three…" But Lil' Woby was smiling too hard so that Plunkett relented with a "Good job!" He then tapped the watch face once; it lit in green. He tapped is again, to yellow. With the third tap Plunkett thought to make the noise himself and did; but Lil' Woby only heard "Vooo!" the remaining "o"s and hard ending "p" lost and gone following Uncle Brother Plunkett.

Left behind was a hole in the room that readily filled with spindrifts of new essence. Lil' Woby sneezed and coughed at the same time, then farted, then cried.

As Plunkett launched from his bedroom into the unexplored paths of time travel, leaving the little Lil' Woby on the launchpad awash in the exhaust of his negative thrust, the massive dog and minimalist pygmies were on the kitchen floor in abeyance and reverence of Alchemista as he made magic with some baking soda; the others had turned on the TV for some party music; and Woby himself returned to the couch to talk to the two professors, those who were "sent" for that purpose.

CHAPTER TWENTY-TWO

Sunday, AUNT. In which Plunkett's plan is revealed.

As Lil' Woby bathed, with help from three of the more nurturing guests, Plunkett was time-hopping and following a seven-step "Six-Step Process" that he had planned with the guidance of Applemon's time-traveler's watch-wearer's owner's guide.

By now he was up to the fifth step and pleased with the progress that day. Things had gone well up to then.

His plan, the Six Stepper, was the Rudimentary, Remedial, Simplified, and Laughably Abridged version of Applemon's much more subtle guide to Accelerated Knowledge Gathering by Learning at the Speed of Instant. A primer for time travel without destroying the world and without making awful changes to your own.

Specifically, as culled and edited from Plunkett's own notes, dumbed-down from Applemon's lofty advanced physics level to second-day-of-inchworm-kindergarten level, the steps were:

Step 0

He needed to make a few trips to the future, to a time reserved for one purpose only: to convince the inhabitants of that era that they were slaves of the Great Man Who Visits and was all powerful, all knowing, all-commanding, a bit self-absorbed, and etc., or something. This part would be fun.

Once there, he needed to show off his vooooooping, vanishing powers in order to convince and cower everyone he met. If this didn't suffice, he could bring knowledge back to them from an even further future, or whatever.

Step 1

Once the people of the future were convinced of his power, the light-metal dressed fools, he would command them to look in a small safe, one placed in a certain location, and to look every morning—and if the safe was not empty, then they should do whatever was instructed on the paper within. It would be a question that needed to be answered or else it would piss off the gods—gods who, on a good day mind you, are entertained by famine and mutations.

They should answer the question no matter how many centuries it takes. "What if it is empty?" some would ask.

"Just put it back and wait. Gosh Damnit you guys, just use your heads." Plunkett would answer. "I am in a hurry here. Just put the answer back in the safe and put it all back. Geez."

Step 2

Those of the future were also instructed that—when the "Glorious Task from the Magic Safe" was done—they'd have to change their family name to begin with the name of the month, day, and year that they finished the task, had answered the question. And to instruct their children to keep the same name forever, through all generations, or else it would be thunderbolt-time for them, and acid-rain-with-locusts for their friends.

"Ummm, and pretty much do that forever," Plunkett would tell them.

"What if we are given more than one task?" some might ask.

"Just relax, I know what I'm doing," Plunkett could then say.

The future-people would assume that the notes would explain everything, and hopefully their instructions would be clearer and less testy than the voice of the Great Plunkett.

Step 3

Plunkett might then write his question on a piece of paper and place it in the small safe—an odd little accoutrement that looked stronger than Torito and more secure. A short and squat Rottweiler of a cube, it had three-inch thick walls of a grey material that seemed to scowl with strength. An item that until then had seemingly no time travel use and in fact Lil' Woby had used to collect his dirty tissues and the mechanical parts that fell off Chatarra the alloyed idiot, dented and dilapidated dork descendent, and ferrous farrago, whom Plunkett noted he hated more and more every few hours.

Plunkett would then put the safe in the place named in Applemon's documents: a footlocker in a strange, small, bunker of a room at the back of an office in the physics building on campus. Applemon's office. It had very thick walls; in fact, under the wallpaper it looked like a larger version of the safe. Plunkett would put a blanket—as provided at the safe location, it turned out—on top of the box, not ask questions, and be gone.

(Note: At this point Plunkett would check the time since he would want to get back to Lil' Woby before he woke from his afternoon nap.)

Step 4

Plunkett then very simply went to the future to see what the people were named (potentially repeating this until it he found inhabitants that were indeed surnamed with calendar dates).

Step 5

Plunkett would then very, very simply go back to the named date and get the answer from the box.

Step 6

Enjoy, Plunkett would think, you have just gained information from the future without having to go there, hang out there, and risk bodily annoyances of the type Woby barely lived through.

CHAPTER TWENTY-TWO, STEP 4

| In which we refer to Chapter Zero.

G entle readers might want to refer to Chapter Zero, the scene with Sally, the first of the book. Full name: Sally November Thirtieth Two Thousand Five Hundred And Nine.

CHAPTER TWENTY-TWO,
STEP NEGATIVE ONE

| In which Nancy adds a step that calls
| for further explanation.

"Okay...but..." Nancy asked in heaving bursts of breath, "how do these steps...help...rescue...your brother?"

Plunkett began to answer, but Nancy's index finger raised from her bent form. "Appl—"

Plunkett began his answer, but Nancy's other fingers raised from her bent form. "—emon?" she finished, and twirled her hand to indicated that Plunkett could answer now.

The two just returned from Step 4, having taken advantage of Applemon's "safe for two" time travel wristwatch. It simply required them holding hands, a price nearly too steep for Nancy but her adventurous side, and suspicious-of-Plunkett side—a large side—took over. They met Sally, but the process was going too fast for Nancy's nausea to keep up.

"That's the especially clever part, thanks to me," Plunkett said. "Next we go back and get the belt remote-control codes. It works like this..." Plunkett explained the now eight-step Six-Step Process of Applemon's that the professor used to get information from the future—in this case the codes Plunkett needed to regain control of the belt—and how Plunkett expanded the ideas to be able to communicate with Applemon across time.

He would use the steps to tell the great, helpless Applemon

what to do and when to do it in order to be rescued by his heroic, younger, biological brother.

Nancy stood upright and twirled her hand again for Plunkett to continue.

"I already inspired awe in the people of the future," Plunkett began. Nancy bent over again holding her guts in place, and Plunkett went on. "Which was easy, and fun—Step Zero. Then I gave them instructions, created my question, and put it in the safe—Steps One, Two, and Three. I asked for them to find out the belt device remote- control codes."

Nancy unfolded slowly. She looked pale but she steadied enough to ask, "What if they didn't know the codes?"

"They probably didn't," Plunkett responded, "but they had forever to find out, and were definitely motivated since an angel of pretty high rank—me—commanded them."

Nancy's cheeks puffed in a spasm; she recovered, and Plunkett went on.

"So we went back to the future, far enough so the future-people had enough time to get the codes. And based on Sally's name we now know when to go get the answer: November 30, 2509."

"Got it," Nancy nodded, "but why not just get the answer then, when we went to see Sally?"

"I am not sure, but I think it makes it easier to clean up time-messes if the answer is retrieved in a different step. And if there is a lot of time between—Sally lived a millennium after the question was answered, right—a lot can change in the world in that time. They might screw with the answer, enemies might have time to screw it up, stuff like that."

Nancy considered this. Plunkett continued.

"So now, Step Five: we go get the answer: the remote-control codes we need are ready."

"You, please. You go. Not me." Nancy didn't look prepared for a trip through the next sixty seconds let alone to the twenty-sixth century. "But still, how does that help Applemon? We don't know where he is, right? Only the year, and that might not even be true."

"According to Apple, the remote codes could move the belt-wearer's location hundreds of miles. So yeah, normal people would just have to give up. But not me. I figured how we can use the safe to get a message to Applemon."

"How?" Nancy motioned with her face and hands.

"I go to 2999 and leave a message in the box that commands the future people to name the continent '*Wear Clean Underwear and Shaving Cream on Ronald's Birthday Land.*'"

Plunkett decided he should give Nancy time here to fully appreciate his genius.

She didn't need long. "That's the stupidest thing of all time."

"I will ask the people from 2999 whether that's true and get back to you." Plunkett's smugness grew to new heights.

"It won't work. It's so inane." Nancy shook her head.

"When Apple hears the name of the land he is in, he will get the message and turn the belt on that date, when I will go and activate the codes to bring him back. That part is easy, it's in the manual. You use the little box, and—"

Nancy interrupted. "It will never work."

"You're still a freshman time traveler. 'Never' is not in our vocabulary. You doubt me? Will your kind never learn?"

"What if Aris goes to the answer-safe?" Nancy asked, pointing one finger upward as an indication that she had more than one objection.

"Well, he can't be everywhere at once, right?" Plunkett said.

"Unsatisfying," Nancy judged. She straightened a second finger. "Why not just ask the future-people to just find The Great Applemon?"

"He might be dead by then. But the codes don't die, so they can take their time with that."

"Why such a silly message? Underwear? And who is Ronald?"

Plunkett answered. "The underwear is code for the belt, it's a private joke between us geniuses. Otherwise Applemon won't be wearing the belt since Aris controls it, right?"

"Better," Nancy judged, refolding three of her four tally-fingers. "And who's Ronald?"

"Someone whose birthday he knows. Don't worry about it. And when I'm in the year 2999 I will check to see whether you have had a better idea yet. Otherwise this is the plan."

Nancy smiled. "Okay. I actually kind of like it, the improbable weirdness of the solution all fits the problem somehow."

"Sure, whatever..." Plunkett said, preparing. "Now I need to go do Step Five. And hopefully Six."

CHAPTER TWENTY-TWO, STEP FIVE

| In which, Step Five.

So: Plunkett was now—"now" during "AUNT"— feeling good at Step Five.

So far, it had all worked, and he was very proud. The world had obeyed. He was ready next to activate the wondrous wristwatch and retrieve the safe. The very safe safe! Plunkett smiled.

He vooooooped himself to the precise date, and he only had to walk the half-mile from where he launched in the dorm hallway to the safe's mythical hiding spot.

He appeared in the future, and gave the usual cataract daze a moment to pass from his ears and eyes; "landing" in a different time was always like crossing a busy street with your eyes closed, or going over a waterfall in a barrel, or watching spiders come toward you as you sit constrained in your underwear.

Thrilled, Plunkett opened his eyes and ears again. He found that he was outside. There was no hallway about him, no walls near him, just a dim but undeniable sunlight. He lifted his head up high, and stood tall, his plans ripening, his breath quickening. He had the mastery; it was all working. Soon enough, he mused, he would be eating champagne with a fancy fork and paying off all his credit card debt with a Black Titanium American Express, hiring two financial advisors, and giving them conflicting objectives.

But first: to the safe. The thick grey cube, as per prior arrangement with the people of the future, was within Applemon's office in the Physics building of what was, is, today, a minute ago, the university campus. But centuries beyond the AUNT world that Plunkett was used to, the university grounds were unrecognizable.

About him sat one big park-like museum hallowed in dedicated memory to the first time traveler. Woby. A bad taste invaded Plunkett's mouth, and he spit.

All about Plunkett hung a thin but foul-smelling mist within an otherwise beautiful and spectacularly sculpted garden. Sunbeams darted between patches of haze as a breeze blew, but soon enough the mist returned to wrap him again and settle back between the ornate shapes of dark hedges and bushes. Moving and muttering, he had to weave around many, many statues of his brother, each capturing in bronze stiffness heroic feats of pioneering exploration. Columbus, Pisaro, Cortez, Magellan, Amundsen, and Armstrong now had Woby for company.

This did not bother Plunkett unduly because he knew that all this misguided reverence was a direct result of improper initial planning that let Woby run amok. It would soon change; Plunkett made a mental note to have Applemon help him fix this future.

History is told by the winners, he thought, and he was about to win. The statues would all be of him by the time Lil' Woby woke from his nap.

Plunkett's youthful stride lengthened. The rank, peppery taste in his mouth returned, had risen up his throat to his nose, and started to burn. He screwed himself into a good spitting pose and spit.

His focus shifted to the management of his sense of direction. Nothing of the old buildings or University roads and paths remained. Increasingly he had trouble breathing the air. It smelled vaguely of nasty acidic spices and of something else. Hmm…oh yes: deathly poison. That's what it must be, he thought.

His optimism overcame all, however, and he pushed onward, keeping one thought above his sickly phlegm: that he was minutes, just a few steps, from completing his task. With his forearm to his mouth he thought of his own future, the party he would throw. And how at the party he would ask Ariel to be his girlfriend, and then take back the offer once someone famouser appealed to him. Payback time, baby. He pictured putting out bowls of caviar and twenty-dollar bills for his guests to help themselves to. Class all the way.

And what he would buy Lil' Woby, and where they would live.

The smelly mist was getting into his clothes and hair as he hurried adroitly around hedges and benches and statues. He practically danced among them, keeping the direction of his best compass-less guess. In fact, he was targeting a cube-shaped shadow a few hundred yards ahead, the only structure in the estimated direction of the old Physics building. Thick walls, square shape: must be the place….

Then crowds came, just as they had come in his first trip, with Woby to the future, where odd creeping beings reached out and forced their way.

These people rose from benches and diverted their own headings to collide with his; there were now dozens in his train. They jogged to keep up as Plunkett increased his pace. In front, the word had spread, the questioner of legend had come, and people circled and wheeled round to cut him off.

There were no mittens this time poking at him, and no attempts to feel for his time travel machinery as if it was the hem of a holy garment, but the figures were wearing masks, covering their mouths and noses, and had the same pale, purposeless aspect in their eyes and brows. They did not moan but spoke to each other in short, mask-muffled, panting sentences. All of it alarmed Plunkett, who kept his mind on the cube within the cube, ahead—and on the end to this nightmare of a future.

He tried not to, but overheard exclamations of recognition:

"The Brother of the Great Hero!"

"It is him! The Great Assistant!"

"How he Breathes!"

Plunkett fought them off, not gently, using his risen elbows on them as he continued to protect his face from the burnt taste of the air. Toward both these purposes, he also energetically swung the sweatshirt he held.

Plunkett was glad he had brought it, and made mental notes for additional improvements should there be another Step Five: Wear a disguise, with a mask; and do not show up exactly on time: go a year or so out, avoid the crowds....

The population did give way, however, as they did not quite know what to do, or what to expect, as Plunkett reached the cube-shaped building. He pushed open a green, round door, and emerged, after two broad and down pitched steps, into a small chamber, a square inner sanctum, a holy of holy of knowledge, the waiting—and waiting, and waiting—sacred receptacle of his own genius. Wherein, as he knew, the box lay, covered in a lush purple fabric and tied with a bow of golden ribbon.

The room glowed nobly with candlelight, and the air was fresh and breathable and smelled sweetly of green apples and fresh maple wood. All was gilded.

"Nice touch," Plunkett mumbled with genuine gratitude.

He shut the door in the faces of several wide eyed, mask-wearing gapers, and sucked two deep lungfuls of the cleanly sweet air of the room.

Plunkett tore the ribbon and lid from the box. Folded beautifully within, in the shape of a capital R, with gold leaf and perfumed plentifully to hide the smell of toxic fumes, was the paper. He first saw his own handwriting and the words of his request.

On the other side, so close now, would be the answer. Then he could leave.

Plunkett straightened his clothes and fingered his hair in preparation of a pose he had practiced in his mind all day.

There he stood, one arm raised: Plunkett. Master, Owner, Fisherman. God. Brother, Unkie, Future Statue. Lawgiver, Hero. Time traveler, Ridiculer of the Universe.

Why? Because this was his trip to get what *he* wanted—not to save Applemon, he had already gone to 2999 and set the belt code for his escape. Not for Trice yet, either. But for Plunkett: his own well-deserved reward for being, succinctly, terrific.

And patient.

So that he was here now for his own plan, and this plan had its own question for the future, and he was ready to retrieve the answer.

Who is the richest man in the history of the world and when did he graduate elementary school and where?

He had asked, via the Steps. *This*, his thinking ran, *will cut to the chase.*

He had words prepared for this moment, the revealing of the answer. Pumping one hand to the air, the watch shining aloft, in a grand, booming, echoing voice Plunkett spoke—no, in fact, in a grand, booming, echoing, voice Plunkett *spake*:

"Today, I…"

As he turned the paper over to see what the future people had written.

But all motion stopped at his shocking recognition of familiar handwriting, and he read on the page words directing him to "Knock it off and come back, you idiot—Nancy isn't impressed."

And it was signed.

"Applemon."

Plunkett tipped and smashed his head against the giant circle of the green door and spit once more even though the air was sweet and his throat clean, and his mouth clear, and even though he didn't need to.

I shouldn't have saved him first, he thought, meaning Applemon who had, apparently, deciphered Plunkett's kooky message, and put on the belt, which received the codes, which Plunkett had discovered and set before redoing the steps again for his own benefit. *I should have done this first, gotten rich first, THEN saved Applemon.* Plunkett thought. *Why is it so hard for me to be selfish?*

Plunkett tipped again, in the other direction, and smashed his head against the small circle of the green button on the wristwatch to return to earlier "today."

Here is a list:

Sweaty mongoloid dwarf cretinous eunuchs, all in a row.

CHAPTER TWENTY-THREE

| Sunday. In which there is a regathering of the forces of good.

P lunkett did come back, defeated, again, to the dorm room. The frolickers were rollicking, but he was a torpid ode to dejection.

They—Applemon, Nancy, Woby—forced him to pretend to listen to Applemon as he explained the new predicament.

"I don't care. I saved him. Isn't that enough?" Plunkett asked. The Uroboros hissed at him, raspberry style.

"Screw you, too," Plunkett said.

But he listened, and Applemon did tell: How, after he escaped using the belt, he was able to keep track of Trice via the location and selection of those who swapped places with her when she escaped to the QOV. This she did often as Aris pursued her, and as, unwittingly, Woby pursued her so rashly when listening to Ariel's psychiatric advice.

"'Why is Woby doing all this?!' I asked myself many times," Applemon said, one professorial finger in the air. "But soon enough I understood—though too late, and too quickly, when I saw Aris' awful, dull gray eyes in front of me at the playground where I had found Woby. It served as a perfect trap."

Woby asked sullenly, "Is Trice going to be okay? What do we do?"

"I am getting to that." Applemon went on. "She certainly was forced to the QOV many times, as the couch here, and Aris' office, attests. This is what he wanted, of course, to learn more of her 'still place,' the modern cosmologist's Holy Grail. I'm sorry to say that, because of Plunkett and Woby's numerous time travails, Aris was able to start all this trouble in the first place. And eventually, using Ariel to use Woby, he trapped Trice in the QOV once he learned enough. This he did to dispose of her, and thereby thwart my research, and the goals of others, his rivals for learning and power. Petty physics professor politics run amok."

"All this for what, a published paper?" Old Woby said mournfully.

"More than that, Wobe, there is a lot more on the line, in fact my colleagues are just starting to analyze the new data, and they say—"

Other partiers gathered round; Plunkett paraphrased what he read in Nancy's blazing eyes: *Who cares? Get on with it.*

Applemon smiled after declining an offer to dance with a small person dressed in oversized professor clothes. He pointed his finger aloft again and continued.

"While trapped in the year 3000—not a bad era for reading material, but awful for food, and music, by the way—I immediately set about to consider, and calculate, what that last, most desperate, most awful, development meant: Woby kidnapping his younger self. Why would Aris want this? What could I do about it?"

"Weren't you," Nancy asked, "more concerned with how to escape and get back here, to AUNT, and us?"

"No, because of the Copernican Principle, and the exponential probability distribution, and my experience of humanity's reaction to time travel so far, namely the few trips made by us in this room, plus Aris and Trice herself: that I would only be spending a few days there at most. Think about it."

Nancy found herself nodding, Ariel-style, and reproved herself for it with a dark frown. "I will, later—just go ahead."

Applemon smiled. "It just means that my life would change either very soon, or never, since my fellow-time travelers knew to find me at that date in 3000. Sure enough, in a few days, once I met others, I learned where I was, and the funny name of the whole country, and knew what to do."

"You're welcome," Plunkett said from far underneath a scowl.

"You finally used your family brain, so yes, congratulations and indeed thank you very much. Now shut up." Applemon said.

"I had a question about that, too," Nancy said. "Why did Aris put you in the future? Why 3000? Why not 30,000 BCE with only primitive tools? And a serious language barrier?"

"And rock fights for your eyeglasses and cardigan," Plunkett added just because.

"Good questions, Nancy," Professor Applemon declared, his finger really wagging now. "Aris knew that if he put me in the past that I am far too clever, too able…that it would be too easy for me to mess things up for him. I could muck around with births and deaths, his lineage, the slave trade, economics, inventions, language, religion. I would make it my life's work to damage AUNT and mess up Aris' nice life. It is hard to time travel without chaotic changes, as we have seen. In fact most of the ingenuity of our devices is that it limits this kind of damage. Who would want to win the world, but only a world so changed that it is not worth winning?"

"Ah," Nancy said.

"And that would be all I would do, eventually, after realizing that I wasn't going to be saved. I could not invent time travel in the past with all the limitations of living among savages, and I of course would not put on the belt with Aris controlling it."

"Told ya!" Plunkett said to Nancy. He rose noisily to get a beer, walking directly through a lively dance floor to the kitchen area.

Nancy waved for Applemon to continue. "Well? What do we do?" Woby looked on with no expression but his legs bouncing with expectant energy. His younger self was playing Twister with the Uroboros and losing, by far.

"Yes, well," Applemon said, "I figured much out, I think. What is going on, and why, and the Trice dilemma, the Woby-Woby dilemma, and what we need to do." Applemon's tone was graver, his voice grown powerfully clear. He put a hand on Woby's shoulder. "I have more to do, now that I'm back and can use my resources.

These are complex matters, I need to look into a thing or two, verify some calculations, run some simulations, get the latest QOV data, map it to Trice's swapping of people."

"Don't give up hope," Applemon went on after a pause during which he stared earnestly at Lil' Woby stretched and wriggling among circles of color. "I think there will be good news. But some bad news also…which for now is that we have to wait for the good news. I will get to it, excuse me…" he trailed off, his voice ending lamely, uncharacteristically.

With another glance at Lil' Woby but without another word, Applemon walked off to his bedroom.

Nancy found herself in charge, somewhat, and perked Woby up, reminding him that very little has ever been a match for his brother's ferocious intellect. Woby nodded, and was approached by the visiting physicists, whom Applemon had brushed aside, considering their decades-old ideas unworthy of him and they unworthy of enlightening.

Woby felt otherwise, so Nancy made the introduction. "Men of science!" she said grandly, "I bring you that Star of the Past, Scourge of the Future, Ghost of the Present, Woby!"

There was a small cheer from the guests, always eager for excuses to drink to Woby's health, and dance it, and sing it, and shout it. The contemplative robed ones, in silence, wandered over as well.

With Woby occupied, Applemon sequestered with his analyses, and Lil' Woby seemingly, and seemingly *always*, happily contented, Nancy moved on to Plunkett.

"Let's join the party," she said. And they did. *What* they did is the kind of aside that gentle readers would find in an Appendix.

CHAPTER TWENTY-FOUR

In which Applemon has a plan that no one likes, though Aris would.

Applemon's bedroom door opened, and the common room hushed. Only Lil' Woby could be heard, counting quietly while facing a corner either as part of a game someone was playing with him, or because no one wanted to play and this was a strategic move.

The expectant crowd watched as Applemon walk to the center of the room hurriedly, and, wasting no time, immediately explained his solution. "I won't sugar coat it. Woby has to die."

Shock. Gasps. Chokes on inhaled carbonated drinks.

"Oh—and be killed by Lil' Woby. Thanks."

Only exclamations, and the beginnings of abandoned questions, and Nancy's one-word request to "Explain." So Applemon still had the floor, as it were, and went on.

"This will unlock Trice from the QOV, it will put the other dimensions back into her life. So that's good."

"What? Is there no other way? Can't be!" most said, supported by nods from all. All except Lil' Woby; he had been shooed to Plunkett's bedroom with his nanny-bot Chatarra.

"Well, there is one other thing I can try. Hold on," Applemon said and went around the room, once more interviewing summarily some of the couch guests, then caballing with the guest physicists for a short time. He worked quickly and checked his new data against numbers he carried on a computer printout.

Then, with a satisfied sigh, he put on the time travel watch and disappeared in a cloud of black smoke.

Actually, as the room soon learned, Applemon *reappeared* in the cloud of black smoke—when it cleared through newly opened windows via newly turned on ceiling fans, Applemon stood there, having returned from a time travel junket that obviously had not gone well. His hair was singed, his clothes charred black.

"Okay, yeah," he said, "I didn't think that would work. Wormholes are bullshit. No, as I said: Woby has to die."

CHAPTER TWENTY-FIVE

| In which Applemon explains more.

The chorus asked Applemon: "Are you sure? How can this be? You must be wrong, it's a mistake, can't be right!" Physicists also chimed in, offkey but with conviction. The monks very slowly said nothing.

Applemon—confronted, affronted, insulted—stood tall, and in the middle of the room and in the midst of the detractors and doubters—doubters of his ability to answer, doubters of his scientific acumen, his calculations, his legendary prowess—he spoke.

"Yep," he affirmed, with strength enough to shut them all up.

Until: "Does this mean that Lil' Woby will also be killed by himself at the same age, or not? Why not? Can you verify that such a horrible deed will collapse all wave equations, and level the consciousness of the universe, if this is indeed why the younger Woby must do it? Does this align the cubes-of view? And optimize Trice's happiness?" Voices were raised. Any snakes in the crowd rose menacingly, the dogs stiffened and growled, and the humans didn't dance.

The physicists waved pages of their own research and presented doubts that were precise to many decimal points.

"What about pseudo-Riemannian manifolds? And invariant-hyperbola, Galilean abductive transformations?" they argued. "The arrows!"

Applemon sighed. It rivalled a lion's roar. He removed and unfolded a paper that Plunkett recognized as the arrow diagram from their talk the day before.

Applemon pointed at it, rotated it, held it aloft, waved it like it was the final peace treaty that would unite all of mankind forevermore, or at least delay it a few months. To emphasize Trice's relative position in her many-leveled existence, as well as Applemon's own confidence, he tore his thumb through the page where the squiggly origin spiraled outward, giving his presentation a visual flair, his mathematical conclusions a physical finality, and his slew of condescending insults a three-dimensional feel.

"You're this sure?" came one last query.

"I think so," Applemon said indignantly, with a surety of voice and strength of stance that should shut them up, he deemed. "And that should be good enough for you."

"How can you be so calm?" Nancy asked.

This was a much better type of question for Applemon's ego, so he answered, one hand raised "Because it is very simple gauge symmetric transition wave spectrum analysis. It's like you people never heard of baryogenesis, for God's sake! Listen:" They did, as Applemon continued donnishly. "To save Trice, the sentient being that caused all the trouble must—for reasons that live in the space where theoretical physics and Nagarjuna's Buddhism meet, though there is active debate on this—" A monk bowed, but Applemon shook his head and continued, "that sentient being must remove his spacetime ripples, those created when he met himself, those wavelets that behave like four-dimensional, exponential dominoes, those that are impossible to fix, only to kill at the source. And one does this at the point of earliest reflexive consciousness, that is, by having self kill self, the younger removing the older. This removes the duplicate, recursive point-of-view issues and also unwinds all the time spent with Trice, despite their equilibrium it was such time that banished her to the QOV. I guess."

The room redounded in the many definitional and philosophical issues, such as whether this would be murder, suicide, egocide, somacide, "Felo de se"—as Nancy contributed—or plain supercilious, though eventually no one could rebut the Professor's logic, mostly since they had no idea what he was talking about.

"See? Trust me, this will do the trick," Applemon gloated, "the girl will be, shall be, saved. I suppose."

Heads nodded in silence.

Applemon then reminded everyone of the much-honored axiom, that meeting your younger self leads to danger and death and is hard to undo. "So this is the only way. I'm pretty sure."

Plunkett sat and mulled this new development. He was visibly agitated, but so was everyone else. He didn't act, didn't question his older brother, even now when it meant the demise of his younger brother. The guests commented on his silence, none too gently nor too quietly, using phrases like "cowering wimp" and "could never be a bullfighter" (nor "astronaut" nor "watchdog") and "perdedor sudoroso y decepcionante".

Eventually he rose, not to defend himself, but to have a meeting with Nancy, Applemon, and a Woby that looked ready to expire due to lethal cocktail of pure confusion mixed with woe begotten unluck.

Plunkett, calmly, offered to kill Woby, to spare Lil' Woby of the pain and horror, the guilt and trauma.

Woby spoke like an overheard ghost, in a near-silence only slightly louder than the panting of Torito or the slither of the Uroboros. "Thank you, Plunkett," he said, "but strength requires at least once to have been strong. Don't bring this on yourself."

"Wow," Nancy said, "that's almost Wordsworth."

Applemon noted that it wouldn't work anyway.

CHAPTER TWENTY-SIX

Trice in the Omnium of Qualia
and Umvelt, the Quali-Omnium-Velt,
the QOV.

When Woby sat on Ariel's couch, all those hours and decades ago, and as Ariel parroted Aris' instructions and enabled Aris' ambitions, Trice:

I can't control it. I keep going there. To be still, to be calm, to be and have everything be still and calm, maybe.

Woby. I can't get to him. He comes to me but it isn't like him. He isn't being him. His being isn't him. There is force, and pressure, question, and probing. When it's him he is ease and rest, and we balance.

And I can't go to him. I go still, I go to stillness.

Woby obeyed, but for his own reasons, and with his own will and heart. Trice:

But what is this! What is this? This time! This time? This is not the same. What did he? What did he say that put me here? This time? What did he do? It's good! But I am still here....

This was love.

A feeling that made Woby remember, and seek, his youth, his self. Trice:

And…now…I see. Clear, pure, and I can move freely. I can leave! Anytime, the time I want. I can leave and be still, but still leave. Freely! Mind first, heart first, I go.

I am infinite, and I can be in peace, or not, and go, and be. Be one.

Or I can meet myself, like Woby did, without harm or fear. It makes the world of time three-dimensional, and I can see all, and forever. Somehow…but it's true.

Trice found herself free, and so…

I can, and I must, fix Woby's world for him, that existence he also loves, with his brothers. They can't. I have to. Or these will all just be possible pasts!

Which she did until…

What's this! A cry, his cry! To me. To his sacrifice. To me, to us.

Trice had heard Woby hugging Lil' Woby's blanket, and offering a prayer to eternity, for her to come to him; "Give me what I love, Trice, since my love was your gift."

Trice:

I hear him, everywhere, and all the time. Like loving words, his are eternally abiding. But I can leave the still place again and be in time.

I can get to him. I can go to him. I am good, loved. I will be in one place, and feel from one heart.

CHAPTER TWENTY-SEVEN

| In which there is acceptance.

Any remaining debate ended, and Applemon hurried them all, stating that by his calculations Trice was at risk of being completely "undone" as he phrased it, as she was growing younger and younger, faster and faster, the Woby-time-ripples multiplying, and she reversing in age exponentially—"which means 'hurry up' in math." He said. "Get Lil' Woby to do the deed soon, or else Trice could dissolve into nonexistence. And Lil' Woby will have killed himself for no reason and have to live with that his whole life."

When, monk-like, no one made sign of hurrying, Applemon showed them his notes. "Do you see where it says $W \leq 1$? That shows how many copies of themselves people are allowed during any one actual ray of time. Idiots. Hurry up!"

Applemon wondered aloud why people argue and rage and get emotional in the face of a mathematical fact. Woby needed to be destroyed or the universe as they knew it would die. Or worse.

Plunkett nodded. He was resigned to this, if befuddled, as many still were since the proposed murderous act seemed to have a zero-sum: Lil' Woby would just grow up to be Big, Old, Woby. And probably, when this great life experience happens, it might yield a better Woby, perhaps even a strongly mediocre one.

That glass now half-full, the full group were resolved. Sad, but resolved, to be witnesses to the crime and to let it go forward.

The guests presented Woby with chaplets of coral, wearing them like the martyrs of old, as Nancy pointed out. He was given knives and kitchen poison, and other sharp or dangerous things that were solemnly collected or donated by the couch guests.

"Anything with a warning label," Plunkett advised. "We don't know how it will happen yet. Woby will have to teach him."

"Yes," Woby said, his voice as thin as if it came from centuries in the past. "This all helps, thank you."

Plunkett patted him on the back, he and Nancy willing to let physics take its course.

Lil' Woby's face was licked cleaned by Torito the Rottweiler as the boy entered the bedroom, and the door was shut.

Soon, the dorm was stunned when a tremulous shudder shifted their perceptions briefly, that recognizable wobble that pulled and pushed at everyone's stomach. By habit the guests started a cheer; this feeling usually presaged a reason to toast another partier.

But the hurrah died quickly. Crashes, a muffled cry, and noises of steel clashing with steel hushed the crowd but only in time for them to hear nothing; a shroud of silence covered all the dorm. No more sounds came from the bedroom, the presumed scene of the crime.

Nancy buried her head in Plunkett's chest but listened with the downhearted rest.

After a few minutes of AUNT, the bedroom door opened. The crowed exhaled then inhaled as one as a little girl emerged, a little girl wearing a little yellow robe. In a comically sure and melodious voice she stated that her name was Trice.

Woby had done the deed, as all thought, and as some said aloud.

A smug Applemon soon confirmed that this Lil' Trice was in fact six years old, as he predicted.

"Who gives a rat's ass?" Plunkett said rudely, and though it made those with literal experience of rats hiss and howl—the Uroboros and Torito Azul, respectively—many agreed with the sentiment, and Applemon left the common room shaking his head at the continued disrespect of hard science. He went to the bedroom.

Nature soon took its course, the partiers returned to their

normal mode and began to celebrate. This was, as all soon admitted, a reason to rejoice. Woby was a hero, and technically he still lived, and Trice was saved.

And, in fact, here they were, Woby and Trice, young but together, about the same age in fact, with the girl already laughing at the boy with a keen smile and curious flashes of her onyx eyes.

It was a selfless act of heroism, an act of pure love, that won in the end.

"Or did it?" Applemon said as he returned from his bedroom. "There is nothing in there but those silly instruments on the floor." The physicists, competing with the monks in the jockeying for position in Applemon's train wherever the great man went, nodded.

They all looked at Lil' Woby, a guilty-looking Lil' Woby, and asked him in baby talk what had happened.

"He put a blanket over my head. I counted in my head under the blanket to ten, ten times."

"And then?" the guests said together in a sing-song voice that made Lil' Trice laugh hysterically.

Lil' Woby answered. "Then he hugged me and was gone."

"Obviously he has no idea what was going on," Applemon said.

"But we heard a scream, and noises," Nancy said softly, coming closer to the boy.

"Me, too," Lil' Woby said while being pulled away by Lil' Trice.

The Asian woman said something that sounded like "love"—the bullfighter agreed with her, and explained his belief "that romanticism wins the bull's ear," that the time-conquering emotion of Woby's self-sacrificial act was what rescued Trice from the QOV.

Applemon harrumphed at this, almost pushing two smiling monks over in his effort to press ahead with fact-based methods. After confirming that there was no sign of Woby, and noting that the time travel belt and watch were secure in his desk drawer, he went off to recalculate, unhappy with sappy answers and his own possible error. He also wanted to have a look at the windowsill, and the ground below.

Plunkett said, "Well I guess that's that." He patted Lil' Woby but quickly turned and faced away, toward a kitchen cabinet. Plunkett offered Lil' Woby and Lil' Trice something to drink and asked whether stale saltines would suffice for a midday snack.

"That's a sad snack," Nancy offered quietly, her attempt at lightness thudding heavily.

Plunkett's little little-brother looked up to ask gently "I'm gone?" His words blew through the flakes of cracker crumbs.

Nancy said, "The poor little guy has seen too much." Plunkett hugged the child tightly, pulling him close and burying his own eyes in Lil' Woby's oversized university sweatshirt.

"Yeah, that's that..." Plunkett said.

CHAPTER TWENTY-EIGHT:
WOBY AND TRICE'S FINAL ADVENTURE

> Trice and Woby's Final Adventure.

The shuddering wobble felt after the Wobies went to Applemon's dorm bedroom, nauseating to all but the most experienced time travelers, was familiar by now; it of course signified unnatural jumps in the natural temporal order, the tearing of spacetime.

But it was not, as the partiers assumed, a result of Trice's escape from the QOV.

No. It was due to her most recent act, the last of a long series of efforts at repair. Repairs necessary to undo damage, damage caused by undulating ripples of spacetime, ripples caused by Woby and Lil' Woby hanging out together in the dorm.

Fixing it required some quick-thinking and fast-acting time travel, similar to how Applemon tracked and revised Woby and Plunkett's initial time travel trips. But when self-meets-self things are much worse, much more complex, and exponentially compounding, as Applemon had explained.

What Applemon had wrong was the effect on Trice. She was not younger from being trapped in QOV, but older, quite a bit older, having to spend much of her own time fixing Woby's mess, Ariel's meddling, and Aris' awfulness.

Next, the QOV-escapee, the Elder—much elder—Trice, searched for, and found, her younger self in a here-we-go-again act of seeming lunacy.

But the elder Trice had new understanding and rare command: over time, over its life, and over her own. Self-meeting-self makes ripples in spacetime, and in the QOV the ripples have an extra dimension, that of point-of-view. The stillness Trice experiences within this expanded reality is then disturbed, and these disturbances are shortcuts to eternity. Trice mastered these, like signposts in the fabric of existence itself they oriented her, led her to anywhere, to anytime, to any mind.

That's the best she could explain it, at least, given the little cosmology, physics, Buddhism, psychology, and esoteric mysticism that she knew.

And Trice had a plan, even when trapped, much as Applemon had a plan when he was trapped, and Plunkett had many plans when trapped in his own life in his own time. And the woman's plan was not forgotten through all the time she aged while fixing existence. And the little girl remembered it, too.

The two Trices, nodding to each other many times in silent understanding, went and found a little boy they would need. They spied on him for a short time, then let him be.

Then they heard a cry, *the* cry, from Applemon's bedroom.

So they went and removed Woby the Elder from that awful pickle he found himself in, of having to die at the hand of his younger self so that the latter might live, and one existence be solidified, and do it all without touching each other too much. Empathy abounds.

Indeed the scene that the Trices found—of murderous weaponry laying around, of the older Woby trying out scenarios and practicing with implements of death while at the same time trying to keep Lil' Woby's clumsy and then blanketed curiosity away because my goodness who knows what would happen should any other combination of deaths occur other than that prescribed by Applemon—was awash in pathos. Both Trices just had to laugh. They laughed harder when they startled the older Woby, making him shriek, drop a knife and a potato peeler, and turn a bright pink, replacing the deathly, almost translucent-of-life pall he had worn of late.

Indeed, seeing Trice the elder made him feel, and look, much younger. They left Lil' Woby under his blanket, counting his eighth "eight..." and continuing slowly.

The wobble that the dorm room denizens felt was this last step, Woby and Trice and Trice vooping out of Applemon's bedroom.

Woby found himself on campus, just outside the university's Physics building, its stucco bricks and dark windows quite familiar. He and Trice—elder version—hugged. When Woby turned to Lil' Trice, he paused to ask, "What for her? A high-five?" But they decided that a kiss on the little girl's cheek was best.

Then the older Trice took charge, her movements those of a large, red-robed hummingbird, her words a torrent. "Woby," she directed, "you need to find Aris. He's in the present for sure. Check his office, I guess, first. Don't do anything. Just find him and keep him in your sight."

Trice did not believe in commas; her style brought back good memories, and Woby smiled broadly. "I can do that," Woby said. "But what if Aris starts vooping around?"

Lil' Trice laughed.

"Then just remember exactly when he disappears, and from where, and I will deal with it."

"Okay," Woby said. "What are you going to do?"

"I have to bring this little one," Trice said, patting herself on the head, "back to the dorm, and run one other errand to pick someone up, and I will meet you wherever Aris is. Goodbye for now my Penthos!"

"How will you know wh—" Woby tried, but Trice's words had concluded so swiftly that his own were too late. Both Trices were gone. Woby finished his sentence to a shrub and a squirrel, then entered the Physics building and climbed the stairs to the sixth floor to Aris' office.

The professor was there, in continual motion in trying to calm many transtemporal transfinite couch-guests. They overflowed into a small reading room adjacent to his office. Woby waited nearby and surveilled. He felt he was good at this.

As his legs tired, and he positioned around a hallway corner to slide down for a sit, the grey tiles of the wall opposite turned into the folds of a red robe. Trice was before him. Woby scrambled up.

"He's that way," Woby said, pointing toward Aris' office. "Who's this?" he added to a doubletake as Trice held hands with a small, portly boy with large eyeglasses who held a very large book under one arm, but as it slipped, even as Woby watched, the need was to switch arms continually. It reminded Woby of the Woby he left behind in time and at the dorm, but of course wasn't.

"Pretty good likeness, right?" Trice commented on the resemblance.

"Except for the book, yeah. But why? Who?" Woby asked, and kept asking, as Trice clasped his hand also and led a swift march down the hall.

Soon enough, Aris caught site of them. He held a chicken in his hands, its cackling panic hugged tight to his chest. He large, eyes, battleship gray, widened diabolically. He threw the chicken into his office, shut the door, and came toward them.

Two pairs of gripped hands awaited him, and the three stood firm in the hall.

Aris, his oversized time-travel wristwatch aloft and gleaming brightly, laughed loudly. "Trice! And what's this, a Woby army?" He had also mistaken the boy for Lil' Woby. "Fools! Trice, you should know, meeting oneself is annihilation. At least one of you has to die! Do the calculations!"

Trice and team remained silent.

"That doesn't worry me, physical laws will take care of them, the little potatoes..." Aris scoffed, pointing a wiggly, bony finger at the two males, then moving that finger direct to Trice, and coming nearer to her face. Woby squeezed Trice's hand in anger at this rudeness, this insolence; Trice squeezed back as a sign to keep cool.

"And for you," Aris went on with an evil sneer as he held up his watch high, "for you, girl, I have made improvements!" He twisted the device about his wrist, it indeed looked very complex compared to anything they had seen. "Yes, Woby, you taught me much in the name of psychology. Your girl won't escape again. Now, for the last time, I will put your time at an end."

Unspoken was Trice's taunting, her invitation to the chase. The three, chained by sweaty palms, disappeared, as did Aris just as he attacked.

CHAPTER TWENTY-NINE

Back at the dorm, the most famous dorm of all time(s).

Lil' Trice was introduced to the gang, even given an honorary spot on the couch, the others drawn to her guileless, coal eyes that were bright with darkness and eager friendship.

Lil' Woby was forgotten for the moment. Nancy and Plunkett had checked Applemon's room for any other travelers, but there was no sign of anyone else, let alone any other Wobies or Trices. Nor was there expected to be.

Plunkett was quiet, Nancy guessing that he missed the big dope, his older younger timeless brother.

"Yeah," Plunkett said, "but I have the little dope to think of."

"Where is he?" Nancy asked when they heard a rumble in the hall, the back hall toward the back staircase.

At the heavy door Lil' Woby struggled to enter, dragging his blanket, falling, and trying nonetheless to hold the way open as a copy of him, seemingly, also came in, holding a very large book using two child-sized hands and forearms.

Nancy and Plunkett came to help, with Applemon running to join them. He cleared the confusion.

"Ha! Do not fear! That is *not* another little Woby!"

"Praise the lord…" Plunkett muttered.

"Then who…?" Nancy looked to Applemon.

"Ha!" Applemon repeated louder, holding the door wide and peering down its hall. "Look!"

Nancy, Plunkett, and Applemon heard a scream, and saw a man running away.

"It's the great Professor Aris!" Applemon said. "Ha! Doomed! Run, Aris!" The professor laughed as the others continued to shriek and echo his footsteps from the stairwell with every leap away.

Nancy couldn't resist adding, "Hey! Chatterton! At a loss for words?"

"I was wrong? I was wrong! Oh! Ohhhh!" Aris squelched as if the W-word caused him pain.

"You aren't wrong, you just aren't right yet!" Applemon shouted as the last word. He simultaneously petted the small boy, the new visitor, on his head.

"I don't get it," Nancy said. "Why is Chatterton running away?"

Applemon answered, "Well, take a good, close look at our newest guest."

The small figure juggled his book in order to rub his eyes, twisting one small fist at a time. Without his glasses each eye shone a steely grey. He spoke then, his voice deep and sure and quite unlike Lil' Woby's squeaks. "He dropped me when he found out it's me."

"Ha!" Applemon repeated again and again until it was a fully formed laugh. Then, he announced to "everyone!" as partiers began to come near, "Say goodbye to Professor Aris, and meet Lil' Aris!"

"What? How?" Nancy asked.

"Ha! Think what you want," Applemon said, "but this must be Trice's doing. Big Trice, that is. Aris will keep away now, as she must've known."

"How clever!" Nancy said. "So Trice was rescued. And somehow brought Aris to his younger self, or vice-versa, right? But poor Woby…Big Woby, that is."

Plunkett relieved undersized Aris of the outsized book, none too kindly. "Plotinus?" Plunkett read the lone word of the cover's title.

Applemon relieved Plunkett of the outsized book, none too kindly. "It's Greek philosophy, third century, but not the useless kind. It is sort of a combination of morality and cosmology."

Plunkett said, looking accusingly at Lil' Aris, "and he blew it with both subjects. Or he will."

"No. I'm sorry," the boy said. "I know what I did, but I won't ever do it. It is privation of good. I'm learning."

"That's in the book, that evil is privation of good," Applemon said to the group, then turned to the boy again. "I believe you, and you're doing very well. Keep learning, and we can talk when you're ready. I'll find some math for you. But this is a good enough start." He handed the book, with his blessings, back to his little ex-adversary.

"Trice gave this to me. I see why," Lil' Aris said, his words mellifluous if a bit pompous, cold and remote like the grown Aris, but like a sunrise, not a prison wall.

Lil' Trice giggled from the couch. Everyone else looked to Applemon to solidify their joyous astonishment. Was Trice really okay? Saved?

"Aha! Yes! Told ya. Trice lives!" Applemon answered. "She lives. Free of the QOV. She conquered it somehow. Somehow…." Satisfied on some things, Applemon quickly turned his mind to others. He made that face they all knew, indicating he was anxious to get to his pens and pads and laptop and to calculate until the world made perfect sense again.

Plunkett said, again, "Well I guess that's that…" And, as before, he patted Lil' Woby, this time smiling. "I think everything is okay, thanks to me, Can I get on with my life now?"

The little little-brother looked up, as before, to ask, as gently as before, "I'm not gone?"

Lil' Aris laughed but kept reading his giant philosophy book, his eyes intense though bloodshot red.

Nancy, similarly as before, said "The poor little guy reads too much…"

But there was no hugging as before; Plunkett left the room to make his own plans.

CHAPTER THIRTY

| In which, The End.

The dorm room continued to buzz, each guest contributing opinions, observations, words, ideas worth commemorating, and proffering new holidays they wanted to combine with those of their beloved AUNT-based friends.

Lil' Trice laughed at whiles, and her dark eyes grew big for short moments, but otherwise she was silent as the Buddhists, clearly preferring to smile than do anything else. It seemed her way of partying, to enjoy linear time, to live it with one thought at a time, with clear subjects, objects, causes and effects.

Lil' Aris, putting a bookmark in his giant philosophy book in a place—which, some noticed, indicated significant progress—listened for a time to the discussions that Applemon and Plunkett had rejoined. The professor moved his seat regularly as the two monks kept trying to sit nearer to him. The visiting physicists had given up trying to be Applemon's friend.

"So we think Woby—the elder—is okay too?" Nancy asked the group. "Why? I'm confused." She looked at Lil' Woby, beseeching him for more information.

"Stop, Nancy," Plunkett said, "you are going to confuse his head off."

The group all gave opinions.

Lil' Aris had returned to his reading but overheard the many questions and loose ends and answered as best he could, though he didn't see the need to stop reading while he did so.

"Woby meeting the younger Woby," he said in his deep voice and reassuring way, "makes a 3-D, so actually a 5-D, presence-hole in the QOV. It's kind of like eternal omniscient omnipresence realized. So it's okay."

"The understatement of the millennium, but yes, that's one solution," Applemon nodded, "though there are others. I hope that's right, since it means when big professor Aris ran from our little Aris here that he was also running away from his dream of taming and controlling the QOV!"

The crowd shook their heads at Lil' Aris as if he was big Aris. This was pretty weird, to be remonstrating against a little kid's future that for sure already happened, yet he was so cute and innocent still and he hadn't done it yet. They all agreed at the benefit of having no lawyers present.

"Leave him alone," Applemon said in support of Lil' Aris who raised his right thumb but said nothing and kept reading. "Anyway, I assume Trice is with Woby, as they always wanted."

"Yay!" squeaked a voice from, apparently, under one of the couches.

Plunkett searched the direction of the voice and said, "But they can't come here, I guess. Or won't."

Lil' Aris walked with his book open-faced atop both hands, heading to the couch where Lil' Woby's ankles and feet protruded. "No," Lil' Aris said, as Plunkett playfully pulled his youngest brother free by his shoes, "they won't come here, but Woby and Trice live on together, if you can call it that, enlightened and eternal, in the QOV. Even ask those guys." Lil' Aris nodded briefly toward the robed monks, who had squatted behind Applemon.

Applemon would not ask the monks, but others would and did. Much whispering commenced.

"How do you know this?" Nancy asked, the last to be convinced. Applemon explained, supported with nods and assenting baritone hums from his Lil' Nemesis, that Lil' Aris was with the two Trices and Big Woby, in the hall of the university Physics building, where they confronted Big Aris, and ended up in different hallway, the one off the back staircase of the dorm, Aris having followed Trice and her trap: presenting the two Aris' with each other.

Which made Aris the older shriek and run away. "He of little understanding," Applemon concluded.

Lil' Aris laughed. He didn't seem to be taking any of this personally, and indeed his apology earlier was proving sincere, promising that what he did previously in his future he would never do now, again, for the first time.

"Then," he added, "Little Woby found me and Little Trice, but the big ones were gone."

"Smart little guy. Geez," Plunkett said, noticing that Lil' Aris was near the end of his giant book, and seeing many, many dogeared pages plumed with multicolored Post-it notes to serve as flags for important passages.

Nancy still had questions and tried to follow the break-out discussions among the partiers—who, indeed, unanimously believed a new celebration was in order—but she was told by many to "relax."

"Well," she said to that, "what about Ariel?"

Lil' Aris pointed a small finger toward the back dorm entrance. His eyes remained down on his 'Plotinus' book; he had started it again from the beginning.

Lil' Woby ran in the indicated direction, followed and soon passed by Nancy, Plunkett, and Applemon. Opening the bulky backdoor they saw Ariel at the end of the hall, her back to them and with one step on the downward steps. She had paused, as if uncertain how to answer the many calls of her name. She turned to face the others. Reason and wit had left her eyes.

Ariel stared blankly, dressed in all the colors of the rainbow except those that aren't brown. On her previous visit, invigorated with the possibilities and definiteness of breakthrough success, she had looked like a walking springtime garden. Now she looked only like the dirt.

"Ariel, wait." Nancy said, coming through the brothers.

A defiant and definitive "No!" then came in answer, Ariel wavering no longer. She plunged down the stairs, her echoing, clicking heels sounded like biting teeth, a scurrilous effect.

Nancy moved to follow, but slipped on a single, folded sheet of pink paper, a letter from Ariel; Nancy stopped, stooped, backed away from the strength of the perfumed scent of the paper, then read it aloud:

While I was looking in the mirror, and cleaning my forearm of the black ink of hasty notes, I wondered why the reflection showed a face of remorse. I felt like I had made a huge mistake and debated whether I had.

I came over myself when I realized something Aris had said at the end of my session with Woby. "Yes superb, Trice is trapped, and Applemon too."

He smiled and I didn't like it, and now I realize why. There is no way Aris could have known this if it was all in Woby's head, if it was psychological I mean—because Woby didn't mention it.

So I think I understand now, but am moving on. I have decided to make changes, and to get away to do it. I am changing majors, changing clothes, and changing mentors, friends, and schools. I know of a true polymath—Astrophysics, Neurology, Comparative Folklore, Neoplatonic Philosophy, you name it—and his offer has been there for me, and I'm going to take it. Bye. Sorry. I don't want to talk about it.

No one wanted to be the first to laugh, it seemed.

"Well," Nancy said at last, "there was a rumor of her with someone else. I didn't see where she could have found the time, but there was talk of her with someone brilliant…it was a long name, began with J or something. Whatever. So strange."

Applemon smiled curiously, but when confronted he, like Nancy, concluded with an apathetic, "whatever….but I hope she's okay. Middle Eastern redheads are always worth knowing."

"Yes, so it's a shame she's Jamaican-Irish." Nancy said, squinting at Applemon while Plunkett squinted at them both. "I'll keep an eye on it if I can. If I want," Nancy went on, conflicted, but promising to try to maybe promise at a later date to maybe try to care.

"But…" She began and led the others back to Lil' Aris. He was on a couch reading, Lil' Woby next to him having collected the discarded, multicolored Post-it notes between his fingers. "How did he know Ariel was here? And all that other stuff? From books already?"

Applemon, ignoring the notetaking physicists who gazed on stupidly, answered. "Perhaps when one crosses self-paths it caused each self to gain information from the knowledge of the other. It is one possible solution to some new equations I was fiddling with. Fascinating."

The house guests were stirring, percolating, their conversation and movement growing livelier. The practical implications of life with time travel began to sink in, though Plunkett grew tired of such real world talk as he always did—talk, for example, about how there was an awful lot of responsibility given their new knowledge, and that the implications for science and society were complex and nearly infinite, and the risks were abundant, tricky, and geopolitically charged, and that things were far from…blah blah blah. Plunkett excused himself and retreated to his bedroom.

He came back.

To the rousing cheers of the couch guests.

Because: he came back fully dressed for time travel. The belt was cleaned and sashed across his shoulder and chest, its control box was in hand, his notebook under his arm. His favorite T-shirt and jeans hung loose in academic scruffiness.

"Where are you going?" Applemon laughed.

Nancy said, "Yeah, you have three kids to take care of!"

"I," Plunkett said, "have a plan." Some cheered, some laughed, Lil' Aris gave a thumbs up, Lil' Trice smiled, Lil' Woby asked if he could come.

"Nope," Plunkett said, "but I'll be back and take care of everything. I need to talk to Grandpa first...." he trailed off.

"Ha, and nice!" Applemon enthused, then looked around the dorm. "Then who is going to clean up?"

"And shouldn't someone put all these QOV-swapped people, your guests, back?" Nancy added.

"I will. It's on my way." Plunkett said. Some cheered, some raspberried, some barked, some snapped their fingers and danced.

"Even the monks?" Nancy asked. "And the physicists?" The latter looked sad. "They said they were 'sent' remember? By who?"

Neither the monks nor the physicists knew for sure. The guests looked alternately toward the diminutive Trice and the small Aris, but neither admitted to anything.

"I'll find out." Plunkett replied. "But not yet." He moved to Lil' Woby, forgotten as he was among the feet and paws and robe-ends of the sashaying guests. Plunkett pulled his little brother to his feet, with an avuncular warning that once the sashaying turned to rock 'n' rolling that it would be dangerous to be face down on the floor. "Listen to Unkie Plunkie, he knows a lot about these things."

Lil' Woby laughed.

Plunkett gave him a hug for an *au revoir,* saying, "We have to say goodbye, and I feel like we are still saying hello, but I will be back soon."

"AUNT, Uncle?" Lil' Woby said.

"Yes. Very good! Wait here. I won't be long. Take care of the snake. Maybe we will keep it...if you are good."

"Eww!" Lil' Woby said.

Plunkett asked for and was handed a cold can of beer. He quickly scrawled a note on a clean page of notepaper, copying from another that was tattered almost beyond legibility. He pressed a few buttons on the device then, alone, placed the belt on the kitchen counter and taped the note to the curtain—soon enough Plunkett was hiding in his dorm bedroom waiting for Woby to read it.

THE END

(Agreed Upon Normal Time)

APPENDIX:
CHAPTER TWENTY-THREE AND ONE-HALF

Sunday, when Plunkett and
Nancy mingled.

"Let's join the party," Nancy said. Woby declined, looking tired from the attention. He and his Lil' self, also tired from losing at Twister, went to Plunkett's bedroom for some quiet play of the arts-and-crafts type.

Nancy and Plunkett mingled, and were soon in close observation of the dorm's common room and swallowing a bubbly gulp of the swirling, mingling, and varying activities. It was a two-couch circus.

Nancy asked Plunkett how long he thought such a costume party could avoid suspicion and the University authorities.

"Forever, as long as the fire alarm doesn't go off. This is college." Plunkett said.

Nancy had a follow up question: how long could it last, other things equal?

Plunkett didn't think the ongoings were out of the ordinary for a men's dorm, except that in this case the guests were from different centuries, so his guess was "seventy-two hours, give or take."

Their first stop on the walking tour of time-bending mayhem was the front door, where two characters—one a fellow University student that Nancy vaguely recognized—were sitting opposite each

W.W MARPLOT

other on stools repurposed from the kitchen counter. The familiar one was wearing the time travel belt, Nancy saw.

"Isn't that the time belt? Isn't that a little risky?" she attempted to verify.

"Shush—just listen," Plunkett said, "and you might want to hold my arm."

Nancy paused at Plunkett's offer, but soon accepted it gladly: riding a reflex she grabbed his elbow and felt her knees buckle while her head experienced a moment of existential insecurity, as if a rock was plunked into the stream of her consciousness.

Her thoughts ping-ponged backwards to previously thought thoughts, and then ahead to something she knew she wanted to think later, and ended back to the current mindset wherein she wanted to know why someone was wearing the belt and apparently paying for the privilege: the young man in the belt was handing money to a long haired, poncho-wearing, somewhat filthy stoner who had wilting yellow and pink flower petals stuck about his head and chest.

Nancy recovered from the strange sensory wobbling, as others had done before her, and heard Plunkett speaking.

"We let them pay afterwards, and they always do," he said.

"Pay for what?" Nancy asked.

She was answered by the hippie, after Plunkett formerly introduced him as *Flormeleno, the Ultimate, Eternal Dropout.*

"For the trip, dude. The best trip ever. Wobifying, man, all out, and far out, and…"

"Shut up." Plunkett interrupted; Nancy glad he did. "How many more can we get?" he asked the anachronistic hippie.

"Oh man, word got around quickly, man, and like forever, they keep coming, a lot of bread, man…" Flormeleno drawled.

Nancy attested to this; the front door hall was home to a buzzing crowd of, well, *those type of people.*

"Good." Plunkett said. "Raise the price then, and keep it going. Don't make me regret leaving a hippie in charge of my predatory capitalism."

The young man who was wearing the time-travel belt droned, "Fine with me. I'll pay whatever…give me one more…."

Plunkett nodded to Flormeleno who took the rest of the youth's cash and spun the time machine's dial with a safecracker's skill, then pressed the green button. This trip was smoother than the last. There was merely the minutest bump felt in the room, followed by a small pulse of jerky perception that expanded outward from the belt-wearer. To Nancy, this was like a rock skimming across the pond of her mind.

"They only go back a few minutes, or forward, but it really jolts them." Plunkett explained, looking very satisfied. "Finally one of my plans is in paying off; finally a worthwhile use of the belt."

The tripster—whom Nancy now recognized as one of the undergraduate students of a class on the Lake Poets she helped teach, a student who showed up to one class out of thirteen—landed, figuratively, and said, "it's like that Bob Dylan song, *The Times they are A'nnoyin.*"

Plunkett whispered to Nancy. "Dylan didn't sing it that way until Woby got there." Then to the time-rider Plunkett said, with caffeinated, cerebrally vasoconstricted sarcasm, "Yeah, great, man, like electrical bananas, dude…just send the next guy in."

"Isn't this," Nancy asked, "a little dangerous, with everything going on? Is Woby ok with this? Is Applemon?"

"What Woby doesn't know," Plunkett answered, "can't hurt him, which means nothing can hurt him, which is how he survives. And Apple didn't say it wasn't okay."

Before Nancy could protest—and point out to Plunkett that this double-negation interpretation of others' assent is what got Ariel in trouble—Plunkett pulled her toward the first couch to continue the tour. He stooped to help old Alchemista assist the even older Flotadora up from the floor. The fragile and ethereal Eastern woman had fallen off her perch—the sofa arm—with the room's recent jolt. Her metal-shingled kimono now had a few bent pieces, and these ruined the flat and perfect interweaving of the stretches of odd, wonderful, futuristic textile. Alchemista promised her a cure, in Latin, and Flotadora nodded politely.

Plunkett made the two introductions, which Nancy funneled zestfully into her memory, closing her eyes to crush the names into a fully packed mental space. She wished she had time to grab a pen and paper.

Just before moving on, the next belt-rider had been propelled—vooooped—back to the hall and made to return. This time Nancy self-steadied on her feet like an experienced subway rider. But the shock did seem to create a disturbance in the bathroom, where she and Plunkett now turned and readied for whatever would come.

First came a crash of the door opening and slamming back against an inner wall. Then came a large, dynamically flamboyant man in full—and authentic—bullfighter costume. As he yelled "Ay! Pamplona!!" and before Nancy could ask for it to be defined, the man was followed at his heels by two small children dressed quite authentically—as was presumed—as savage natives from long ago. They spoke a strange tongue.

Last came what was either a black baby rhino or the largest Rottweiler of all time, growling and sprinkling spangles of saliva to left and right.

Nancy wished again to take notes, especially of all the exotic dialogue, but had to commit it only to memory for now. Nonetheless she wrote in her mental pad with such zeal that her real fingers and palm cramped.

"Chatarra! Get the door, hurry! It will get out!!" Plunkett yelled, and the scratched, dented metal and spaghettied wires of the forlorn robot rolled past as daintily as a burning, busted, defeated army tank, and proceeded to shut the bathroom door. "You know that thing is not allowed out here anymore!" Plunkett admonished the robot aggressively. "And where are your clothes? Put them back on!" he ordered. Nancy noticed there was now grey duct tape placed in an X pattern across where Chatarra usually spewed his printed output; there was paper jam noise coming from it.

Nancy had two different questions that happened to have the same answer.

First, she asked, "What's that stink?"

"Uroboros urine," Plunkett answered, "you don't get used to it."

Obvious enough. Then she asked, "what '*thing*' can't come out of the bathroom?"

"The Uroboros."

"Ah." Nancy said.

Plunkett then led Nancy to what he considered the main attraction, and another money-maker. As he explained, "I knew there had to be a way to cash in on the science-geek visitors, they looked wealthy. And everyone's view of Woby as hero has potential. So I am charging them to listen to a lecture."

Self-impressed, Plunkett brought forth some tokens gathered from Applemon's various academic awards, a collection of jokey, or trophy, versions of real donnishness: a fake white beard, an oversized mortarboard cap with fluffy tassel, an absurdly large-bowled, droopy pipe, black regalia robe, and a walking stick that would double as a warlock's staff.

"Have those dorks all paid?" Professor Emeritus Imposturus Plunkett asked.

"Yeah, man," was the answer.

They had paid, and they had gathered.

"I told our science visitors," Plunkett told Nancy, "that I was authorized to relay the awaited and wanted words of Woby. They will lap it up. Easy money."

So Plunkett took his place: aloft two interlocked comfy chairs that were in turn precariously stacked atop the second couch. He looked out and down on the room like the Pope's Holy See—and yet was Wholly Other, a large white wizard in black, his head, shoulders and beard bent at the ceiling.

The physicists and mathematicians were a rapt audience. More had arrived; whether a result of the for-profit hippie trips or from Woby and Trice's misadventures in spacetime, Plunkett cared not.

He winked at Nancy as she approached with zero reverence. A bifocaled latecomer banged her into the side of a couch on his forceful way to a good seat.

"Oh!" Nancy puffed involuntarily like Dorothy when landing hard in Munchkinland; and like so Nancy was resigned to a spot on the floor.

In front of the chairs on the floor two levels down from Plunkett were numerous grey-haired and serious people in a row, each scribbling into pads. They looked uncomfortable but appeared undaring to move. Most were kneeling, some sat cross-legged.

Plunkett spoke. No—Plunkett *speaketh*:

"I have been given wisdom by the wise, wizened Woby the wandering wizard."

And:

"Hear me!"

Plunkett raised his stick aloft.

Nancy moaned a sigh, and sighed a moan, but was hushed and scowled at by the audience of smart people from the past and future.

They begged Plunkett to go on.

"A wolf may be a sheep inside a man—but big brother is each other." He waved a finger down at the listeners, and each peered into the air in front of them, for a second or two, then scribbled.

Plunkett pulled escaping pieces of beard out of his mouth and winked again at Nancy.

He continued with some made up guesses at how the universe works. It sounded like Aris-speak, but with a few "*like, you know*"s thrown in.

One of the attendee's heads craned up the harsh angle to Plunkett The Wise, and poised to speak, then decided against it and scribbled some more. The others looked at her, and scribbled some more.

Nancy frowned. Then frowned some more. She peered over shoulders to look at their notes, and shook her head at the Greek-looking scrawl and what it might mean when these people returned to wherever/whenever and tried to build machines based on the nonsense Plunkett was spewing from the unlit pipe between his teeth.

"This I have been told by Woby." Plunkett now said, and there was much more scribbling, with hard underlining and intense circling.

Nancy did not hear the question asked, hesitatingly, by the shy professor who rocked upward on bony knees, quill pen in hand, to speak. She did hear the answer, however, and the sudden, random attempt at a German accent in Plunkett's voice.

He pointed his staff at the ceiling for effect.

"You are *alvays* making *uber*-assumptions! *Sieben* times!" He began, with authority, as if addressing impetuous and hasty youths, and he added a short, Rhine Valley, upper-class laugh. His voice then changed back to that of a great orator, lecturing the obsequious masses he pictured in third century robes and sandals though he stuck with his nineteenth-century German. "*Unt* hear *vat* I say! How do you know *ze* equations *vere alvays das* same?"

"What do you mean?" some in the audience cried.

Nancy worried—Plunkett seemed stuck. A specific example was called for. Plunkett scratched his mortarboard.

"*Bundeslieger*! He exclaimed at last. "Listen to *zis* example! E equals MC-squared, as *vee* all agree! *Ya*? But in the past maybe *sings ver* different! Maybe *eet vas* E equals MC-squared, plus nine!! *Neun*! *Sprechen zei* wasp?"

There was a hush. Not counting Nancy's moans.

"Hear *vat* I say!" Plunkett threw his cap upward and pointed his staff outward, his robe waving with authority.

It worked. There was an aroused flurry of scribbling and for-eign-accented humming among the intellectual throng.

Professor Plunkett eased, satisfied and grinning, and then spoke/speaketh, dropping the German accent. "After all: Somebody has to steal, to protect us from robbers…while the Queen is subject to her subjects!"

He ended. And climbed down.

Nancy had seen enough, heard enough, laughed enough, and her head hurt from shaking it. She rose and stretched.

Torito the Dog appeared and was actively shaking its own cinderblock of a head. Its barrel frame bucked past Nancy while its teeth gripped and tore at an astronaut's helmet, shaking it loudly to a certain inanimate death. Chatarra the Mute Robot followed, grasping a feather duster in one clamp-hand, and wearing a backwards facing sign that read *"Danger! Kick Me!"* and, under that, *"Danger! Push Me Over!"* With the robot's other clamp it picked up pieces of drool-drenched foam that flung from the chewed gear like wet sparks.

Nancy carefully stepped around all that and made it to Plunkett's bedroom where she stared with great curiosity at some preschooler artwork, a picture made of small curls of uncooked macaroni and cheese shells pasted in place by what looked to be—though Nancy was not an art student, she could only guess—sticky chocolate. Many little yellow smiles set against a world of brown stripes and finger-painted rainbows.

Which would have been fine if it had been on paper or cardboard and not been instead on a small child's face. Lil' Woby was sleeping in Plunkett's bed next to a hand mirror.

He was smiling, curled up, and looked like a slumbering number 2.

Nancy woke him gently, and brought him to the kitchen to clean up. They passed Unkie Plunkie, who was counting cash and upset with his hippie Chief Financial Officer for bypassing the simple rule that payments not be in currency from the future, nor in seventeenth-century German Reichsthalers.

"Do I have to think of everything?" He said as Nancy came near. "Well that's the end of the tour anyway. Applemon should be ready soon. Don't tell him anything."

REFERENCES

1. CHAPTER ZERO: "Sample Spots of Time" recalls Wordsworth, *The Prelude* (1805) XI 257.

2. CHAPTER THREE: "Lysic archetypes." Lysis denotes dream resolution in Jungian Depth Psychology.

3. CHAPTER THREE: "Behmen" is an older spelling for (Jacob) Boehme.

4. CHAPTER FIVE: "Plunkett is not undertly anti-social" shows Aris' neoplatonic, apophatic influence upon Ariel.

5. CHAPTER FIVE: For "Resembling-outcomes is at play" see, e.g. https://repository.upenn.edu/cgi/viewcontent.cgi?article=1301&context=oid_papers

6. CHAPTER FIVE: "Enoptromantic" is divination via mirror-gazing, as the internet tells us. Though he may mean this, Aris most likely used the term because it ends in "-romantic" since he is clearly playing games.

7. CHAPTER FIVE: "You are unbolting wisdom's door!" Is from the real Chatterton's (Thomas, 1752-1770) *Journal 6th*.

8. CHAPTER SIX: "Penthos" means misery, grief — just as Woby is short for woe-begotten. One of Marplot's books in progress has a sub-theme near to that of Pentheus, who tried to banish Dionysius and found himself dismembered. There is no relation to that here.

9. CHAPTER NINE: In *The Silmarillion* (J.R.R. Tolkien), Ungoliant, when trying to collect a promised reward of Valar treasure from Melkor, says: "Yea, with both hands shalt thou give it."

10. CHAPTER NINE: "NOW" is capitalized as another bow to the prince of fantasists as it also is capitalized when used at the end of Bilbo's farewell speech in *The Fellowship of the Ring*.

11. CHAPTER ELEVEN: 1834 denotes the year of S.T. Coleridge's death.

12. CHAPTER ELEVEN: Trice's eyes recall the mystic title *The Cloud of Unknowing*.

13. CHAPTER ELEVEN: The London hospital, and vista, described must be in the vicinity of Guy's Tower, though Marplot only visited the city once and as an unco but wee lad.

14. CHAPTER ELEVEN: "Animalcules" is how they referred to bacteria and microscopic organisms in the 19th century, so this might be a slight exaggeration.

15. CHAPTER TWELVE: With "Lamtayle" etc. Aris is extemporizing, and doing it well. I.e. "lamb tail" — as in "two shakes of a lamb's tail" — denotes a short period of time, as does "Trice". And note that, much more lazily, "Queen Atoi" is simply a matter of spelling "iota" backwards.

16. CHAPTER TWELVE: Who knows what Aris really means to convey, but his use of the latin "volo ergo sum" and "isum aliter deo" translate to "I want therefore I am" and "it seemed otherwise to god."

17. CHAPTER TWELVE: "Knowledge without action is death!" Aris slightly misquotes Plotinus here.

18. CHAPTER FOURTEEN: "What it's like to be a bat" refers to Thomas Nagel's famous essay on consciousness.

19. CHAPTER FOURTEEN: Applemon in his turn summarizes Plotinus (with his "stream" description), see for example *Enneads* 3.8.9.

20. CHAPTER FIFTEEN-E: "Haruspex, or bibliomancy!" Aris is continuing to throw Ariel off by the mention of divining techniques from ages past. Haruspex is the reading of entrails of sacrificed animals. Bibliomancy does so by interpreting book passages selected at random.

21. CHAPTER FIFTEEN-E: "whether she is a God or a pig I won't breathe for her" is Coleridge, from the Preface to *Aids To Reflection* (whose full title continues *In The Formation Of A Manly Character*), 1825.

22. CHAPTER FIFTEEN-N: Flormeleno once "rode a white swan," or so he claims, but he could be convoking the Marc Bolan song from 1970.

23. CHAPTER TWENTY: Woby was "surprised by various joys" but in the William Wordsworth sense, not in C.S. Lewis'.

24. CHAPTER TWENTY-ONE: "RTFC" is computer-geek-speak for "read the f-----g code!" and used when a software developer accuses another of being lazy.

25. CHAPTER TWENTY-ONE: W.W. Marplot wishes it to be known that Plunkett's reference to "a cat eating a wasp" always makes him laugh.

26. CHAPTER TWENTY-THREE: Plunkett being a "slumping ode to dejection" recalls Coleridge, *Dejection: An Ode* (and also harbingers a future Marplot work):

we receive but what we give,
And in our life alone does Nature live

27. CHAPTER TWENTY-FIVE: "Galilean abductive transformations" is in homage to Charles Sanders Peirce and his three syllogisms for induction, deduction, and abduction.

28. CHAPTER TWENTY-FIVE: Nancy's contribution of "Felo de se" comes from her knowledge of Medieval Latin and means "felon of himself."

29. CHAPTER TWENTY-FIVE: The partiers' Spanish insult of "decepcionante" is an attempt at calling Plunkett a sweaty, disappointing loser.

30. CHAPTER TWENTY-FIVE: Nancy is right, Woby almost summoned Wordsworth. The actual quote is "diversity of strength attends us, if but once we have been strong" from *The Prelude* XI: 327.

31. CHAPTER TWENTY-SIX: Woby's call to Trice are quotes of Augustine's *Confessions* Book 11.

32. CHAPTER TWENTY-SEVEN: They dress Woby in "coral" as the Christian martyrs did in similar moments (according to *The Epicurean* by Thomas Moore, 1827).

33. CHAPTER TWENTY-NINE: Plotinus is not "sort of a combination of morality and cosmology" but that is how Applemon perceives it. Lil' Aris would call it (more correctly, in Marplot's view) a combination of mysticism and cosmology.

Made in the USA
Middletown, DE
07 March 2023

26304447R00172